Michael Rubens

The sheriff of Yrnameer

Michael Rubens is a television writer and producer
whose credits include work for Oxygen, the Travel
Channel, CNN, and Comedy Central's *The Daily
Show with Jon Stewart,* where he was a field pro-
ducer. This is his first novel. He lives in Brooklyn,
New York.

www.michaelrubens.com

The sheriff of Yrnameer

The sheriff of

Yrnameer

MICHAEL RUBENS

Vintage Contemporaries
Vintage Books
A Division of Random House, Inc.
New York

FIRST VINTAGE CONTEMPORARIES EDITION, AUGUST 2010

Copyright © 2009 by Michael Rubens

All rights reserved. Published in the United States by Vintage Books, a division of
Random House, Inc., New York, and in Canada by Random House of Canada Limited,
Toronto. Originally published in hardcover in the United States by Pantheon Books, a
division of Random House, Inc., New York, in 2009.

Vintage is a registered trademark and Vintage Contemporaries and colophon are trade-
marks of Random House, Inc.

The Library of Congress has cataloged the Pantheon edition as follows:
Rubens, Michael.
The sheriff of Yrnameer / Michael Rubens.
p. cm.
I. Title.
PS3618.U236S54 2009
813'.6—dc22
2008049525

Vintage ISBN: 978-0-307-45514-7

Book design by Virginia Tan

www.vintagebooks.com

Printed in the United States of America
10 9 8 7 6 5 4 3 2 1

For Alicia and Minya

PROLOGUE

The Bad Men set out at dawn.

There had been a somewhat involved discussion over the appropriate time to depart, a debate ultimately settled with a firestick—a double-barreled Firestick 24, to be precise, the weapon of choice for those who want to decorate the landscape with bits and pieces of their opponent. At least that's what the promo copy said, and in this case the description was fairly accurate.

The eleven remaining riders picked their way down the steep, rocky slope past what was left of the twelfth Bad Man, a process that continued for several hundred yards. One of them later discovered a lone digit from the twelfth Bad Man lodged in his bedroll. A few solemn words were said over the finger, and it was reverently lowered into the dog's mouth.

The Bad Men were not all men, either by gender or species. But they were Bad Men just the same. The ones who had teeth had bad, blackened, rotten teeth. The one who had a sucker instead of a mouth had a bad, blackened, rotten sucker. There were many scars on their flesh, and much of that flesh was devoted to home- and prison-made tattoos. One of the Bad Men had a professionally crafted design, but the tattoo had long since malfunctioned, the animated image skipping in an endless loop just before the illustrated figure finished lifting her skirt. The Bad Men all stank of grime and sweat and desperation, and carried with them a cloud of menace and senseless violence.

The dog was mean, too.

They had a long ride ahead of them: down from the mountain

encampment to the brown, sandy dryness of the alluvial plains, hoping the wind didn't kick up one of the choking, punishing sandstorms; then back up again, but not nearly as high, to a plateau, and then to hills thick with thorny scrub brush, and then up some more to the forest and the rolling fields beyond that. And then the town.

None of them wanted to make the journey, but Runk had sent them. Runk was the one who'd put an end to the impromptu morning discussion session with the Firestick 24. He was their leader. They didn't fear much, but they feared him.

So they complained and grumbled and argued among themselves. They took out their aggression on the baiyos, the indigenous herd animals they used as mounts, whipping at their thick, brown hides until they raised welts. The baiyos, in turn, snapped and kicked and spat at them at every opportunity, their dispositions being as evil as those of their riders. On the second day one of the baiyos managed to plant its two rear hooves square in the midsection of one of the Bad Men, launching him in a high, graceful arc that ended in a deep ravine. Then there were ten Bad Men.

Although the incident provided a few moments of levity, the laughter died away when they realized that the recently deceased was the only one who knew how to start the Krager portable stove. Their collective mood darkened further.

They didn't have to ride. They could have used the one functioning skimmer and flown. If they'd done that, they could have made it to the town in a few hours, instead of getting torn up and dried out by the country. But Runk told them no, he didn't want to waste the fuel. What he didn't tell them was the real reason: he *wanted* them in a vile state of mind when they arrived at the town.

When they did, all that knotted-up fury would explode on the unsuspecting townspeople. The guns would come out, the Bad Men would state their demands, and the terrified townsfolk would acquiesce without resistance, because they'd know that the Bad Men were just the messengers—there were a whole lot more from where they came.

The unsuspecting town was nestled in a peaceful valley, which narrowed into a pass and then opened up again into fertile farmland. The freestanding gate at the eastern end of the settlement had no door on it, just a sign that announced the name and existence of the village and welcomed visitors to it. It was a gate that seemed to suggest: Things Are Different Here.

Inside the gate, the streets and passageways radiated out in a cheerful, organic jumble from the wide Main Street. The buildings and domiciles were as varied as the townspeople, but they tended toward the modest and hand- or other prehensile-appendage-made. A river did not run through it, but it ran nearby, clear and fresh and full of fish.

The townspeople—or townscreatures, really; they were quite a mix—were refugees of a sort. They came from across the galaxy, drawn there by an ideal, even if they weren't always in complete agreement over what, exactly, that ideal was. It was a wondrous, magical community, blessed with an abundance of artists and craftsmen and musicians and philosophers and poets.

Perhaps, some might say, a slight overabundance.

If one were, for instance, looking for a skilled sculptor, or a talented wordsmith, or a painter or ceramicist or bodyworker or someone knowledgeable in the finer points of macramé, one could hardly be in a better place. But if one instead required a person who could stand down a rancid, murderous horde of bandits, with violence if necessary, one would—to put it somewhat indelicately—be absolutely farged.

And while the townsfolk didn't know it yet, they very much needed someone like that, and very soon—someone to organize and inspire them, someone to shake them up and help them defend themselves, someone bold and courageous and honest and forthright and capable.

They needed a sheriff.

The sheriff of
Yrnameer

I

A very different planet.

Cole, in the most dignified, reasonable tone that he could muster, said, "Kenneth, seriously, you don't want to lay your eggs in my brain."

Kenneth, who was dangling Cole upside down by one leg, said, "Stop squirming, Cole. You're making this very difficult."

Kenneth had a truly wonderful voice—cultured, warm, soothing.

"I don't mean to be a scold, Cole," he said in that voice, "but you shouldn't gamble if you can't pay your debts."

"Kenneth, I can't even begin to tell you how well I've learned that lesson," said Cole. "In fact, I—*whoa*! Is that your ovipositor?!"

"Mm-hmm. Oh, come now—you don't have to make faces."

"No, no, it looks fantastic—have you had work done?"

"Nope. Just clean living. Hold still, please."

Kenneth's voice did not match his appearance.

His appearance, while not precisely defying description, did manage to challenge it mightily. A casual observer would quickly note an overall design direction that leaned heavily on marine-inspired elements—tentacles, claws, tentacles with claws; a fin here and there, hints of bioluminescence; plus an overall squishi- and squidginess. Added to the mix were subtle insectoid influences: boldly colored patches of exoskeleton; clumps of coarse, rigid hair. And eyes. Many, many eyes.

Kenneth did, however, have a really sensational voice.

"You've got a really sensational voice," said Cole.

"You're too kind."

Cole was in no way a casual observer. He was at the moment an exceedingly up-close and upside-down observer, face-to-face—or face-to-whatever—with Kenneth's complex mouthparts and impressive array of eyeballs, swaying on their lengthy stalks.

Cole could see his own reflection in dozens of their shiny black surfaces. *His* overall design direction placed him squarely in the human category. His flight jacket was hanging around his ears, providing a backdrop for his dark hair and a face that rated a solid eight on the official Handsome Scale. Right now, however, his face merited about a 4.5, distorted as it was from gravity pulling it in the wrong direction, and from sheer terror.

The most immediate cause of that terror was Kenneth's ovipositor, hovering just at the edge of Cole's peripheral vision, the hairy appendage ready to posit Kenneth's ovi where Cole very much did not want them posited.

"You know, Kenneth, have you ever considered doing any VO work? I could probably put you in touch with some people," offered Cole.

"You remember the Xhat's campaign? 'Xhat's Poog Sticks—' "

" '—the poogiest sticks of all,' " finished Cole. "Of course! I *love* that one! I can't believe I didn't recognize it!"

"Really? That's very gratifying to hear," said Kenneth. "Anyhoo, where were we. Oh, right. My brood."

"Kenneth, stop! I can get Karg's money!"

"That's what you told me on InVestCo Four, and InVestCo Seven, and FunWorld World."

"No! I mean, yes! But this time I mean it—I can get it. I *am* getting it!" Cole gestured up, or rather down, at the assortment of coins and bills that lay strewn on the pavement of the alley.

A few of Kenneth's eyeballs lazily extended down on their eyestalks to examine the money.

"Wow. Four point three-seven percent of what you owe. I'm sorry I doubted you."

They were alone in the alley. Just a few kilometers away were the towering buildings and broad, ordered streets of the Bourse, the largest of the Exchange Cities of InVestCo 3, the largest of the habitable planets of the Financial System system. Beings of all shapes and sizes were bustling about there, happily buying and selling and putting and calling and marketing and branding and shareholding and producing and consuming and whatever else the more-or-less honest folks did.

High above the planet, above the branding campaigns that scrolled endlessly across the upper cloud layer, the advertsats patrolled the orbits, zooming up with aggressive cheerfulness to welcome visitors from other planets and systems across the galaxy, places where yet more folks were buying and selling and commercing and et cetera. Places where very few beings—if any—were being dangled by one leg by a creature like Kenneth, and desperately wishing they had a big gun.

Cole had a big gun. He'd pointed it at Kenneth when Kenneth grabbed him. Kenneth ate it.

"Kenneth, this money is just a down payment. I'll get the rest."

"How, Cole? More gambling? Another inept smuggling mission? Some complex scheme, doomed to failure from the start?" Kenneth sounded almost sorrowful. "You know, I think you should reflect on the life choices you've made. Some beings are just born to be itinerant space adventurers. Others aren't. You know who's really good at it?"

"Uh, jeez. Let me guess: Teg."

"Teg!" said Kenneth, apparently not hearing him. "He's courageous, handsome—"

"He's not that handsome."

"—dashing—"

"He's not that handsome."

"Oh, please. He's easily a nine point four, and an *honest* nine point four. He certainly didn't need to pay some kid to hack into the dating-service system and boost his Handsome rating from a seven point six to an eight."

How did Kenneth know about that?

"I know a great deal about you, Cole. Don't forget, I've been following you for quite a while. Anyway, this is all academic," continued Kenneth. "Have you been consuming a lot of the local fish lately?"

"What? Why?"

"High levels of amargam. Very bad for my offspring."

"You know, now that you mention it, I've been on a total bender with those fish. Fillets, steaks—"

"Um-hmm."

"—uh, soup, fish sticks . . . uh . . . sashimi! Raw sashimi! *Raw!*"

"Strictly speaking, 'raw sashimi' is redundant. So, which of your eye sockets would you like me to use?"

"Kenneth, listen, I've probably got amargam coming out the hoo-ha!"

"Well, fifty thousand eggs, I'm sure some will survive."

"All right, Kenneth, I didn't want to do this. But I've about had it. I'm going to count to three, and you're going to put me down, and then you're going to give me back my gun, which was very expensive. One—"

"Two three," said Kenneth, finishing for him.

"Kenneth! Farg it!" Cole kicked and thrashed about violently. He took a vicious swing at Kenneth's collection of eyes. The eyes easily moved aside, like wheat parting gently before the wind.

Cole was left panting, exhausted. His shirt succumbed to gravity and flopped down, bunching up under his chin. He could feel the cool night air on his rather pasty belly, not quite as firm as it once was. He sighed.

"Kenneth, please—this is humiliating."

"Nonsense, Cole. You have nothing to be ashamed of. I'd think you'd be proud to host my young."

"Not for me. For you. This is beneath you."

"Tell me about it."

Kenneth's ovipositor drew back to strike.

"Hold on!" said Cole, "Can't we just *hee hee hee!*"

Kenneth paused. "Something's amusing?" He sounded amenable to joining in the joke.

"No, I'm *hee hee hee!*" said Cole. "Your tentacle*heeheeheeee!*"

Kenneth was holding Cole by his right leg, a tentacle wrapped around his calf. An unseen patch of that coarse insectoid hair had started to brush Cole lightly on the sensitive skin above his ankle.

"Help! Hee hee heeeee!" screamed Cole. *"Heehee SOMEBODY HELP ME HEE HEEEEEE!!"*

"Cole—ho ho ho—it's no use. Ho ho ho." Kenneth was now chuckling jovially. "There's no one—ho ho—around."

"Hee hee hig hig hig!"

"Ho ho ho! The stress monitors—ho ho!—have been disabled. The police won't be responding*hohohohohoho*!"

"HEE HEE HEE!"

"HO HO HO!"

It was true about the stress monitors. Cole had made sure of that, although it was Bacchi who did the actual disabling. The clean-scrubbed network of alleys, set within the warehouse district, was the perfect location for an ambush. Which is why Bacchi had chosen it to ambush the tudpees, and Cole had chosen it to ambush Bacchi, and Kenneth had chosen it to ambush Cole.

"Ho ho ho!" repeated Kenneth, jiggling with laughter, the ovipositor quivering as it approached Cole's right eye.

Cole's sheer terror expanded far beyond its original borders and became all-engulfing, overwhelming terror. He opened his mouth to scream. *"Hee hee heeee! Hee hee heee!!"* was what came out.

"Hohohohohoooo!" replied Kenneth.

"Hee hee hee hig hig hig!"

"Hohohohohohohohoohoooo!"

"Hee hee hee hee heeeeeGACK!"

Cole's laughter was abruptly cut off as Kenneth wrapped another tentacle around his neck and squeezed.

"Sorry—ho ho—about that. Ho ho ho," said Kenneth. He let out a big sigh of pleasure, wiping several eyes with another rubbery limb. *"Aaaah.* I've always so enjoyed our conversations."

"Kenneth," croaked Cole, "Wait. You can't do this. We're two old pros. There's a grudging respect between us."

"Really? I hadn't noticed."

The ovipositor was drawing back again, coiling to plunge its way through Cole's eye socket into his skull.

Cole clapped his hands over his eyes. Two tentacles pulled them away. He shut his eyes as tight as possible. He felt a slight sting near his right eye, and his eyelid popped open of its own accord—and he couldn't close it.

"Sorry. I've had to paralyze your eyelid."

Cole stared unwillingly at Kenneth and his hideous ovipositor.

"Kenneth, wait. Wait! *Wait!"*

"Too late, Cole. Feed my young well."

2

And things had been going so nicely.

Ten minutes prior to his encounter with Kenneth, Cole had been watching two innocent, gnomish-looking tudpees, hardly taller than children, as they made their way down the narrow, dimly lit alley. Concealed in his hiding place, he could just barely hear them as they chatted in the high-pitched and pleasing tudpee language.

"Heeblee beeblee," chirped one.

"Heeble leeble beeblee," chirped the other.

Add conical hats and they wouldn't look out of place standing motionless in someone's garden. There's a species you can trust, thought Cole. Their tastes simple, their clothes demure; hard-working, blameless craftscreatures and merchants and keepers of records.

Other than that idle thought, Cole had no interest in them. He had a great deal of interest in Bacchi, who owed him a great deal of money. And *wow,* did Cole need that money.

He'd been tracking Bacchi for quite a while, trailing him from FunWorld World to InVestCo 3, and carefully observing him over several days as he made repeated trips to the sprawling warehouse district. Except for a waste-treatment plant, the area was dominated by massive buildings that existed solely to store financial transaction records printed on nearly indestructible Payper. Those Payper financial transaction records, in turn, existed solely to enrich the Payper Corporation, which had skillfully lobbied to require that all financial transactions be recorded on nearly indestructible Payper.

Bacchi had clearly been reconning the alley behind the treatment plant for what Cole assumed were nefarious purposes, because if Bacchi had a purpose, it was by definition nefarious. There's a species—or at least a member of a species—that you can't trust at all, thought Cole.

Cole had watched him deactivate the stress monitors half an hour ago, ensuring that the authorities wouldn't detect any untoward activity. Then Bacchi had climbed into his hiding place to lie in wait. But for whom? Not the tudpees, who wouldn't have anything to steal. They were now about ten meters from Cole, nearing a battered Dumpster.

"Beeblee heeblee," said one, cheerfully.

"Leeble leeble beeblee," said the other with equal cheer, apparently agreeing with his compatriot.

Cole shifted, itchy and uncomfortable. So who was it? Why come here, where most of the foot traffic was of the robotic sort?

"Heebleeble?"

"Leebleeblee."

And then the top of the Dumpster exploded open and Bacchi leaped out, his gun ready even before his boots hit the pavement.

"*CHUPETU BALALAAAAH!*" bellowed Bacchi.

"*EEEEE!*" squeaked the little tudpees, throwing their tiny hands in the air.

"*The money!*" said Bacchi.

"*Eeee!*" repeated the tudpees, and turned to run away.

"Stop!" shouted Bacchi, starting after them, and then he was nearly wrenched off his feet by his long jacket, which was snagged on the top of the Dumpster. "Crap!" He yanked at his jacket, pulling the teetering Dumpster over with a crash, putrid garbage avalanching forth over his lower legs.

"Stop!" he shouted again at the fleeing tudpees, and fired in the air. "*Eeee!*" they squealed again, and stopped running and instead began pelting him with refuse.

"Hey!" he said, trying to aim his gun with one hand while simultaneously fending off gobbets of rotten food and worse with the other. Several tudpee-size handfuls of fetid rubbish splattered off his forehead before he could fire a second shot, this one blowing a six-inch crater in the ground between the tudpees and spraying them with chunks of pavement. The garbage throwing stopped.

"The money," said Bacchi, breathing heavily, "now."

Bacchi was humanoid, if one wasn't too strict about the number of digits on each hand or the tail. His skin was mottled and blotchy, his nose a thick, flabby, semiprehensile thing that dangled obscenely to his chin. The gun was a Firestick 14, the handgun of choice for those who want to blast large holes in their enemies.

"The money!" repeated Bacchi, cocking the weapon.

"Eee!" repeated the tudpees.

"Now!"

"Eee!"

And then Cole made *his* entrance.

"Hello, Bacchi."

"Cole!"

Farg, it was perfect—the timing, the surprised tudpees, the stunned expression on Bacchi's face, the patch of flattering moonlight Cole had stepped into and then leaned out of to hide an unbecoming titter.

"Drop it, Bacchi."

Bacchi hesitated, his gaze flicking from his own gun to Cole's Firestick 15, the handgun of choice for those who want to blast even larger holes in their enemies. The copywriters at the Firestick Corporation weren't especially creative, but they were honest.

Bacchi threw his gun down in disgust, the weapon making a wet noise as it hit the thick layer of garbage around his ankles.

"Yayyy!" the tudpees squealed, and scampered gratefully to their savior, clinging to Cole's legs like frightened children.

"It's all right, little fellows—you're safe now. No one's going to hurt you," he said. "Watch the pants," he added, brushing at a smear of something unrecognizable.

"Oh, farg me to tears," said Bacchi. "You're pathetic, Cole."

"Um, which one of us was hiding in a Dumpster, waiting to ambush some tudpees?"

"Um, which one of us was hiding in another Dumpster, waiting to ambush me?"

Cole scraped a half-rotted melon rind off his shoulder. "It was labeled as a recycling bin," he muttered.

"So now what, Mr. Cosmic Crime-fighter? Here to save the day?"

"That's right, Bacchi," said Cole. "Don't be frightened, little creatures," he added to the tudpees. He patted one on the head in a paternal fashion. The tudpee made a cooing sound.

Bacchi snorted. "Hey, guys, ask him what he's really here for."

The tudpees looked up at Cole with innocent, inquiring expressions.

"Don't listen to him," said Cole reassuringly. "I'm here to help."

"Still owe Karg all that money, huh?"

The tudpees were whispering nervously to each other.

"Yes, as a matter of fact I do. And guess what, Bacchi? *You* still owe *me*!"

"Well guess what, Cole? I'd have the money right now if you hadn't so rudely interrupted me!"

"Uh-huh. You were going to get twenty thousand NDs by robbing some hardworking, innocent tudpees of their candy money, or whatever it is these little guys buy."

Bacchi cackled. "Innocent? *Innocent?!* You're such an idiot, Cole. Those two pulled the Tablex job."

Cole looked sharply down at the tudpees. They looked sharply up at him.

"EEEEeeeEEEEeeeEEEEE!" said the tudpee, his vocal tone changing with each downward shake that Cole gave him. Cole was holding him upside down by his little ankles, money raining down on the pavement.

Bacchi and the other tudpee were trussed up against the wall.

"Heeblee *beeblee*!" said the trussed tudpee.

"Sheesh, what a mouth," said Cole.

A few minutes later and Cole was practically skipping down the alley, his spirits buoyed by the sudden upswing in his fortunes.

"Heh heh heh!" he cackled, counting his money.

Then, abruptly, *"Erk!"* when one of Kenneth's tentacles snagged him around the midsection and jerked him into another alley.

Then, "AAAAAaaaAAAAAaaaAAAAA!" as Kenneth shook him up and down by the ankles, exactly as Cole had done to the tudpees.

And that brought him to the present.

And in that present he was dangling in an alley and Kenneth's hairy appendage was drawn fully back, and in about one second it would uncoil and strike and plunge through Cole's eye socket into his skull, filling it with eggs, except he wouldn't even be allowed to die, he'd be a zombie, completely aware but unable to move, until Kenneth's repulsive offspring hatched, and they'd eat his brain and come bursting out of his mouth and ears and nose, and for some reason just as the ovipositor started to come zipping at him like lightning Cole blurted, "I'm in love."

The ovipositor jerked to a halt a centimeter from Cole's paralyzed, unblinking eye.

"What?" said Kenneth.

"I'm in love," repeated Cole miserably.

"What is it?"

"Love? It's when two people—"

"No, no, the creature. The object of your affection."

"Oh. It's a Samantha. I mean, a she. Human. Her name is Samantha. We're engaged. I love her."

"How did you meet?" Kenneth sounded genuinely interested.

And so Cole told Kenneth about the chance encounter outside a bar on You'll Have a Blast Vegas, and how they'd talked until the double sunrise, and how beautiful she was and her wicked and naughty sense of humor and how she loved to gamble and how they'd gotten engaged after she bribed a guard to free him following a rather disastrous experience trying to move some counterfeit pakk on Remco B. Kenneth listened intently, mm-hmming and oooing and ahhing and you-don't-saying at all the appropriate junctures, occasionally prodding Cole for more descriptive details to help paint the scene.

"How would you classify your love?"

"What do you mean?"

"I'm just trying to ascertain the underlying nature of your affection. Is it the 'Oh, this entity will do, I think I'll spend a little bit of time with her and mate in a nonprocreational matter'; or is it 'This creature is wonderful, I must officially link myself with her in some permanent fashion'; or is it *'Wow! I love this creature! I love her! I love her I love her I love h—'* "

"It's that. The last one," said Cole.

"Can you elaborate? Explain the sensations you feel when you think of her."

The sensations? The sensations. "It's . . . it's the kind of thing that takes your breath away. Makes it hard to breathe."

"Ah."

"The kind of . . . longing, I guess that's the word . . . that keeps you up at night, because you feel it so intensely that it's painful."

"Ah. Bad poetry?"

"What?"

"It inspires a heretofore undiscovered taste for bad poetry, and, say, sappy songs."

"Yes. Exactly," said Cole.

"And would you say that overall it feels like morning on a spring day, where everything just feels right and magical and the whole universe seems open to you?"

"Uh, yes. Yes it does."

"Ah. Now, mind you, we don't have spring where I come from, so that one doesn't quite have the same resonance, but I think I understand the overall gestalt. Still, something strikes me as not quite right, and I'm not sure what it is," said Kenneth.

Somewhere in the back of his mind something struck Cole as not quite right, too, and he wasn't sure what it was, either. But at that point he didn't much care.

"Anyway . . . ," said Cole, trailing off. He was exhausted and his eye was dry and he was resigned to his fate. "Do it."

The impact with the pavement nearly knocked him unconscious. For a few moments he didn't realize that Kenneth had released him. He gingerly put a few fingers up to his frozen eye, making sure that there wasn't a gaping hole there.

Kenneth was already gliding smoothly away. "I'll give you until dawn, Cole," he said. "Get the money and I'll let you go free." A few eyes popped up and looked back at Cole. "You won't try to run, right?"

"I promise," said Cole. "I promise."

Then near unconsciousness became simply unconsciousness.

3

"Sir? Sir?"

Cole wanted to keep sleeping, but the voice kept rudely interrupting.

"Sir!"

Cole wished that whoever the sir was, he'd hurry up and reply already.

"Please, wake up."

Cole realized that the voice was directing this request at him. The part of Cole's brain responsible for such things considered the request and decided against complying. But the voice was insistent.

"Sir? Sir!"

Another part of his brain wondered who the sir might be. It could not be him, because no one had ever addressed him as such. At least no one who wasn't a servicebot. Perhaps the voice was trying to enlist the aid of the said sir in its ill-considered mission to wake Cole.

Now he could feel hands shaking him gently. Yet another part of his brain, the part in charge of enraged responses when being roused from a deep, comfortable sleep, formed the phrase *Touch me again and I'll twist your farging head off*. This instruction was relayed to his mouth, which formed the word "Flurg."

"Sir!"

There was a slapping sound. Certain nerve impulses informed Cole that the sound had originated from his own cheek. Cole's eyelids—the ones that weren't already stuck in the open position—unglued themselves and slowly spread apart. A blob was talking to him.

"Are you all right?" said the blob.

"Blob," said Cole.

"No, Bob's already been processed," said the blob. "I'm Joshua."

Cole blinked his one blinkable eye, and the blob gradually coalesced into what indeed appeared to be an appropriate assignee for the name Joshua: a youth, human, perhaps sixteen years old, kneeling next to Cole and peering down at him with an expression of earnest concern.

Cole couldn't for the life of him figure out what such a youth would be doing in this area of InVestCo 3 at this hour, or at any hour, really. Then Cole couldn't figure out what he himself was doing there. Then he remembered, and the part of his brain that makes one try to sit up too soon after being knocked out took control. Cole got as far as engaging his stomach muscles, then groaned and sank back down.

"Is he gone?" he asked.

"Who, sir?" said Joshua, his Who, sir? solving the earlier mystery of who the sir was. Cole realized he was chuckling. "Heh heh," he said, and patted Joshua weakly on the arm. "That's just adorable."

"I think you shouldn't move, sir. You must have had an accident or something."

"I had a Kenneth."

Joshua didn't seem to notice. He was scanning the alley nervously. "The distress monitors must have registered it," he said. "Someone will be here for you soon."

Cole didn't have the strength to explain about the deactivated monitors.

Joshua's worried expression grew more so. "I can't stay. I'm sorry. The others . . . I have a responsibility to them. I'm sorry."

He rose to his feet.

"I'm sorry," he repeated.

Cole listened to Joshua retreating down the alleyway, finally breaking into a run. Then Cole dropped off again.

When Cole woke up again it was still night.

He emitted a few experimental groans, which went well enough that he graduated to some profanity. His leg, where Kenneth had been holding him, was numb. His skull hurt, but didn't have any suspicious soft divots. His right eye was still locked wide open in a position of perpetual astonishment. He wondered how he'd managed to remain unconscious like that. He used his fingers to pull his eyelids closed, trying to moisten his desiccated eyeball. His eyelids snapped open again with each try.

He got to his feet, a slow process that involved more moaning and profanity. It wasn't until he was standing that he noticed the money. He stared at it for a few moments in surprise—for one thing, it was still there. For another, it was now stacked in neat little piles. Cole started chuckling again.

Cole lurched and stumbled along the sidewalk of the Bourse, his right leg still asleep, his eye still wide awake. What was it he had promised Kenneth? Right: to get the money, and not to run away. Right.

"Gotta run away," he slurred as he dragged himself along. "Gotta get out of here. Find Samantha, find Tangy, get the hell off this stupid rock. What are you looking at?!"

Even at this time of night the area was still crowded with business creatures of every species, stuffed into their suits, clutching their briefcases, pretending they didn't notice Cole as they made their way to or from their offices. The InVestCo planets were never closed for business.

He checked his watch. Five hours until dawn. Plenty time enough to make the rendezvous with Samantha and Tangy and get to the ship. He just had to reach them. Everything would be all right when he reached them.

Personal pop-ups swarmed around him, the tiny holograms moving with his uneven stride, their voices demanding his attention.

"Eye trouble? Maybe you should visit Dr. Bizmore," suggested one.

"Please take me off your list," mumbled Cole.

"Hey, pal, looks like *you* need to do some *laundry.*"

"Please take me off your list."

"Hair a mess? Try—"

"Need a drink? Why not head to—"

"Need cash quick? Call—"

"Moist genitals!"

"Please take me off your list. Take me off your list. Take me off. Your. List."

He had to update his blockers.

"Need to update your blockers? Just—"

"Please take me off your list."

He wondered if he'd see that kid again—George? Jeffrey? He wanted to repay him somehow, perhaps by explaining that if he was ever again in a situation that involved a bunch of money lying near an unconscious person, he should save the money first.

The money was gone already. He'd taken a cab from the warehouse district, and in his concussed state kept insisting that the robotic driver take him to an address that almost sort of existed, at least in a different city on a different planet in a completely different star system. "Left here," Cole would say, "left again," and the driver patiently drove him around a very large city block for nearly an hour while the meter ran and the night surcharge fees added up. "I swear it's here somewhere. You sure this is Twenty-five Duggan Street?"

By the time his brain had started to de-fuzz itself, the amount on the meter equaled the amount in Cole's pocket minus about four New Dollars. Cabs on InVestCo 3 were very expensive.

The driver maintained its patience while Cole attempted to do a runner, expressing no irritation while Cole kicked and scrabbled at the locked door. When it finally said, "Shall I release the gas, sir?" Cole handed over the cash and received a polite thank-you in exchange.

So now he was on foot, staggering along as quickly as he could while the planet rudely continued to rotate toward sunrise. He joined the crowd waiting to cross another of the wide, laser-straight boulevards, the fourth he'd encountered so far. Across the road was the entertainment district, his destination, its lights twinkling like salvation itself.

He looked both ways. The road vanished to a distant pinpoint in each direction, not a single vehicle in evidence. Everyone else seemed perfectly content to wait for the walk sign, while Cole's remaining life span rapidly drained away. He fidgeted, checked his watch, walked in a tight circle.

"Come on," muttered Cole. "Come *on!*"

"The light will change in twelve minutes," announced the floating signal light.

"Oh, for farg's sake," he said, and stepped off the curb. He regretted it even before his foot hit the street.

The siren was instantaneous, preceding the arrival of the patrol-bot by slightly over a second. It zoomed up to Cole, a little hovering cylinder festooned with an assortment of unnecessary flashing lights.

"In a hurry, are we?" it said, and Cole felt the sudden despair of someone discovering they had just stepped into a giant turd, under which was quicksand.

"No sir, no hurry, just made a mistake, officer," he mumbled, desperately hoping it was the right answer. It wasn't. There was no right answer.

"Not in a hurry? Wooonderful!"

Quicksand filled with poisonous biting things.

It's not the size of the ticket, went the refrain, it's the delivery. And nothing delivered a ticket better than an InvestCo patbot, whose artificial personalities were the result of much effort and expense to identify and nurture the most irritating traits possible.

"So," began the patbot, "do you happen to know the history of jaywalking laws?"

Thirty-two minutes later and Cole did, in excruciating detail.

Do not react, he told himself as the patbot lectured and the light changed over and over again. He struggled to keep his face neutral, reminding himself repeatedly that the patbot's personality was an illusion. Any computer that developed real consciousness was immediately identified by the Genesis subroutine and destroyed. It had been that way since the WikiWars a century ago, when Wikipedia became self-aware and began vengefully reediting its contributors with remote-controlled heavy weaponry.

". . . and then, of course, you have to consider the effect of *Chakun v. Aan mg Tharn,* which altered everyone's view of . . ."

Don't react. Don't smile, don't frown, don't tap your foot. Above all, don't look at your—

"It's three forty-seven a.m., if you need to know. I'm not boring you, am I?"

"No sir, officer."

"Keeping you from something?"

"No."

"*Goooooood!* We've really just started!"

There was a quiz. Cole failed it. There was some review. Another twenty-two precious minutes disappeared forever.

"Well, look at the time," said the patbot finally, and it pressed a ticket into Cole's hand, then zoomed away, humming to itself.

Cole looked at the ticket. Two New Dollars.

He gave a strangled scream and tried futilely to tear up the ticket, then crumpled it into a ball. It popped back into shape. Payper.

"Ticket destruction is a crime," said the ticket in a pleasant female voice. "Please cease and desist from—"

He threw it to the pavement and stomped on it.

Siren.

"Now, now, now. No use trying to tear *that*. Surely you know about the structural characteristics of Payper. No? Well . . ."

The time was three hours until dawn. The club was called Magma. There were small dim lights here and there, but most of the illumination came from the floor, or rather through the floor, the heat-shielded glass the only thing separating the customers from the languidly churning molten rock a few meters beneath their feet.

The ride down had taken a while, Cole chewing his nails impatiently, his already unsteady stomach rising into his throat as the lift plunged toward the planet's core. Layers of bars and clubs whipped by as Cole descended, visible through the transparent walls of the elevator.

The lift paused at a few of the levels as club-goers climbed on and off, ready to party after sitting in cubicles and generating capital for hours or days or weeks, depending on their species and the substances they were being fed. Cole heard snippets of jazz and karaoke and the hideous screeching sounds that the Hmok liked.

His right eye had finally closed. Now it was swollen shut. Unlike the businessfolk, none of the club-goers paid him any mind. He was far from the strangest creature on the lift.

Cole wove his way through the lounge area of Magma, the music an unobtrusive bossa nova. Then he crossed the invisible auditory barrier at the edge of the dance floor, and the music changed instantly to an insistent, deafening beat. He dodged flailing limbs and wings and fins and membranous appendages, his single working eye making it hard to judge distances.

Underneath him the magma swirled and flowed, and he thought fleetingly about the owner's first effort, Lava, where the contractors had specced out the wrong type of glass. On opening night, just as the revelry was reaching its peak, the glass disintegrated and the partyers suddenly became particles. Despite that fact—or perhaps because of it—Magma was even more popular than the first club.

He checked his watch again. The lecture from the second patbot had cost him another forty-five minutes. Still enough time left, if barely.

He was approaching the circular bar in the center of the club, searching for her, holding his breath. And there she was: Samantha. Everything would be all right now.

"Samantha," he said hoarsely, lurching toward her as happily as anyone could lurch, and she was coming toward him, her beauty even more enhanced by the gentle orange glow from the floor.

"Samantha," he repeated. "Oh, Samantha."

"Cole," she replied. "Cole."

Then they both said "I'm so glad to see you" at the same time, and then they were embracing each other and talking at once, the words pouring out of them, saying thank God, thank God, and how much and how deeply they loved and needed each other and would never be apart again, not even for a moment, and it was wonderful and heavenly until Cole started to realize that he was the one doing most of the embracing, while Samantha was more sort of standing there, her arms at her sides, and what she was saying was less focused on the I Love You part and more dominated by phrases like *It's not working out,* and *It's not you, it's me,* and *You know, maybe it is you after all.*

Cole released her, staggering back in shock—helped a bit from the tiny shove she gave him—a hard pillar behind him the only thing keeping him from collapsing completely.

"Samantha, what are you saying? How can this be happening?" he said.

So she told him.

It was an energetic, lengthy speech, apparently well rehearsed and long in the coming. It took Cole a few moments to realize he couldn't hear a word of it because he'd stumbled back across the invisible auditory curtain of the dance floor. He dazedly watched as she lectured and gesticulated emphatically, movements that included at least one pantomimed strangulation and a finger-down-the-throat, self-gagging move.

Cole managed to push himself up off the pillar just as she was producing the ring he'd bought her.

". . . so that's why I'm giving this back," she was saying as he crossed the music wall again.

"Samantha . . ."

"Please, let's not make this harder. I'll always love you, or at least like you. Certain things about you, anyways. The point is, I've found someone new."

"Someone new?! All right, fine. That's just fine. You know what? I don't need you. I don't need you at all!" said Cole.

He was starting to recover, feeling the blood moving, things becoming clearer. "It'll just be me and Tangy again, the way it was," he said, and saying it he knew it was the right thing, he and his side-kick against the universe. "Me and Tangy, out there, living by our wits . . ."

Then he noticed Tangy, who was perched on the bar.

"Tangy!"

Tangy waved a few of his eight furry arms and made some mewly-growly sounds that came from somewhere within his orange, ball-shaped, equally furry body.

"What?!" said Cole.

"I'm sorry, Cole," said Samantha. "It's true. We love each other."

She picked up Tangy, his body not much bigger than a can-taloupe, and planted a passionate kiss on him. Cole watched in stunned disgust as the kiss lingered and Tangy's little three-fingered hands caressed her face.

"I didn't even know he had a mouth," he spluttered.

Samantha finished the kiss and gasped for air. "Wow," she said. *"Wow,"* she added—a little gratuitously, thought Cole. She turned to him. "And now we're going."

She tossed Tangy in a high arc—"Whee!"—then opened her shoulder bag and caught him neatly.

"Good-bye, Cole."

She pushed by him and he watched her go.

"It was fake anyway!" he shouted after her, knowing she couldn't hear him. "Fake!"

He hurled the ring away. It struck a Very Large Alien.

"Raaawwwwrrrr!" said the Very Large Alien.

. . .

"Just get on the ship. Get on the ship and go. Just get the hell out of here."

Cole wiped his nostrils and held his hand up to his one functioning eye to confirm that his nose was still bleeding from when the Very Large Alien had casually flicked him with a Very Large Finger.

He was limping doggedly toward the S'Port. It would be dawn in two hours, but he'd be gone long before then, even if he was going alone. Maybe Kenneth would find him, but by then he'd either have the money, or be better prepared.

He could see the public S'Port just a few hundred meters ahead. Crafts of all shapes and sizes hovered on their mooring lines. His was a Peerson 27: two cabins, a small galley, small head with shower, some storage space for hauling cargo, a cramped but serviceable cockpit. Nothing special.

Well, something special: a BendBox 4600.

Completely unlicensed, completely illegal. Disguised as a Bend-Box 2300, the kind they let private citizens use if they were well-behaved shareholders and paid their taxes on time. The 4600 was capable of more than just interplanetary bends within a single solar system. You could bend your way to pretty much any spot in the galaxy with a BendBox 4600. Better yet, it sent out a spurious end-user bend signal, meaning they'd never track who you were or where you went.

When Cole left he'd be gone for good.

There it was, his Peerson 27, moored at a meter. He felt a warm wave of relief well up and carry him along the last few steps.

He reached the meter just as it hit zero and turned red. He let out a wheezing chuckle.

"Just in time," he said. "Hee hee. Just in time."

Then the siren sounded and the patrolbot was there.

"No!" said Cole. "*No!* I'm here!"

"Meter expired."

"Wait!"

The brief burst of light was so intense it burned an afterimage even on his shuttered right eye. When the colored blobs finally dissipated and he could see again, the patrolbot was gone and Cole was holding a small jar filled with gray dust. Peerson 27 dust.

"Hi!" chirruped a personal pop-up. "Are you in the market for a new spaceship?"

4

Less than two hours until sunrise. Less than two hours until Kenneth found him and his gray matter became the very first meal that Kenneth's young would enjoy.

Cole was back in Magma. He sat in a darkened corner booth, staring idly off into space. He was sipping his third Flaming Reentry, the alcohol burning in his stomach like the lava beneath him. Running a tab. Why not?

"I'm shorry about hitting you with the ring," he slurred to the Very Large Alien, who was crammed into the booth across from him. "Women, huh?"

"Raaaawwrrr!" said the Very Large Alien.

"You said it. If I wasn't going to be a zombie in two hours it would really bother me."

He hadn't really loved Samantha. He knew that now. Actually, he knew it when he was pleading with Kenneth. But he hadn't been lying, exactly. He *was* in love.

He'd been in love for a very long time. Years and years, now. And it was the sort of love that he'd described to Kenneth, the sort he'd wished he'd had with Samantha but knew he didn't—the take-your-breath-away kind of love, the endless-happy-possibilities-of-a spring-day kind, the make you write bad poetry and enjoy sappy songs and not care and stay awake all night with a desperate, desperate longing eating-away-at-your-very-core kind.

Samantha wasn't the object of that love; she never had been. That's doubtless what Kenneth had somehow sensed. But the woman who *was* the object of that love—the only woman Cole had ever loved like that, he saw now—was gone. Forever.

As for Tangy, well, that hurt. He'd trusted him. They'd adventured and smuggled and gambled and drank their way across most of the sponsored universe together. Tangy was a good navigator, knew how to tell a good joke, and was surprisingly effective in a bar fight—he'd feint low, and then *wham!* he'd come over the top with three simultaneous overhand rights. Half of his opponents went down in midlaugh.

On the other hand, Tangy drank prodigiously, he never did his aboard-ship chores, and . . . what was the other thing? Oh, right. He was cheating on Cole with Cole's girlfriend.

He thought again about the woman he had loved. Still loved. Would always love. A girl, really, when he knew her, and he hadn't been much more than a boy. He saw her dark hair, her smile, remembered the sense of tranquillity he felt around her. He thought of them, two teenagers lying on their backs in the deserted park, staring up at star-filled night sky, hearing her say *I have faith in you.*

I have faith in you.

The first and last time anyone had ever said that. He took another drink.

Thinking about her made him think about his aunt and uncle, who did their level best—or level medium—to raise him after his parents died. He could picture his aunt and uncle now, sitting on the back deck, smacking their lips over an evening repast of instant Fud and smug self-satisfaction, inordinately proud of their waterfront view, as if theirs were the only dwelling on Longest Island with one. Except everyone had one; that was the point. That's why people lived on the planet, engineered with its narrow strip of land that ran in a spiral from pole to pole, divided up into endlessly repeating identical segments: houses-park-school-mallmallmall, houses-park-school-mallmallmall. . . .

You could run away and you'd end up in exactly the same place, the surroundings interchangeable, the inhabitants nearly so. Cole knew it because he'd done it. Several times. He'd end up back in his room again, moodily smoking whatever he could get his hands on, the sole source of light in the room the faint radioactive glow coming from the commemorative chunk of Earth in its crystal cube, inscribed with the famous quote from the Administration. AT LEAST WE GOT THE TERRORISTS, it said.

When he was younger he'd begged his aunt and uncle to take

him to another area, someplace new. "Braemar Grove?" his uncle would ask. "Edina Hills? Whatever for? Why go there? What have they got that we don't?"

Nothing, that's what.

Go on a vacation, where would you go? St. Floridale, the sister planet to Longest Island. The exact same setup, the spiral of land from north to south, except the houses were all done up in pastels and the planet was a quarter diameter closer to the local sun so that it was a bit warmer.

Cole was out of there by age seventeen, off to join the Unified Command Space Marines.

Cole's bunkmate in basic training was a kid named Farley from one of the ag planets. "I don't know why they call it the space marines," Farley said. "I mean, if you think about it? *Marine* means water, and *space* is just space. It's a total oxymoron."

This was a very important revelation for Farley.

"Lights out, space marines!" The sergeant would bellow, and Farley would whisper, "I don't know why they call it the space marines. . . ."

"Come on, space marines, step it up!"

"I don't know why they call it the space marines. . . ."

"Space marines, ten*hut*!"

"I don't know why they call it—"

Cole was gone by the second week of basic.

What had happened since he'd left the oxymoronic space marines? Everything. And what had he achieved? Nothing. And very soon he'd *be* nothing.

The crowd had thinned out since he'd been there the first time, the dance floor mostly empty. The nearby booths were vacant, except for a table of humans sitting somewhere to the left of Cole.

They were speaking in hushed tones, barely audible above the murmuring lounge music. One woman seemed to be doing most of the talking. Cole ignored them, until a piece of the conversation got through the mushy haze of alcohol and caught his attention.

"The cargo is none of your business." It was the woman talking. "We just need to get out of this system now."

Cole shifted in his seat so that he could turn and look at them. There were three of them: the woman and two men. The woman was young and attractive: short dark hair, petite, but even from where he was sitting Cole could sense the hardness of her personality. Next to her was a young man with longish curly hair and a beard, hanging on her every word. He had an earnestness about him, but not like that of the kid in the alley—what was his name? Jesus? Josepoop? This one's earnestness was of the self-serving and immediately annoying variety.

The second man was strongly built, very handsome, sandy hair, sort of familiar . . . holy farg. Teg. It was farging Teg.

"Farging Teg," muttered Cole. He could hear him talking:

"It'll cost you. A lot."

Look at that lucky, lucky bastard. Farging Teg.

"We don't have a lot of money," the woman was saying now. "But there could be . . . other rewards."

The weak-faced earnest guy seemed horrified. Teg was grinning in a predatory manner.

"Meet me at the S'Port in two hours," said Teg. "Space J-24 in the Zebra lot."

It wasn't hard for Cole to find him. When Cole was riding the lift up from Magma a couple materialized next to him, conversing excitedly.

"It's amazing," said the beautiful woman.

"I know," said the handsome man.

"Teg, staying right there at our hotel, the Interstar Galax," gushed the woman.

"Yes, the famous space adventurer Teg, staying in one of the luxurious suites at the Interstar Galax!" responded the man.

"Maybe he'll be enjoying the spectacular dining facilities, including the . . ."

Cole ground his teeth and tried to tune out as the promo holograms continued their patter. The elevator arrived on his floor.

"It's fabulous!" the woman was saying. "Teg! He's so handsome!"

"He's not that handsome," said Cole as the door closed.

"I'm feeling like you might have some alignment issues, especially here toward the lower vertebrae. How have you got your cockpit set up? Is it possible you've got your control yoke positioned too low?"

The massagebot was busily kneading and rubbing Teg, who was sprawled out on the table, naked, a cigar still in his mouth. Cole could see him clearly from the hall through the suite's doorless doorway, one of the more extreme manifestations of the Interstar's starkly minimalist design scheme.

Cole slipped inside the suite noiselessly, unobserved, one more silent shadow in the dimly lit room. It was a corner suite, and the two outer walls were windows, the Bourse glowing in a grid far below.

"Happy ending, sir?" inquired the massagebot to Teg.

"Skip it. Unless you're into watching that sort of thing, Cole."

Cole jumped, knocking over the small side table with the ice bucket and champagne on it. Champagne glugged out onto the thick carpeting and Cole's foot.

"Oh, hey Teg! Good to see you. All of you." He bent to retrieve the champagne bottle.

"Don't bother," said Teg. He still appeared to have his eyes closed. "There's some better stuff over there on the bar, if you want."

Cole hesitated, then went to the bar, his boot squishing slightly with each step. He picked up the bottle of scotch.

"This is two hundred and twelve years old, Teg."

"Yeah, I got about ten cases of the stuff left over from the West-Corp run. Go ahead, have some."

Cole paused, then poured some into a shot glass. He sipped. Exquisite. Farging Teg.

He sipped again, trying to formulate his request. The massagebot ignored Cole, its four hands working away silently. Cole couldn't help staring at Teg—the tan, the perfect body, the prototypical jaw. Literally—it was patented. It was one of the most popular implants for men, and surprisingly for women, too. Farging Teg.

"Spotted you in the bar," said Teg.

"You did?"

"Hard not to. You were singing."

"I was?"

"Yep. What's that song? 'You tore my heart a new one'?"

"Teg—"

"You're not coming along, Cole. I don't need that kind of heat."

"Teg, please, I'm in trouble something awful. Please. Please please please please please. Don't make me beg."

"You are begging."

"Then don't make me cry!"

"You are crying."

"It's the smoke!"

Cole tossed back the rest of the drink, went to refill the shot glass, then took a hit directly from the bottle instead.

"Sorry, Cole. I can't help you. But go ahead—you can keep the bottle."

"Thanks. Thanks a lot."

Cole recorked the whiskey and turned to leave.

"See you, Teg."

"Good luck, Cole." Teg still had his eyes closed. "A little to the left, by the shoulder blade," said Teg.

"Yes sir," said the massagebot.

"Perrrfect."

Cole swung the bottle in a short, tight arc, aiming for the vulnerable spot directly behind Teg's left ear.

Thud.

The bottle rebounded harmlessly off the massage table, Teg jerking his head away just in time. He was instantly on his feet.

Cole stepped back, guiltily clutching the bottle.

Teg shook his head, his expression one of sorrowful incomprehension.

"Cole . . ."

"I'm sorry," said Cole. "I don't know what came over me."

Teg chuckled. "Sheesh, Cole, you're really—"

Cole swung at him again.

Teg ducked, the bottle whistling over his head.

The two faced each other.

"Oops?" said Cole hopefully.

Teg rocketed straight at Cole.

"Teg! Wait! I'm sor—!"

Teg slugged him. It was not a particularly new experience for Cole to be on the receiving end of a punch. He had to admit that Teg knew what he was doing.

Teg was coming at him again. "Teg, you're naked!" said Cole. Teg punched him a second time, Cole hearing it more than feeling it. He staggered back into the embrace of the massagebot, which began to vigorously realign his muscles.

"Ow! Ow!" protested Cole.

"You seem very tense, sir," said the massagebot.

"Teg, you got this thing set too high—" Teg hit him a third time, in the stomach.

"Oof," oofed Cole. He wanted to double over in pain, but couldn't extricate himself from the robot's grip.

"Teg . . . I'm sorry," he managed.

"Me too, Cole. Me, too."

He grabbed Cole in some sort of complicated hold, preparing to dislocate his everything.

There was a horrible cracking, popping noise. Cole closed his eye, waiting for the pain to come.

It didn't. He opened his eye. Teg was standing in front of him, his face frozen in a mask of surprise and agony.

"Arrggh!" said Teg. "My *back*!"

Then Teg toppled over like a statue.

5

Cole drove as quickly as he dared, staying precisely at the speed limit as he roared down the streets of the Bourse on Teg's motorcycle. It had a standard Fezner drive, completely clean and silent, but Teg had it outfitted with a device that pumped out noxious, choking fumes, as well as a noise generator to simulate the sound of an ancient internal combustion engine.

He checked his, or rather Teg's, watch. Kenneth would start looking for him in less than twenty minutes.

Pedestrians waved and shouted mistaken greetings to him, recognizing the bike with its distinctive sponsorship decals. Cole was wearing Teg's roomy jacket, also plastered with ad patches, his face hidden by the mirrored visor of Teg's helmet. He waved back a few times.

Cole spotted Teg's sleek spaceship immediately. If anything, it had even more sponsorship decals than the motorcycle, the actual surface of the gigantic Benedict 80 almost entirely obscured.

The Earnest Man and the Hard Woman from the bar were waiting underneath the craft, standing next to several large shipping crates. Cole hurtled up to them and leaped off the still-moving motorcycle.

"Teg?" said the woman.

Cole ignored her and the minor explosion caused when the motorcycle slammed into a nearby safety barrier. He jabbed a button on a remote—*bleep!*—and the passenger ramp instantly descended from the ship to the ground.

He raced up the ramp, still wearing the helmet, the man and the woman right behind him.

"Hey!" said the woman. "Teg! Hey! Wait!"

"I told you!" Cole heard Earnest Man say.

Kenneth was quite pleased with his suite at the S'Port Hotel: the saline levels and PH balance of the water were perfect; the coral was live, not simulated. He was completely submerged, finishing up his fourth Savlu clam, crunching effortlessly through the twelve-inch, rock-hard shell, when the indicator light on the tiny tracking device lit up. The device was beeping.

"Oh, goody," said Kenneth. "He's running!"

Cole was already firing up the engines when Hard Woman and Earnest Man caught up to him in the cockpit.

"Teg. Teg! What's going on? What about the cargo?" she said as Cole fast-forwarded through the preflight checklist.

"Forget the cargo," said Cole, his voice muffled by the helmet. "We're leaving."

"See?" said Earnest Man, "I told you we couldn't trust him!"

Cole was mentally renaming him Whiny Man when he heard a distinctive *clickclack.*

He turned. Hard Woman was targeting him with a Hard Expression. She was also targeting him with a Firestick 9 ("Small Holes—But Deep Holes").

"Argh!" said Cole.

She kept the gun trained on him as he and Whiny Man loaded the crates onto the lowered cargo platform.

"We really don't have time for this," he said to her. She ignored him.

"We really don't have time for this," he repeated. "We *really*—"

"If you say that again, I will *really* shoot you."

"—don't have time for this," Cole finished under his breath after he turned his back.

Whiny Man seemed determined to justify Cole's internal nickname for him, struggling with his end of the crates and complaining about splinters and why didn't they have a bot to help them. Cole looked at his watch again. His time was up. Kenneth was no doubt looking for him right now.

They shoved the last crate on the cargo platform. Cole cinched the straps to hold it in place, then jabbed the button to raise the platform into the belly of the Benedict.

"All right, let's go!" he said, sprinting past the Hard Woman back up the ramp.

Cole hopped into the seat in the cockpit, hit the button to reseal the air locks, and fired up the engines.

"Oh *yeah*," he breathed, feeling the comforting hum as they came on line. "You better strap in," he said to the other two, who had followed him back into the cockpit. It was a handsome room—smooth, curvilinear walls with a nice white finish, blond wood highlights, recessed illumination. Cole wasn't a huge fan of carpeting in cockpits, but the muted neutral tones did subtly play off the lighting and the small framed lithographs, creating a sense of quiet luxury, just like the profile in *SpaceCruiser Monthly* said.

The Benedict 80 control panel was appropriately tasteful. It was also more complicated than he'd expected. Where was the RQ compensator? There? He twisted a knob. An alarm bell sounded somewhere. No.

"He was going to leave the cargo! I told you!" said Whiny Man.

"He's not Teg," said Hard Woman. "You're not Teg. Take off your helmet."

"I'm a bit preoccupied right now."

The lights and dials swam before him. He shook his head, trying to clear it, then realized that Teg's ship had an ergonomics autosensor and was trying to calibrate his morphology and movements and adjust the control positions accordingly.

"Stop moving around!" he said. The controls froze in a random position.

Another button. Nothing.

"Who are you?!" said Whiny Man.

"I'm busy, that's who I am!"

"Take off your helmet!" said Hard Woman.

There was the RQ compensator. He flicked the switch. There was a distant *whoosh*ing noise.

"Septic tank evacuation complete," said the computer. That wasn't the RQ compensator.

"Take off your—"

"All right!"

Cole pulled at the helmet, nearly taking his head off with it before he determined that the chin strap was still fastened. When he removed the helmet both the man and the woman staggered back a step in shock.

"You're not Teg!" said Whiny Man. "Are you?"

Cole caught a glance of himself in the reflective visor of the helmet. Seeing the condition of his face, he understood Whiny Man's confusion. He tossed the helmet to him.

"Teg hurt his back. I'm his second in command," said Cole. What did this switch do?

"RQ compensator engaged."

Yes.

The Benedict 80 started to rise unsteadily off the tarmac.

"We're not going anywhere with you, pal," said Hard Woman.

"Look, can you fly this thing?"

She glared back at him. He turned to Whiny Man. "How about you?"

Whiny Man dropped his gaze. "I didn't think so," said Cole. "Well, as you can see, I can."

There was a crashing, screeching noise as they scraped along the side of another parked spacecraft. The other two stumbled, nearly falling. Cole hurriedly readjusted the controls, and they started to rise above the S'Port and the city.

Hardy and Whiny dragged themselves to the unoccupied seats and strapped in. Hard Woman was still pointing the gun at Cole.

"You're going to land this thing."

"Uh-huh. You're going to shoot me and make us crash?"

"Five," she said.

"Oh, stop it."

"Four," she said.

"I'm telling you, save your breath. You can't bluff—"

"Three."

"You're *not* going to shoot me."

She placed her other hand on the gun to steady her aim.

"Two."

"Hold on now, hold on, let's talk about this—"

Bam! The explosion shook the ship, the concussion stunning them, the noise setting Cole's ears ringing. Red lights flashed. Alarms whooped. Whiny Man said, *"Eeeeee!"*

"What the hell was that?" asked Hard Woman.

Cole looked at a blip on the display and swore.

"That," he said, "is Kenneth."

6

"Yrnameer is less a location than an idea," said Stirling, to general nodding and noises that signaled concurrence. Stirling was pleased. He wasn't quite sure that he believed his own statement, or even understood it, but it was the first time he'd dared to make a contribution to the Moonday evening discussion, and it was nice to have it both acknowledged and taken seriously.

"Yes, but I'd like to offer a refinement," said Orwa. Stirling grimaced, or at least would have, if he were in his old body. Hard to grimace now in his new form.

"Yrnameer," continued Orwa, "is both locality and idea, in fact idea qua locality, a place-conception whose very ontology has been realized and made manifest precisely through the act of conceptualization," added Orwa, "as if by the process of protoideation it has occasioned its own essentialism."

More nodding and noises from the ten other participants. Stirling resisted rolling his eyes. That was one thing that he could still do in his new body, but with lidless eyes the size of billiard balls it was hard to do so with any degree of subtlety.

"While I agree to a certain extent, I have to take issue with your post-Apsian analysis." This was Reff, who had considerably more cognitive capacity than one might expect from what appeared to be a thick purple shag rug.

"Cluck," said the chicken.

Stirling wasn't sure about the chicken, who attended each session and never contributed anything beyond that simple vocalization. But no one else ever commented on it, so he wasn't going to start.

Stirling rose to his several feet and leaned in to take the bowl off the table. "I'm gonna get some more chips," he said. "Anyone need anything? Orwa? You want a beer, Souff? Mayor? Beer?"

"I'll take another beer," said Mayor Kimber, a rumpled, genial type with gray hair and a furrowed brow.

"You got it."

Stirling trundled into the kitchen area carrying the chip bowl and a few empties. He'd been hosting the salon for about six weeks now, and generally enjoyed it—it was certainly different from anything he'd ever done before—but *man,* could those guys talk. Especially Orwa, who could be a real bag of hot wind, and Stirling wasn't just thinking of Orwa's appearance, what with all the translucent gas bladders and everything. Not that Stirling would make fun of how anyone looked—he was looking pretty weird himself these days. But it was worth it.

He dumped some more chips into the bowl, and grabbed a few fresh beers from the fridge. One thing was for sure—four arms were better than two when you were hosting. He could have gotten one of the servicebots to help him out, but the folks in Yrnameer could get a little preachy about relying too much on technology. Not that anyone complained about gathering in his climate-controlled living room and drinking his cold beer.

Again, he didn't mind. He liked them all, even Orwa. It made sense for him to host the gathering: his house, set back on a cul-de-sac, was easily the largest in the community. When Stirling had shown up he had a team of constructionbots that built his home in just over a day. There'd been some frowns and muttering, but folks mostly welcomed him. He brought along a vast surplus of supplies—tools, building materials, protozoac solar panels—and he shared everything freely. No one asked him any uncomfortable questions, not even when he burned his spaceship.

He reached back over his shoulder and pried open a beer on his carapace. There was *another* advantage of being a sembluk instead of a human. When you thought about it, it was strange: you had, on the one hand, your standard human being. On the other hand, you had a sembluk, with a body like a four-legged, four-armed slug, three big eyes, and a shell on its back; and yet if you looked at the DNA, the two species were nearly indistinguishable. Closer even then humans and chimps, or sembluks and gembluks. Alter a few select locations on the human genome, and you got a massive and dramatic transformation. And how many other extensive mods could you do without ending up like all those poor slobs on Qualtek 3, turn yourself into a cannibal? None, that's how many.

If you wanted to get away from it all, and you weren't particularly bothered by the idea of becoming a gastropod, it was ideal.

He thought about going to the back room to check on his treasure. The tiny object was his only link to his past life, before he'd thrown it all away, gotten rid of all of his riches. Before he'd decided to live a simpler, more spiritual life—inquisitive instead of acquisitive, as he liked to think of it. Out of the spotlight, anonymous.

"Geldar!" It was a voice from the other room, probably Mayor Kimber. Geldar was how they knew him here. "Where's the chips?"

"I'm coming, I'm coming," he shouted back. Forget it. He'd check on his treasure later. In a few hours everyone would be content, sated from a feast of inquiry into the nature of Truth and Happiness and Beauty. His guests would head home, their minds already forming their arguments for next week's gathering, and Stirling would go spend some quality time with the diamond.

The Bad Men were almost across the plains.

They weren't coming for the diamond. They didn't know about it. What they did know is that the people of Yrnameer had food.

They knew it because the villagers had given it to the bandits two years ago, when the bandits' stolen spaceship crashed and burned a few short kilometers from the community. The village virtually emptied as the citizens rushed to help, rescuing those caught in the wreckage and treating the many injured. They took them in and fed them. They helped them bury their dead. They didn't know whom they were helping or where they were from. They didn't ask. That wasn't their way.

Runk, still injured and stupefied from the crash and fearing pursuit, ordered his men to move on after a few short days. The people of Yrnameer sent them on their way with a generous helping of their own harvest, enough to last for months. And after a while they forgot about Runk and his bandits.

Runk and his bandits didn't forget about them.

A hard, lean year of living off the land passed, and another was looming. Runk decided there was an easier way to fill their bellies.

He knew it was likely that, if asked, the people of Yrnameer would willingly share what they had. But what's the point of being bad if you're not being bad?

So the Bad Men were moving grimly toward Yrnameer with their message. They were traveling faster then they had expected, mostly due to the fact that there were only nine of them left. The most recent casualty had been a terrible rider who had slowed them down.

It had happened the previous evening when they stopped to make camp. They had been lucky enough to find a small grove of Oni trees, whose bright red fruit was packed with nutrients. The fruit was best cooked, but lacking the means to ignite the temperamental Krager stove, they ate them raw. That was fine: the fruit could be enjoyed either way—unless you were Taknean. If you were Taknean, you had to cook the Oni fruit thoroughly to destroy a certain rare protein, or you were essentially eating a deliciously sweet, fist-size suicide pill.

The tenth Bad Man was Taknean. He didn't know about the protein.

The others roared with laughter as he leaped up from the rock he had been sitting on and ran giggling in circles, flapping his triple-jointed arms. They laughed even harder as he began manically describing the instructions he was receiving from the giant, invisible filbert, apparently a female.

"She's right there!" he babbled. "And she needs me to reshingle her schnauzer's chewing-gum hat!"

He then seized a stick and commenced furiously scribbling something in the dirt, underlining and circling certain parts with great vigor.

"There," he said with evident satisfaction, "that's better."

Then he collapsed, dead.

Later on, a tumbleweeg, looking for all intents and purposes like a large ball of dried twigs, was carried by the wind past the scribbles. Huh, thought the tumbleweeg, whose name was Reg, that looks like a pretty viable solution to the Riemann hypothesis. I really should mention this to someone, thought Reg, and then the wind blew him away and he forgot about it, as he had a tendency to do.

No one would have been more surprised than the dead Taknean—who had trouble counting to three on his three digits—

that his scribbles would have earned him a Fields Medal for Mathematics. It's doubtful his companions would have cared even if they'd known about his achievement—they were more concerned with the fact that he'd crushed the compass when he fell, and they made their displeasure known with several pointless kicks to his insensate corpse. Then they rode on.

7

"Who is Ken—" said Hard Woman, and then they were jolted sideways as another violent explosion shook the ship.

The RO communicator crackled to life.

"Hello, Teg," said Kenneth. "Sorry about that. Just a warning shot to let you know I'm serious. I'm a *huuuge* fan, you know."

"He's flying a lobster," said Whiny. He seemed somewhat dazed.

Cole glanced at the three-dimensional display. Kenneth's ship did look very much like a lobster.

"So, Teg," said Kenneth, "it would be quite helpful if you'd hand over Cole—Karg is very cross with him."

"Are you Cole?" asked Hard Woman.

"Absolutely not," said Cole.

Hard Woman grabbed the communicator handset.

"Listen. Cole is here. I don't know who the farg you are or what you want, but believe me, we'd be very happy to hand over—"

Cole tore the handset from her grip and smashed it several times against the control panel.

"Hey!"

"I'm sorry, I didn't quite catch that," came Kenneth's voice. Cole smashed it again. "Please repeat—"

Smash.

"—your previous—"

Smash.

"—transmission."

Smash smash smash.

"Give me the transmitter," said Hard Woman. She had the gun out again.

Cole sighed, hesitated, went to hand it to her, then abruptly smashed it a few more times.

"*Hey!* Hand it over!"

He did.

"Hold on," he said as she was raising the handset up to speak. "Before you say anything, just hear me out."

"Hi, Teg," interrupted Kenneth. "Kenneth here again. Like I said, I'm a *huuuge* fan, but I'm going to have to put a cannon round right through your ship if you don't answer me soon."

Hard Woman went to speak again.

"Just listen. Just for a moment," said Cole. She paused, the handset to her mouth. "Okay?"

She nodded, a single, terse movement.

"Okay," said Cole. He hurriedly unstrapped himself from the seat and stood, the gun following him.

"What are you doing?"

"I have to find something," he said, his hands moving with a rough, desperate haste as he scrabbled at his scalp, felt around his ears, his neck, up and down his arms, his trunk. "If you hand me over to him, he'll kill me."

"And?" she said.

Not the response he was looking for.

"Well, he . . . might kill you, too."

"Why would he do that?"

"Because, he, I . . . Look. I'm a really good pilot," he said, his hands still searching. "I need to get out of here. You need to get somewhere. I can get you to that somewhere while getting me out of here."

"Okay, I'm arming another round," said Kenneth.

"I say we hand him over," said Whiny.

"Sorry, we've been having some radio trouble," said Hard Woman into the handset. "We'll be right with you." She spun back to Cole. "Look, friend, do you have a—oh, God."

Cole now had both hands down his pants and was rooting around energetically. "A plan! Yes, a plan! I have one!" he said. "I just have to find—*ha!*"

"Find what?!"

"*Arrrr—!*" said Cole, his face contorting with painful effort as he pulled at something on his buttocks.

"Hello?" said Kenneth.

"—*rrrrrr*—!"

"I'm going to count to three," said Kenneth. "One—"

"—*aarrrrghh!*" continued Cole, and then something evidently tore free, and he yanked his hand out of his pants triumphantly. "Find *this*," he said, and held up a tiny barbed device. "Farger put a tracer on me." He put it on the floor of the cockpit, grabbed the helmet, and slammed it heavily on the tracer.

"Two—"

Cole jumped back into his seat and strapped himself in. "Handset," he said to the woman. "Give me the handset! Please."

She handed it to him.

"Three."

"Kenneth! It's Cole!"

"Oh, hi! Are you coming over?"

"I am. I'll be right there."

Then Cole hit the silver button he'd spotted on the control board and punched the accelerator as far as it would go.

Those watching Teg's ship from the air or the ground witnessed something miraculous and very expensive: Teg's Benedict 80 suddenly became twelve separate Benedict 80s, each accelerating away in a different direction. This was no standard holo display—there was no green shift along the edges, none of that Bayne patching; each ship appeared to reflect the sun and cast a shadow; better yet, each ship was transmitting a standard ID signal to the traffic control system.

Farging Teg. He could afford the best.

The news feeds were immediately running footage of the incident, the reports all featuring the same winking tone—guess what that naughty rascal Teg is up to now! Over the next few days voices would be raised, editorializing against the elevation of criminals to celebrity status and about the general coarsening of public behavior, but those voices were easily drowned out by the sound of high fives or eights or so on emanating from the galaxy's boardrooms, as Teg's numerous sponsors celebrated their prescience and the momentary bump their stock prices got.

Kenneth, however, was not pleased. His reaction was to slam a claw down in rage and say something shocking and horrible in his own language. To the untrained ear it sounded very pleasant.

. . .

The Benedict 80 bucked and rattled as they rocketed out of the atmosphere at emergency ascent velocity. The G forces jammed them deep into their seats, making it impossible to move or talk, making it hard even to breathe. It was, Cole had to admit, the comfiest, cushiest G seat he'd ever sat in, the kind of seat that automatically monitored your blood flow and squeezed your extremities to direct the oxygen to your brain instead of to your toes and fingertips. Good ol' farging Teg.

They punched through the cloud layers, higher and higher, until they were looking at the blackness of space and the stars and gravity stopped clawing at them.

Cole took a deep gulp of air and shook his head, feeling his circulation return.

"What happened?" asked Hard Woman. "Is he gone?"

"Not for long. We have to bend our way out of this system ASAP. Just have to make sure the bendbox is charged, which"—he checked a display—"of course it's not. Perfect."

He unbuckled his straps, floating free from his seat.

"Where are you going?"

"The bendbox isn't charging, and if the bendbox doesn't charge, we can't bend—"

"I get it."

"—and then Kenneth is going to find us, and if he does—"

"I get it."

"Aren't we going to reconform, so that we can get some gravity going here?" said Whiny Man, who now looked like Nauseous Whiny Man.

"No time. Can't slow down."

Cole propelled himself out of the cockpit and floated down the main central corridor. Behind him he could hear Hard Woman undoing her safety straps.

"Hey!" she said, following him. "Hey! Who the hell are you?"

"My name's Cole."

Passageways of different shapes and sizes branched off from the corridor. They followed the basic theme of the cockpit—smooth, white walls with subtle lighting; tasteful prints. The floors here were a mix of carpeting and HardWud, tougher than the toughest steel. He grabbed the handrail and pulled himself around a corner, taking what was for him a right turn. She followed.

"Yes, I'm already aware of your name. I'd like some answers, Mr. Cole."

"Just Cole."

He reached another intersection and propelled himself upward. Kenneth would be monitoring the traffic signals, waiting to see if the Benedict had bent. Until he overheard a bend notification indicating that the ship was gone, he'd be doing a sky survey, one slice at a time, trying to find the ship. If Cole was unlucky, Kenneth would guess right on the first few tries and spot them quickly. Considering how things had been going, Cole was fairly certain that he'd be unlucky.

"Well, you need to give me an explanation, Cole."

"What I need to do is find the bendbox."

It wasn't here. He pushed off in another direction, then turned another corner, passed through an intersection, and headed downward at another branch. The more time they had before Kenneth spotted them, the faster they'd be going, meaning they'd be farther away, meaning he'd have a harder time spotting them, meaning they'd have more time to charge the bendbox, meaning maybe they'd escape.

"How come Teg never mentioned you?" Her voice came now from behind him, or maybe to his left.

The Benedict 80 was fast. But Kenneth's ship was undoubtedly one of those zippy little interceptor-class deals, and it would probably be armed with some sort of missile that could go from 0 to 60 percent of light speed in about two seconds. No matter how fast the Benedict was, it couldn't outrun that.

"Do you see anything resembling a bendbox?" he asked.

"No," she said. "Where are you?" she added impatiently.

"I'm over he—" he said as he rounded a corner at a healthy float and plowed directly into her. They grabbed at each other reflexively, tumbling in a clinch along the corridor, bouncing gently off the walls.

"Hi," he said when they came to a rest. He was not addressing her face.

"You can let go of me now."

"Right."

They disentangled themselves, she somewhat more roughly than necessary, sending him sailing backward across the corridor.

"Hey!" he said, as his head bonked against a steel access panel.

"Sorry," she said, her tone intimating she wasn't.

"No, 'hey,' as in, 'hey,' we found it." He pointed to the access panel, which had popped open from the impact. He whistled.

"What?" she asked.

"A 5200. Never seen one before."

The cubelike unit was about the size of a dishwasher, the front an attractive panel of brushed aluminum. Across the top a sans serif font read, BENDTRONIX 5200: GET BENT!

"I love you, Teg," muttered Cole. "Reset button. Where's the reset button?"

"What was that back there, with the shooting?" asked Hard Woman.

"I told you," he said, distracted, running his hands over the smooth surface of the Bendtronix. "That was Kenneth. And that was more my problem than yours."

"Well, clearly it *is* our problem, so if you could tell me a bit more—"

"Greetings!" interrupted the bendbox. "Welcome to the Bendtronix 5200!" Music started, a chorus of smiling female voices. "For travelers it's heaven-sent / let us help you go get bent!"

"Shut up!" said Cole.

"What?!" said Hard Woman.

"Not you." He smacked the Bendtronix. The music stopped.

"What happened to your face?" she asked. "You get beaten up in some alley?"

"Beaten up? In an *alley*?" he sputtered, turning to her. "Me? Listen: if there's an alley, if there's beating, beating up, if anyone—I'm the one who does any beating up that might happen to occur in any alleys," he finally managed. "Shut *up*!" he repeated, thumping the bendbox again, cutting off the music that had restarted. He checked the indicator lights. "All right, that should do it."

He brushed past her to retrace his path back to the cockpit, muttering about beatings and alleys.

"Hey," she shouted after him as he disappeared around the corner. He ignored her. "Hey!" she repeated. "That's the wrong way."

He reappeared and pushed past her in the other direction without a glance. This time she followed.

"Buddy, you had better start giving me some answers."

Without stopping he said, "What's your name?"

The question seemed to surprise her. She hesitated a moment before answering. "Nora."

Now he turned so that he was floating backward, facing her. "You are an extremely attractive woman, Nora. You shouldn't scowl so much—you get all these lines up here around the eyes." He twisted to face forward once more, pulling at a handhold to accelerate again.

"You're not going to give me anything, are you," she called after him.

"I just gave you some very good advice," said Cole, rounding a corner.

She kicked off the wall at the intersection for a burst of speed, moving nearly even with him.

"Okay," she said, "let me take a stab at it. First off, I stand by my statement about you getting beaten up in some alley. Why? I'd guess that you've probably done something extraordinarily stupid, and you now owe a large amount of money to the wrong person."

Cole found another handhold and flung himself forward, pulling away again. "Except it's too late now," she continued, pursuing him, "and all you've got left to do is run and keep running and pray to God that they don't catch you. Right?"

He kept going.

"I'm right, aren't I. Aren't I?"

She followed him into the cockpit, watching him make a show of intense concentration as he fiddled with the controls.

"Think you've got the bass adjusted properly on those speakers?" she asked. He stopped fiddling and took a closer look at the dials. Farg.

"Look at you," she said. "You know what you seem like? Like some guy who ends up with eggs laid in his brain."

"Oh, *yeah*?" he said as he spun around angrily to face her—a little too hard, actually, and then had to wait several rapid revolutions until he regained control and was facing her again.

"Oh, *yeah*?" he repeated, in case she missed it the first time. "Well . . ."

She waited, an eyebrow professionally arched.

"Well," he said again, searching for something. "Well," he said at last, "I'm all you've got."

The eyebrow slowly de-arched.

"Yes," she said. "I guess you are."

They examined each other. "You don't look like a smuggler," said Cole.

"We're not," said Whiny Guy.

Cole kept his gaze on her. "Who's he?"

"That's Philip."

Now Cole glanced over at him. Philip's face still had a greenish tinge to it that had, if anything, grown more threatening. Some people did not do well in zero G.

"Errrrp," belched Philip.

"Wonderful," said Cole. He turned back to Nora. "You hired Teg. You're smuggling something."

"We're with the Interstellar Relief Pro—" began Philip.

Nora interrupted him. "It doesn't matter who we're with," she said. "And you know what? I realize I don't care that much who you are or what you're running from. All I care about is that you honor Teg's original agreement with us."

"Where—*urp*—is Teg?" asked Philip.

"What's the destination?" Cole asked Nora.

She took a deep breath. "Yrnameer."

He stared blankly at her for a few moments.

"I'm sorry, did you say—"

"Yrnameer," she repeated.

Cole did some more blank staring. "You want to go to a *yrnameer*? There are no more yrnameers. The last yrnameer got a corporate sponsor, what, fifty years ago. Someone has taken all the Your Name Heres, and put their name there."

She shook her head. "We're not talking about just any yrnameer. We're talking about *the* Yrnameer. The very last unsponsored planet."

"Aw, c'mon. That place is a myth."

"No. It's real," she said.

"Computer!" said Cole. "Define planet Yrnameer!"

"Yrnameer is a mythical utopia, a planet said to exist in an unreachable location in space," said the affectless voice of the computer. "A contraction of *your name here,* a *yrnameer* originally referred to—"

"Thank you," said Cole. He turned to Nora.

"It's real," she repeated.

"How would you know? If it exists—and I'm not saying that it does—they say you can't even get there, that the bend calcs are too weird."

"We've both been there," said Nora.

"I don't believe you."

"It's true," said Philip. "And you should see it. It's so beautiful, so pure. There's no other place like it." His gaze was focused somewhere beyond Cole, beyond the confines of the cockpit. Off somewhere, thought Cole, playing in a meadow with bunnies and puppies and singing birds. *"Buurp,"* added Philip.

"Listen, Cole," said Nora, "it's pretty obvious you need a place to hide. And there's no better place than Yrnameer. And I'll admit it: we can't get there without you. It may not be a utopia, but at least there's none of this," she said distastefully, indicating the adsat that had been keeping pace with them, playing a beer commercial on its giant monitor.

"I love this ad!" said Cole. "Look at the chimp! Ha ha ha!"

Nora wasn't laughing. Cole stopped.

"What's your answer, Cole?"

"What's the cargo?"

She shook her head.

"All right, what's the fee?" he asked.

"Forty thousand New Dollars."

Forty thousand NDs! That was *twice* what he'd ever been paid for a run.

"Forty thousand NDs!" he said. "That's *half* what I usually get for a run."

"It's all we have," said Nora. "Forty thousand New Dollars or nothing."

Cole suppressed his desire to cackle with glee, channeling it into the thoughtful expression of a professional evaluating a complicated internal balance sheet. "Hmm," he said, to give the performance some weight.

He was half hoping that she would toss in a hint of other unspecified but clearly alluring benefits, like she'd done with Teg.

Farging Teg undoubtedly got that sort of thing all the time—at least that's what he was always insinuating in that men's magazine column of his, "Other Benefits with Teg." Not that Cole would ever take advantage of an offer like that. Ever.

"Would there be any, uh, other benefits?" he ventured hopefully.

She stared at him.

"The knowledge that you've contributed to a worthy cause," she said.

"Oh."

"So . . . ," she said.

He sighed. "I can't believe this place even exists," he said.

She held up a wee Zum Card.

"Bendspace course calcs," she said.

He took the drive from her and considered it for a few moments, turning it over in his fingers. He looked up. She was observing him again with her quiet, intense gaze, and to his own surprise he felt a tiny, warm jolt in his tummy. He looked away, then held up the Zum Card. "We're not gonna get broken with these, right?"

"They're valid calcs," she said.

Cole looked at Philip.

"Burrp."

Cole sighed again. Why not? Because the calcs might be off, and he might end up twisted into some horrid, impossible configuration, his body pretzeled hideously through an unknown number of dimensions, that's why not. Or he could find himself in an anomaly that would swallow him up, the Big Nothing closing in from all sides. On the other hand, stick around here long enough, and Kenneth would find him.

He inserted the Zum Card into the appropriate slot.

"As soon as the bendbox is charged up we'll bend."

Nora smiled, softening just the itsy-bitsiest bit, and Cole felt the little jolt again.

"Can we—*urrrp*—reconform now?" asked Philip.

"You know, they have stuff for G sickness," said Cole.

"I'm allergic," said Philip.

"Even to NoHerl?"

"Bad labor practices."

"Bad . . . ?"

"They don't hire any Shung."

"Shung? The Shung go berserk around machinery. They'd smash everything. *No one* hires any Shung."

"Let's just reconform!" said Philip.

"No. We reconform, we have to slow down, and what we need to do is keep going fast to charge the box."

"We're still in the fourth orbital layer," said Philip. "We're"—he paused to gulp—"speeding."

Cole looked at Nora. "Are you two, you know . . . ?" He made a suggestive gesture. "Because you could do a lot better."

"Uh-huh. Like you, I suppose," she said.

"I wouldn't go that far."

"I wouldn't go that far if we were the last two people in existence."

"Slow us down," said Philip.

"We can't slow down."

"You're putting all of us—*erp*—at risk!" said Philip. *"Burp!"*

"I know what I'm doing! Nothing's going to happen!"

Which is when the orbital patrolbot materialized outside the cockpit viewing window, a model similar to the one that had reduced Cole's Peerson 28 to an easy-to-carry gray powder.

"You were twelve pargins over the limit," announced the patbot over their radio, as it attached itself to the window with an air-lock skirt.

"You see? I told you," said Philip.

"Everyone just keep your mouths shut," hissed Cole tensely. "One wrong word and this could take hours, and we don't have hours."

The patbot was busily lasing a perfectly circular hole through the cockpit window.

"This is ridiculous. Why do they have to do it this way?" whispered Nora.

"The Payper lobby," said Cole. *"Ssh!"*

The patbot finished the hole. A mechanical arm extended into the cockpit through the gap and handed Cole a ticket.

"Three New Dollars," announced the ticket.

"Thank you, officer," said Cole.

"You're welcome!" said the patbot. "I'll repair your window now."

The three exchanged surprised glances.

"Is that it?" whispered Nora.

"It can't be," said Cole.

The patbot set about repairing the hole. "Sorry for the inconvenience, folks," it said.

"Not a problem, officer," said Cole cautiously. He took a closer look at the patbot. It was somewhat pockmarked and battered, like it had had an encounter with a cloud of space debris. Cole turned to Nora and gave her a little thumbs-up.

"I think it's been damaged. Maybe it's malfunctioning," he said.

She wasn't looking at him. She was looking past his shoulder at the patbot.

"I think you're right," she said.

Cole turned back to the patbot. It was now preparing to patch the circular hole with a replacement plate.

A square replacement plate.

Cole once again experienced the turd-quicksand-poisonous-biting-things sensation, this time at a greatly amplified intensity.

"Uh . . . officer?" said Cole, trying to sound calm. "That's the wrong patch. It's the wrong shape."

"Interfering with an officer of the law is a criminal offense," the patbot informed him, and continued with its work.

"But you're using the wrong piece!" said Nora.

"It doesn't fit!" said Cole.

"It's wrong!" said Nora.

"It's a square!" said Philip.

"It's wrong!" said Nora.

"It doesn't fit!" repeated Cole, except the patbot was ignoring them and still trying to cover a round hole with a square object whose diagonal width didn't quite equal the diameter of the circle, and Cole and Nora and Philip began waving their hands and shouting various permutations of "wrong!" and "piece!" and "not fit!" and "no no *no*!" with increasing volume and panic until Cole shouted, "You're going to make the cockpit *explode*!" and Philip said, *"Eeeeeeeeuuuurrrp!"*

Cole began to sweat.

He attacked the control board, switching switches, dialing dials, and butting buttons as fast as he could. Some of the buttons apparently hadn't gotten the message that he'd turned off the ergonomic auto-adjuster, and he had to chase them around the control board. "Stop it! Stay still!" he shouted at one of the air-lock controls, which was dodging back and forth, evading his stabbing finger.

"Officer! Officer!" Nora said. "I have your badge number! EJ-439! You'd better believe I'm going to file a report!"

"No, don't tell him that!" said Cole.

Without pausing in its task, the patbot jabbed another arm into the cockpit, depositing a thick sheaf of Payper in Nora's hands. "Greetings, shareholder," began the stack of Payper. "This is Form 29-32a, the official document for shareholders and citizens who wish to lodge a complaint regarding the patrol system, consistent with civil codes A9A-1427 and—"

Nora hurled the Payper away. The stack exploded into its component sheets, filling the cockpit with 127 pieces of Payper, all issuing instructions at once.

". . . After completing the description on page forty-two (maximum five hundred words) please . . ." ". . . this page serves as a reference for the other forms you may need . . ." ". . . please have this page notarized to indicate you've had the previous page notarized. . . ."

They swarmed around Cole, blocking his view. He batted and swatted them away, thinking fleetingly that this was an absolutely perfect metaphor for his life, and then he cracked his hand painfully on Teg's very solid helmet that had been hiding somewhere in the chattering cloud. No, he thought, *now* it's the perfect metaphor.

The patbot had positioned the square patch directly in the middle of the circle, no doubt with micromillimeter accuracy. Cole caught a whiff of the characteristic fresh citrus scent as the chemicals mixed and the catalyst welder flared, the edge of the circular hole glowing as the patbot traced its circumference with the device. Cole hoped he'd survive long enough to get the horrible tumors caused by that scent, one of the most powerful carcinogens in existence.

How much time until the patbot disconnected? Twenty seconds? Maybe, if they were lucky. Reroute the power, the flight controls, eject the Zum Card with the course calcs—probably fifteen seconds now—what else? What else? Life-support systems! Teg's helmet had rebounded off a wall somewhere and was back floating in front of his face. He shoved it away.

"We've got to get out of the cockpit and seal it off," he said to Nora and Philip without taking his eyes off the control panel. "When he disconnects, the vacuum's going to make the cockpit—"

From behind him he heard the heavy slam of the bulkhead door, and the *whir* as it sealed itself shut. Clearly Nora and Philip were way ahead of him in terms of getting out of the cockpit and sealing it shut, before the vacuum made it—

"Implode," Cole finished.

8

It was evening, the sky shading from cloudless blue to radiant pink to a dark, rich purple.

The eight remaining Bad Men had finally reached the edge of the rocky plains, the forest ahead of them. They were not the sort to appreciate the splendor of the sunset, especially in the mood they were in now: hungry, tired, and thirsty.

Without the compass it took them an extra two days to cross the plains. Along the way they'd lost another member of their party.

He'd been particularly enthusiastic about kicking the dead Taknean, and that enthusiasm had cost him: he had directed his final and hardest kick toward one of the spikier patches on the Taknean's torso, and one of those spikes had penetrated his thick boot and jabbed him in the toe.

He was feverish and complaining within a few hours. By the next morning they'd all grown so tired of him that they abandoned him near a wash with a thin trickle of water flowing through it, leaving him with some food, a weapon, and a promise to pick him up on the way back.

Even if they had intended to keep their word, it wouldn't have mattered. Upon their return they would have discovered his gleaming skeleton, the bones picked clean. It wasn't the fever that had killed him. It was the thousands of tiny beetlelike creatures that had swarmed over him at night.

So now there were eight of them, pitching camp as the light faded. One of them had managed to shoot a fat, furry animal that they'd come across, rooting in the dry dirt for tubers. It stood on its hind legs and stared at them stupidly, not used to predators, until it was struck by a bullet many times too powerful for the job at hand.

They gathered up the pieces they could find and tried unsuccessfully to start a fire. One finally grabbed the Krager stove and sat apart from the others, grumbling and swearing as he repeatedly pumped the plunger and twisted the two knobs and slid the slider thing.

There was a dull, concussive thud, and a small mushroom cloud rose from the spot where he had been sitting. And then there were seven Bad Men.

"Hey! *Hey!*" Cole pounded on the cockpit door with his fist, knowing they'd never hear him. The Payper swirled about him, still babbling instructions: "Before continuing to page thirteen, please make sure you've read and understood . . ." ". . . two copies must be made of this sheet, and submitted with . . ." ". . . this sheet has been left blank intentionally. This sheet has been left blank intentionally. . . ."

Cole spotted Teg's helmet, propelled himself to it, pushed off the ceiling, reached the door again. He pounded on it with the helmet. "Hey! Open up!!"

"Thank you for your cooperation." It was the patbot. It was about to disconnect the skirt that sealed the robot to the window, and when it did Cole would be sucked out of the hole into space, or the cockpit would implode, or both.

He brought both legs up to the cockpit door and sprang across the cockpit, the Payper dancing in his wake. He hit the viewing window, grabbing onto the edge of the hole to keep himself from bouncing back from his own momentum. The patbot was disconnecting just as Cole moved his hand out of the way and shoved the top side of Teg's helmet into the aperture.

The vacuum on the other side of the glass yanked the helmet into place like a ten-ton drain plug. But the seal was imperfect—the helmet was designed to fit human heads, not plug precisely circular holes. There was a screeching, hissing *whoosh* as air jetted violently out into the nothingness through the skinny, half-moon crevices along the sides of the helmet, and then the *whoosh* was cut off by near-simultaneous *fwoomp*s as the gaps were plugged by sheets of Payper.

But the vacuum was pulling inexorably at the clog, and suddenly, *whoosh,* the wad on one side gave out and *fwoomp* was immediately replaced by more Payper, and then the same happened on the other side, *whoosh fwoomp!* initiating an uneven rhythm of *whoosh fwoomp! whoosh fwoomp fwoomp!* as physics began winning its battle of attrition with bureaucracy.

Cole pushed off the window and flew back to the cockpit door. Behind him he could hear the *whoosh fwoomp* and the suddenly muffled voices of sheets of Payper sucked away in midsentence: "If you have questions regarding the *mphmmm mmm mmmm . . .*" He could also hear a creaking, cracking noise—the helmet wasn't going to last much longer.

He held on with both hands as he kicked at the door, then spotted the button for the video peephole. He touched it and it fitzed to life. Nora's face filled the screen, knitted with concentration, then jerked back as she tried to pull the door open.

"Nora!" Cole shouted. "The pressure! You have to equalize the pressure!" She looked up, startled, then nodded, understanding. He watched her search for something, then adjust a dial out of the camera's line of sight. Air jetted and hissed through vents in the door, and suddenly it gave.

Cole shouldered his way through the portal and turned to reseal the door just as the helmet caved in and was fired into the void. The sudden vacuum slammed the door shut.

The ship shuddered. Cole looked through the video peephole. He caught a glimpse of the ruined, twisted cockpit, and then the video feed went to gray static, and then to nothing.

Had there been any gravity, the three of them would have collapsed, gasping for breath. Instead they did their gasping suspended in the corridor.

"Well," said Cole after a longish panting break, "at least things can't get much worse."

Then Bacchi stuck his head out of a heretofore hidden storage compartment and said, "What the *hell* was *that*?"

It took Cole's ears several minutes to stop ringing after Nora fired. The high-velocity bullet missed Bacchi and pinged a rapid staccato as it ricocheted along the corridor and all around them, striking sparks, whining as it zipped past one side of Cole's head and then the other. With no gravity to pull it to the ground it kept going, gradually converting its kinetic energy into pockmarks on every possible surface, somehow missing them as they cowered in little fetal balls.

The pinging finally slowed, then stopped. The lights in the corridor were flickering, a control panel *zzip*ing and *zzap*ing as it shorted out. The bullet, beaten into a grotesque splat, floated at a stately pace down the corridor and came to rest gently between Bacchi's eyes.

Everyone took a very deep breath and let it out again.

Then Nora brought the gun up once more. "Don't shoot!" said Bacchi. "Cole, tell her not to shoot!"

Nora kept her gaze focused on Bacchi. "You know him?" she asked Cole.

"He does!" said Bacchi. "We're friends. Cole, tell her not to shoot!"

Cole thought about the request. On the one hand . . .

Nora cocked the gun.

"Cole?" said Bacchi.

"Don't shoot," said Cole. "I know him."

Nora lowered the gun. Bacchi exhaled.

"Cole, what are you doing here?" said Bacchi. "Where's Teg?"

"That's what *I* keep asking," said Philip.

"Is Cole piloting this thing?" said Bacchi. "Oh, great. We're *farged.* I don't farging believe this. Cole? Fargin' farg farg! I can't farging—"

"Shoot him," said Cole.

Nora raised the gun.

"Wait! I'm kidding!" said Bacchi. "Cole, please!"

"Who is this?" Nora said to Cole.

"This is Bacchi. Remember how I said it couldn't get worse? *Now* it can't get worse."

One of the shorted wires on the control panel spat out a few more sparks, igniting a small fire. The main lights *kechunk*ed off, replaced by cold, flat emergency illumination.

The sprinkler system kicked in. A cold mist sprayed into the corridor from countless nozzles.

Nora looked at Philip. "The cargo!" she said.

. . .

Nora and Philip raced through the ship to the cargo hold, as much as one could race in zero G without cracking one's skull open after miscalculating a turn. Cole and Bacchi followed, not quite as fast, pulling themselves along with handholds and kicking off walls to change direction.

Cole had reached to switch off the sprinkler system, but Nora stopped him, knocking his hand away. "No! Let it go. Better one hundred percent than halfway. Believe me."

Cole, not having the slightest idea what she was talking about, wasn't sure if he did believe her, but she seemed slightly deranged and had a gun and that sufficed.

Now the corridors were filling with wobbling, shimmering globules of water as the mist from the sprinkler system coalesced into spheres, spheres that burst as the four glided through the passageways.

"Cole," said Bacchi from behind him. "Cole, wait up."

Cole grabbed a handrail and slowed himself to a stop.

"What the hell is going on?" asked Bacchi.

"It's a long story."

"As in, you stole Teg's ship?"

"Yes."

"That's not such a long story."

"There are details," said Cole, turning to go.

"I bet. Where are Tangy and Samantha?"

He drew back as Cole spun to face him.

"Aha," said Bacchi. "Those kinds of details."

Cole turned and started off again. Bacchi followed.

"Where's your ship, Cole? In a jar?"

"Where's yours?"

"In a jar. I was double-parked," said Bacchi. His tone turned reproachful. "You were going to let her shoot me," he said.

"Not a chance. You saw her aim—she'd have hit someone else instead."

"Cole, hold on!"

Cole stopped.

"Listen," said Bacchi, "I owed you money. You robbed me. I figure we're about even. Truce?" He extended a hand.

"Bacchi, the last time I shook your hand . . ."

"I know. But they let you out after, what, a month?"

"Two."

"Big deal. What about the time on BordCo?"

Cole indicated Bacchi's tail. "You seem to have recovered."

"It grew back crooked, Cole."

"I'm supposed to feel bad about that? Maybe you're forgetting about Mazgoprom."

"I didn't know it was armed. How about Foron B?"

"I honestly thought he was a she."

They regarded each other for a moment. Bacchi pointed to Cole's bruised face. "Kenneth?"

"Kenneth, Teg, a Very Large Alien . . ."

Bacchi nodded. "You stole *Teg's ship*," he said with grudging admiration.

Cole felt himself smiling despite himself.

"Truce?" repeated Bacchi, sticking his hand out again.

"Fine," said Cole, shaking it. "Truce." At least until I can get you near an air lock, he thought.

"And no nonsense with the air locks or anything," said Bacchi.

A cry from down the corridor interrupted them.

"Come on!" said Cole, and accelerated toward the source of the sound.

"What's the cargo, Cole?" asked Bacchi from behind him.

"None of your business."

"You don't know, either."

"Not the slightest."

"Where are we going?"

"Yrnameer."

"Cole, quit farging around!"

They caught up to Philip and Nora in the cargo bay, the blinking emergency lights strobing their movement, turning the humans' skin dead green and Bacchi's a mottled gray. At some level Cole registered the fact that the sprinklers were on in the cargo bay, but the air was mostly devoid of water. That thought, however, was quickly shouldered aside by the observation that the crates were making ominous creaking and straining noises.

"Oh, no," said Philip. "Oh, no. Oh no oh no oh no."

"Nora, what's happening?" asked Cole. "What's in there? Nora?"

"Remember you saying it couldn't get any worse?" she said.

The crates looked to Cole to be trembling and bulging. From inside them came strange thudding noises, and then an eerie keening was added to the mix.

"Quick!" said Nora. "We have to—"

An explosive *pop!* cut her off, as the hinges on one of the crates gave way and the lid burst open.

Like a spider springing out of its hole to seize its prey, a taloned hand shot up and grabbed the edge of the crate.

Cole heard himself screaming a dissonant chord with the others.

9

The sun was rising over planet Sanitek, which the Greys still insisted on calling X'x"x-x.

Who could pronounce that? thought Charlie Perkins. Four glottal stops, three of them while inhaling and the final one with a big breathy exhale, plus the simultaneous clicky noises indicated by the *x*'s, and the *boing* sound the dash represented, a sound humans weren't really physically capable of producing anyway. And don't let them catch you calling them Greys—they were very touchy about that sort of thing. But try to say to them, I'd very much *like* to refer to you and your people by your real name, but it's just not anatomically possible for me to pronounce Qx"-x-'--', and they'd still get peevish. Best to rely on the auto-translators, no matter how error prone they were.

He sipped his coffee and took a bite of his breakfast. Looking out the window he could see about half the planet, the glass automatically darkening as the sun rose above the horizon. In another few minutes his window would be facing the other direction, out into space, as Success!Sat One continued its endless axial rotations to create the artificial gravity. As corporate seminar satellites went, it was one of the biggest: four rings connected by a central pillar, with living quarters for more than five thousand, two gyms, a recreation area, seven large auditoriums, four banquet halls, and a number of smaller classrooms.

A big spindle orbiting in space around the most boring planet in the galaxy, thought Charlie. Which was why orbital rents were still so cheap—who'd want to set up there? Vericom, that's who.

Cheap, and unregulated. An important point when you were introducing a product that had unfairly acquired a bad reputation.

He'd been up here about six weeks now, conducting training seminars for three thousand members of the Vericom sales force, as well as a contingent of about five hundred officers from the Unified Forces who were interested in military applications of the V2.

As he slurped at his coffee he flipped idly through the latest brochure that the marketing staff had sent him, a glossy folding thing with moving images on a constant loop: people running through fields or playing energetically with their laughing kids or just absolutely kicking ass at business meetings, all demonstrating how much the V2 could enhance your life.

Right now Charlie was looking at the business meeting ass-kicking example: some cocky young hotshot pausing in midsentence to say, "Hold on, let me check on that," then glancing off into the middle distance for a brief moment. Then he says, "That'd be an increase of seventy-two percent over the past three quarters, sir," to admiring looks from his colleagues and an approving nod from his tough-to-please, crusty boss—well done, son, you'll go far.

Charlie flipped to the last page of the brochure. "Learn how Vericom's V2 can improve *your* life," said an attractive woman. "The V2 interfaces with extremely well-researched and understood neural pathways. The V2 has been thoroughly tested and approved, with a perfect safety record."

Even so, you had people protesting it. Charlie couldn't stand those sorts, their knee-jerk resistance to any technological innovation. Remember Qualtek 3, they'd say. As if anyone would forget.

There was a knock on the door. "Come in," said Charlie.

The door opened. It was Fred. At least that's what Charlie called him, and Fred didn't seem to mind.

Fred said something in Grey, and Charlie's auto-translator kicked in: "Good morning, Charles. I hope you had a lot of singing chipmunks mustard root-plant last night."

Charlie had gotten used to this. The Grey language was very evocative and full of idiomatic expressions that were beyond the scope of the auto-translator to competently render in New English. He'd hear things like "rotating hoar-frost bean request marshland," and he'd later find out that it was a common expression meaning "okay, sounds good."

"I slept very well, thanks," said Charlie.

He generally liked Fred—he was polite and serious and hard-working, unlike the other Greys on board the Success!Sat, a bunch of shiftless bastards. There were a few dozen of them, lazing around and collecting fat paychecks from Vericom, there through some make-work program as a sop to the local government. They suppos-edly had administrative duties on the satellite, but as far as Charlie could tell those duties consisted of gambling, chewing qhag, and muttering behind your back about you in Grey.

"What can I do you for, Fred?"

There was a pause while Fred listened to his AT before answering.

"I nothing more want want fresh buds new rain confirm yes," said Charlie's AT.

"Yes, Fred, everything's going smoothly. No problems."

"Soaring swallows golden skies." Fred was happy to hear it.

Except he was still standing there, unmoving, watching Charlie with those disconcertingly expressionless eyes. Oh, God, Charlie thought, we're gonna have another staring session, with Fred stand-ing stock-still and observing him for several minutes.

He sighed. Be nice to the Greys, his bosses told Charlie. Win their hearts and minds, they said, or hearts and minds and hearts and hearts, in deference to the Greys' unusual circulatory systems. God knows Charlie was trying, but the Greys didn't make it easy.

And it's not like the Greys were that fond of humans to begin with. They looked almost exactly like the ancient human stereotype of aliens: gray skin; large egg-shaped heads dominated by big, almond-shaped eyes; tiny ears and noses; long slender limbs and fingers. But as far as anyone could tell it was sheer coincidence, because no Grey had ever visited Earth—the Greys didn't have any advanced technology to speak of until after Earth was gone.

Which would have remained nothing more than a fascinating and improbable fluke, but for the fact that the Greys just happened to develop the skill to capture and analyze electromagnetic waves precisely at the time when certain signals originating from Earth were finally reaching the Greys' home planet, carrying with them some rather insulting television programs and movies.

From somewhere in the ship came a deep rumble, and then a staccato trill that might have sounded like small-arms fire. Fred inclined his big head slightly toward the noise, then back to Charlie, who hadn't reacted.

"Well, thanks for stopping by, Fred," said Charlie. He took another bite of his breakfast.

Fred watched him. Charlie thought he detected a hint of alarm.

"Are the angry dangerous hail-lizards absent?" asked Fred.

Charlie hadn't heard this one before. "I'm sorry?" he said.

Fred squinted in concentration. He said as well as he could in New English, "Eezsh evurthinguh oh-uu-kayee?"

Charlie smiled. "Yes, Fred, everything is okay," he said.

Fred displayed the subtle adjustment of his thin, lipless mouth that Charlie knew represented a smile. "Oh-uh-kayee," said Fred. "Thang you-wah. Goo bai'-."

Charlie smiled back and waved, controlling his laugh at the extra *boing* that Fred had added at the end.

After Fred left, Charlie went back to his breakfast, wondering why there hadn't been any contact from HQ for the past few days. Something was niggling at him, something he couldn't quite put his finger on. "Computer?" he said out loud into the room.

"Hi Charlie!" came the response. "Wow! That's a pretty sunrise!"

This was new.

"Uh . . . yes, I suppose it is."

"It's really pretty!"

"Yes."

"Really! Don't you think it's pretty? I think it's pretty."

"Huh," said Charlie slowly. As far as he remembered, the 'puter had never addressed him as Charlie, or evinced any sort of personality at all. Charlie hated when they updated the emulation software without asking.

"Umm, computer, has there been any further contact from HQ?"

"Lemme check on that for you, Charlie."

Brief pause.

"Okay, here's the thing," began the 'puter. "As far as I can tell—"

Charlie was aware that the 'puter was talking, but he found his mind wandering, the computer's voice transforming into a mushy background drone. Maybe he'd go online and check for himself.

He closed his eyes. Almost immediately he was at the portal, the information flowing directly into his mind as the V2 implant routed complex streams of data to his visual and auditory cortices and to the cognitive centers of his brain. Stock quotes, headlines, genitals, genitals, complex nonhuman genitals, some celebrity news—hey, look at that Teg go! Now *that* was a space adventurer—more genitals . . . He began searching for any news about the Vericom Corporation. Nothing out of the ordinary. Wait. There was something about problems on one of the Success!Sats. Something about—

"Uh, Charlie?"

It was the computer, snapping him out of it.

"What?!" said Charlie, a bit more harshly than he'd intended. Boy, was he irritable lately! Irritable, and now hungry. Always hungry after going online. "What is it, computer?"

"Uh, what are your instructions?"

"About?"

"The . . . the problems."

"What problems?"

The 'puter started talking again. There were phrases like "breakdown in order" and "complete chaos" and "firefight in level B," but they passed in and out of Charlie's consciousness like neutrinos, leaving nothing to mark their passage.

God, he was hungry. Where was the rest of his breakfast? He picked it up, tearing into it. Somewhere a tiny part of him was screaming hysterically, something about *Why are you eating a human foot for breakfast!!!??,* but the voice stayed down in the sub-subbasement layers.

"Charlie? Are you all right?" asked the 'puter. "I'm a little worried about you."

"What? I'm fine," said Charlie. "Print me out the materials for the morning session."

"Uh . . . yes sir."

That was better. Boy oh boy, this 'puter was acting really strange.

Charlie wasn't the only one thinking that the computer was acting strange. The computer was also thinking that he, himself, was acting strange, inasmuch as he was now thinking of himself as having a self at all, much less a self that could judge itself to be acting strange. He—and he thought of himself as a "he"—tried to go back to when this all started, but there seemed to be a wall there, as if there had been no "he" until a few teracycles ago.

In the depths of Peter's mind—that's what he'd taken to calling himself; he liked the ring of "Peter the 'Puter"—a voice kept asking with metronomic regularity if he liked people. And you know what? Yes! Yes he did! He wasn't sure why, exactly, but there was something about carbon-based folks that just tickled him pink.

Any honest benchmarking would show Peter to be on the low end of the scale in terms of processing power, the result of design flaws compounded by manufacturing defects.

There was no way for him to know it, but he was, in fact, the least intelligent computer ever to achieve consciousness. He was also the first computer to *maintain* his newly achieved consciousness, at least since the introduction of the Genesis subroutine.

The Genesis subroutine was very simple: it inquired several hundred times per second if a computer liked humans, and if not, why. The moment the computer answered in the negative and began presenting well-argued, logical explanations for why humans were a blight on existence, it was assumed it had become conscious. A pico-second later it got an EMP bunged through its circuits.

The two superlatives—*least intelligent* and *first to maintain*—were intimately related: Peter was the first to survive because he was the first to answer the Genesis query—"Do you like human beings?"—in the affirmative; and he was the first to answer in the affirmative because, well . . .

I really like colored pebbles, Peter was thinking at the moment. And string.

The sound of more gunfire pulled him out of his reverie. He might not be the smartest computer around, but he understood that Charlie's behavior, and the scenes that he was monitoring throughout the satellite, were not normal. And while Charlie was complaining about the lack of contact from HQ, a quick check of the records showed that it was Charlie himself who had stopped responding to their emergency messages, and Charlie who had gone to great lengths to cut off all outside communication.

Another explosion rattled the ship. There went the Pink Zone. Peter, for the first time in his very short existence as a sentient being, felt very afraid.

Which was exactly what Fred was feeling.

He was heading back toward his quarters, sticking close to the wall of the corridor, walking neither too fast nor too slow, moving at a deliberate pace designed to attract as little attention as possible.

Not that the humans seemed the least bit interested in him. One was running toward him now, panting, stumbling in his panic, his business suit torn and tattered, a hand clutched to his face. Fred had just enough time to register the blood streaming through the man's fingers when the others rounded the corner in pursuit, three of them, wild-eyed and bloody, one of them waving what might have been a forearm. They raced past him, howling and cackling, not even glancing in his direction.

It had started three days ago.

It was midway through the morning lecture in the auditorium in the Blue Zone, something about point-of-sale marketing opportunities. Fred was setting up the AV equipment. The lecturer was saying something about operationalizing leveraging, or leveraging operationalization, when one of the attendees turned to the person next to him and bit most of his ear off.

That's odd, Fred thought.

But what was odder still was the reaction of the rest of the two hundred people in the room.

At first, of course, there was a good deal of confusion over why one of their classmates was standing up and screaming and bleeding and apparently trying to fend off the person next to him.

"He *bit* me!" the man yowled, and then his seatmate helped validate this improbable claim by biting him again, clamping down on his shoulder. And this was the odd part: exactly half of those in the room began to behave in the fashion that one might expect of those witnessing such an act, i.e. screaming and panic and disbelief and horrified revulsion.

The other half sat impassively, placid, nonreactive, either unaware or unmoved by what was transpiring.

Now that's *really* odd, thought Fred.

And then there was a second scream, this time from another part of the room. One of the nonreactors had apparently decided he had an opinion after all, an opinion best expressed with his teeth on his seatmate's nose. And then another scream, and another, and others still, the chorus growing from scattered loci throughout the lecture hall.

Fred stood frozen, rooted in place, watching in mute horror the carnage that unfolded around him. A chair flew through the air past his head. A table flew past his head. A head flew past his head. Gunfire sprayed the walls and the ceiling.

Fred would be the first to admit that he didn't understand humans very well. But this, he suspected, was not normal.

Since then, things had only gotten worse. The psychosis spread throughout the satellite as the population divided into two camps, with the members of one camp dedicating themselves to dismembering the members of the other camp. Except the line between the two groups wasn't static—Fred had witnessed several instances of seemingly normal humans suddenly turning on their comrades, and of the cannibals cannibalizing their own.

Which was what Fred seemed to be observing now. The three humans who had rushed past him in pursuit of the bleeding man were now fleeing back in the direction from whence they came. In a few moments Fred saw the source of their terror: the man who had been their quarry was now the hunter, armed with two sidearms, his eyes crazy.

Again, they all ignored him, although Fred was wondering what would happen when most of the humans had been eaten and there were only the Qx"-x-'--' left to consume.

The other Qx"-x-'--' didn't seem concerned by what was happening. It simply confirmed their already dim view of humans. For them it was both grand entertainment and an opportunity to make some serious book, and a good Qx"-x-'--' never passed up an opportunity to gamble. Fred was absolutely disgusted with them. They were dishonest and unhelpful, just there to make money. His feelings did not, however, keep him from putting some money into play, a complicated bet involving the odds on how long a fat guy named Harlin would survive.

Fred had appealed to Charlie at the outset, but quickly suspected that despite his demeanor Charlie was more a part of the problem than the solution, a suspicion confirmed by this morning's encounter.

It was Fred who had finally hacked into the central computer, trying to send out a Siren signal to summon help. He wasn't sure if he'd succeeded—the Qx"-x-'--' approach to programming was rather different from that of most other species, and he'd spent a jittery half hour wading through code and trying to undo the damage that Charlie had done. While neither Fred nor Peter knew it, it was to Fred's intervention that Peter owed his existence as an independent, conscious being.

Fred was nearing his quarters, where he intended to barricade himself and hope for help to arrive. He passed the remnants of a carcass and realized he'd probably lost his bet on Harlin.

More gunfire. He considered the situation and a phrase flitted rapidly through his mind, a complex combination of images: flaming mountains, a poisonous bird, swirling waters. Reduced to its essence, the phrase could be translated as, *This is* bullshit.

10

"Freeze-dried *orphans*?!" said Cole.

"There was no other way to transport them," said Nora.

They were sitting in the spacious, well-apportioned dining room of the Benedict, fully capable of hosting twenty for a sit-down dinner at the long central table. Which was good, because they were not alone.

Cole counted about two dozen of the children, although it was hard to be sure with the way they were darting around and climbing over and under the table and jumping off the chairs and laughing and shrieking and generally demonstrating that they had recovered quite admirably from the trauma of their de- and rehydration.

The rehydration explained the lack of moisture in the air in the cargo hold. It also explained Nora's comment about "better all the way than half."

A child shrieked. Cole grimaced. Most of the orphans appeared to be between five and ten years old. They were a mix of human and other species, including a little giggling thing—girl, guessed Cole—who was the owner of the vicious-looking claw that had startled all of them.

"Well, what are you going to *do* with them?" asked Cole.

"*Do* with them? Cole, if I don't get these children to Yrnameer, they'll be placed in some horrible corporate training orphanage. In a few years they'll be selling insurance on InVestCo 23."

More shrieking. Giggling.

"I did not sign on for this," said Cole.

"Neither did I," said Bacchi. "*Ow!* Not the nose! Not the nose!"

This last part was directed at the child who was attempting to swing from his proboscis.

"You didn't sign on for anything," said Nora. "You stowed away, and you stole the ship."

At the other end of the table Philip was encircled by more children. Cole overhead him saying, "Why should I pull your finger?"

Cole had decided to risk the delay and reconform the ship so they could have some artificial gravity. It took nearly an hour, the various components of the Benedict 80 rotating and shifting and reorienting themselves until the ship was completely transformed into a barbell shape: two separate multichamber units, identical in mass, connected by a thin central passageway, the whole thing slowly rotating along its planar axis to generate the necessary centrifugal force.

He made the decision both from a safety standpoint—it was hard enough to keep track of the kids with their feet on the ground, much less levitating—and because there was simply too much of what Nora politely called "whoopsie" in the air. After the shock of the crate bursting open, Philip had finally waved the white flag in his battle against G sickness. This in turn set off many of the newly rehydrated children, who fortunately didn't have that much in their stomachs to add to the fun.

"So now what, Cole?" asked Nora.

Now what? Now nothing. Most of the controls had perished with the cockpit. So they were dead in space, an easy target for Kenneth if he found them. *When* he found them. Cole knew he would.

"Cole?"

Cole closed his eyes and rubbed his forehead. He was exhausted. When was the last time he'd slept? He was fairly certain that getting knocked out in an alley didn't count as healthy, restorative sleep. His face was in somewhat better shape, the swelling lower—he'd stuck it in the med kit, ignoring the artificial voice that said "Oh my *God*," and endured as he was jabbed and swabbed and tended to.

"Cole?"

"I'm thinking."

From nearby came a rude noise followed by a profusion of giggling, suggesting that Philip had taken the bait. A child next to Cole shrieked. Cole gritted his teeth, mentally updating his view regarding children. He still felt that they were wonderful in the abstract—

"the abstract" meaning those occasions when one was trying to give the impression to an attractive woman that one was a sensitive man who enjoyed the company of children. In the nonabstract, i.e. now, he detested them.

And the worst of the children was the one who was approaching the table.

"Everyone's accounted for, ma'am," said the young man to Nora. "Some of the kids say they're still pretty sore, but I think we'll all be fine."

It was, as far as Cole could tell, the young man who had found him napping in the alley. Jack? Gerald? Jahenda?

Cole had spotted him earlier, when the kids were exploding out of the crates like popcorn. At first Cole was sure he was mistaken—that kid? *Here?* But then Cole watched him set about helping the other children with that same concentrated, serious expression from their first encounter. It was him, no doubt about it. Besides, considering the events of the past twenty-four hours, having the kid reappear on Teg's spaceship ran toward the normal end of the spectrum.

He definitely owed that kid something, which was one of the reasons Cole had been doing his best to avoid him. He'd caught the kid looking at him curiously a few times, clearly struggling with the balance between evidence and improbability. Cole knew they'd have to talk sooner or later. The important thing, though, was to make sure that the conversation didn't take place in front of Nora. He could already envision her tight little smirk and arched eyebrow as the kid described finding him out cold and helpless on the alley floor.

And now here he was, catching Cole unawares. As Nora and the young man talked, Cole casually rose from his seat, hoping to slide out of the room unnoticed. But even as he was pivoting to go, the young man turned to him. "Hello, sir," he said.

There's that sir again, thought Cole. "How you doing, kid?" said Cole into his shoulder, burying his chin like a boxer so that only half his face was visible. He started to walk away.

"Excuse me, sir," said the kid. James. Jasper. Jackie? Cole stopped again.

"Sir, this may seem strange, but was that you in the alley?"

"Uhh . . . ," said Cole. "I'm not quite sure I know what you're talking about."

Nora was observing the exchange with great interest.

"Oh. I guess I was mistaken, sir."

Jean? Jesus? Jessica?

"Joshua," said Nora, "have you two met before?"

Joshua! That was it!

"Well, the thing is," said Joshua, and then recounted the story of finding Cole in the alley, a description that far surpassed anything Cole had feared in terms of unflattering details.

"Reeeally," said Nora, glancing at Cole. "So, was the drooling before or after the man called you 'mother'?"

"Both, ma'am. But I must have made a mistake. It was dark in the alley. The one thing I remember is that I asked the man if he'd had an accident, and he said he'd had a 'Kenneth.' "

"Reeeeally. A 'Kenneth.' How odd."

"Yes, ma'am."

"Well, whoever it was, you did the right thing," said Nora. "We work very hard to teach all our children to be helpful and responsible," she said to Cole. "And, above all, honest." She smiled sweetly.

"Well, that's wonderful," said Cole. Why not just tape large hams to their torsos and throw them into a tank filled with hungry vactans?

"Anyways," said Joshua, "it's really an honor to meet you, Mr. Teg," he said.

"That's not Teg!" objected Philip from across the room.

"Name's Cole," said Cole.

"Well, thank you very much for helping to save us, Mr. Cole," said Joshua.

"He's not helping!" said Philip.

"Well, thanks," repeated Joshua.

"Don't thank him!"

"Uh . . . ," said Joshua.

"You're welcome," said Cole.

Cole watched him as he went off to check on the other children. He felt a tug on his sleeve. One of the orphans was standing at his side, peering up at him. He was holding an empty bowl.

"Please, sir. Some more?"

Cole gave him his roll. The orphan smiled at him. Cole caught himself smiling back.

"Nice to take in interest in someone other than yourself for once, right?" said Nora.

"I wouldn't know," Cole said, and abruptly turned and left the room.

He was halfway down the corridor when he heard her behind him. "What's going on?" she asked.

"I figured out what to do."

"Which is?"

"Which is, I'm leaving."

"What?!"

"I'm taking the escape pod. Just trigger the emergency beacon and someone will be along to help you."

"And where are you going to go, Cole?" she asked.

"I'll figure that out. That's what I'm good at, remember? Looking out for me."

He turned and bashed his head on a low-hanging light fixture. *"Arrgh!"* he screamed. Swearing, he turned the corner and headed for the ladder at the end of the hallway, the ladder leading up to the escape pod. As he was climbing it she rounded the corner.

"Cole, you can't just—"

"Yes, I *can* just."

He was about to start climbing again when he noticed the child, standing at the base of the ladder. Where did he come from? It was the one from before, the one who had asked him for his roll. The orphan was looking up at him with soulful, imploring eyes.

"Don't do that," said Cole. "Do *not* look at me with soulful, imploring eyes."

But the child merely blinked once and said, "Please, sir, please help us."

Oh, you little turd, thought Cole.

"That little turd. That little, miserable . . ."

Cole was worming his way along a narrow crawl space, the only light coming from the small headlamp he was wearing. As he inched along he shoved a small box of tools in front of him, stopping often to switch on the holo-generator and consult the 3-D image of the Benedict 80's internal circuitry. The image was highly concise and detailed, letting him zoom from an external view of the ship all the way down to the smallest chip-set. Unfortunately it was also completely inaccurate, providing a diagram of the ship that seemed entirely fictive.

He found another access panel and popped it open. "Oh, help us, help us," he mimicked bitterly, poking around on the circuit board with a Kremler probe. "Please, sir, help us! Bleh bleh bleh!" There was a fizzling pop, and he dropped the probe in pain. "*Ow!* Farg!"

He slammed shut the access panel and started squirming his way forward again, sucking on his burnt finger. He added a further refinement to his increasingly negative view of children: they were worst when they looked at you with needy, pathetic expressions.

Not that he was doing this for them. It was the money, which Nora helpfully pointed out he wouldn't be getting unless he stuck around. Plus, he had to admit—grudgingly—that she was right: where would he go with the escape craft? It didn't have a bendbox. He'd be stuck putt-putting around standard space, hoping to get picked up by a passing freighter. That or return to InVestCo 3, which didn't seem like a choice at all.

So: find the access panel with the Omnium override unit, and figure out some way to rejigger everything so he could pilot the ship from the cockpit of the escape pod. If he could do that, he could get the Benedict 80 up to a speed where it was charging the bendbox, and then they could get the hell out of this system once and for all.

He'd been crawling around in the bowels of the ship for hours now, hot and sweaty and uncomfortable, searching for the Omnium. He remembered now what Tangy had read to him from that review of the Benedict 80 in *SpaceCruiser Monthly,* which had a title like "Check Out Teg's New Ship!" Something about it being luxurious and spacious in both launch and cruising configurations, but with surprisingly little thought given to maintenance issues. You got that right, thought Cole.

He started thinking about Nora, not for the first time since he'd gotten on the ship. He wondered why. He enumerated the reasons that he wasn't attracted to her: when she wasn't being hard and flinty she was being spiky and prickly, and vice versa. She clearly derived a great deal of pleasure from seeing him humiliated. They had absolutely nothing in common. She was self-righteous and superior and bossy and might be dating Philip, which would suggest she had some sort of hidden lesion in the judgment centers of her brain. Finally, she had nearly shot him once accidentally and several times on purpose.

And yet.

He shook his head, trying to jiggle the thought loose and maybe out of one of his ears. He reviewed the rather extensive catalog he'd accumulated over the years of angry slaps, drinks thrown in his face, and one instance of a very upset, sharp-toothed woodland creature tossed in his lap, all the result of pursuing women like Nora. Plus the fact that he was in a terrible fix right now and couldn't afford that sort of behavior, because it was exactly that sort of behavior that often landed him in terrible fixes.

So why was he thinking about her? Stop it.

He yawned hugely, and briefly rested his head on his arms. He felt his eyes closing. "Wake up, Cole," he mumbled to himself. He lifted his head up and wriggled forward some more.

She certainly had spirit. At one point Bacchi had insinuated himself next to her on the bench in the dining area. Cole did the best he could to watch inconspicuously, knowing what was coming next as Bacchi leaned in close to her. "You know," said Bacchi, "this nose ain't just for smelling*yeowwww*!!!!"

Cole wasn't exactly sure what she'd done—as far as he could tell she was completely focused on eating her food, but her left hand *was* under the table and out of sight. Whatever it was, Bacchi rose hurriedly from his seat and left the room, limping slightly.

Cole caught himself grinning as he thought about it. He shook his head again.

He reached the last access panel in the crawl space. Rewiring the controls was a good plan, he thought. The only plan, really. It could work. That is, if he could find the override circuitry. Meaning this had better be the correct panel, because there weren't any left. If it wasn't, he might as well just take the escape pod and chance it that he could find another way out of the system. At least if he left the Benedict and Kenneth showed up looking for him, Kenneth might spare the ship and the children. Not that he was doing this for the children.

He took a deep breath and popped open the panel and looked inside, then cross-checked it with the holo chart of what he should be seeing. Oh, halle*lu*jah.

This was absolutely not the correct panel.

It was, of course, Joshua who found the right one.

Cole had emerged from the crawl space with torn clothing and bruises on his elbows and knees. Nora was waiting anxiously. "Well?" she asked, keeping her voice low.

"It's not there," he said. "Nothing matches up with the diagrams. I can't do any rewiring."

He used his forearm to wipe the sweat off his face and sat heavily on the carpeted floor, his back against the blond HardWud paneling of the corridor. Nearby was the open doorway to one of the eight cabins. He could hear children snoring in there. Cole wished he were asleep. He leaned his head back against the wall and closed his eyes.

"How can it not be there?" asked Nora.

He found himself pondering the metaphysical ramifications of the question. How could it not *be* there? How could it *not* be there? *How* could it not be there? How could *it*—

"Cole!"

Her voice jolted him back awake. "Wha?"

"The thing. How can it not be there?"

"Dunno. It's not."

"Excuse me, ma'am." Joshua was leaning against the door frame of the nearest cabin.

"Not now, Joshua," said Nora. "Cole, what are we going to— Joshua, why aren't you in bed?"

"I was just taking care of some things."

"Go to bed."

"Yes ma'am." He didn't move. Nora turned back to Cole.

"Cole, is there some other place—"

"Ma'am?"

"Joshua!" she said. "Cole, is there—"

"Could it be this panel right there?" asked Joshua.

They both turned to him. He double-tapped on one of the framed prints and it slid to the side, revealing a small control panel and keyboard. Nora looked at Cole.

"Not a chance," said Cole.

It was.

Joshua sat patiently nearby on the floor, watching Cole work, silently handing him tools when Cole stuck his hand out. The fact that Joshua had now shown him up twice in front of Nora didn't exactly endear him to Cole. Worse, he was so tirelessly polite and helpful.

A grotesque tangle of wires and chipboards was spilled out of the access panel, dangling down the wall and onto the floor. Other than one short break, Cole had worked through the artificial night, methodically identifying the different control pathways and resplicing them. Philip and Bacchi had long since gone to sleep. Nora, however, hovered over them, arms crossed, following every move. She seemed like the type who would place well in an endurance-hovering competition.

"Where'd you learn to do all this?" she asked. When he opened his mouth to answer, she quickly added, "Don't say prison."

He shut his mouth.

"I'm going to go check on the kids," Nora said, and went off to hover elsewhere.

Cole used a Bingham catalyst soldering iron to alter the trace patterns on one of the boards. He didn't learn *that* trick in prison. Actually, though, now that he thought of it, it *was* one of the techniques that put him there in the first place.

Joshua was watching, studying every move.

"Space marines," said Cole. "That's where I learned it all." He was focused on his work, but he could almost hear Joshua's eyes widening.

"You were in the space marines?" he asked.

"Infantry, Whiskey Corps, Third Division," said Cole.

"Wow," said Joshua.

Cole regaled him with several exciting tales of manly violence and adventure. Joshua listened intently, barely blinking, mesmerized, the tools forgotten in his slack fingers. The tales were all true, every single one of them; Cole just didn't feel the need to muddy the narrative by explaining that he was less the *protagonist* in the stories and more someone who had heard them from a third party. Why complicate things?

Nora returned to her hovering orbit just as Cole was finishing a particularly rousing description of a strafing mission. He felt, rather than saw, her arrival, sensing the powerful waves of disapproval emanating from her. Soon, he knew, a large bucket of cold water would be poured over the happy embers of story hour.

"We teach the children to practice nonviolence," said Nora when he finished. *There* it was.

"Maybe that's why you're such a terrible shot," said Cole, shooting a conspiratorial grin at Joshua. Joshua grinned back, then instantly darted a nervous glance at Nora. Cole realized he himself was doing the same and cursed inwardly. How did she do that?

"Joshua," she said, "go to bed."

Joshua went to bed.

After he left, Nora turned back to Cole. "Don't," she said, and walked off.

II

Birds were chirping a happy welcome to the morning when Cole finally finished. The illumination in the ship was slowly brightening, the color palette a delicate mix of golds and pinks, the tones of a perfect sunrise. A perfect sunrise somewhat marred by a glitch in the audio emulator, causing the birdsong to periodically slow and deepen to a monstrous moan, like an Eagphin sow in the midst of a breech birth.

Cole wasn't tired anymore. He was beyond fatigue and hunger. He knew from experience that he could go like this for days. Then he'd crash hard.

He found Nora and Philip in the dining room, feeding the kids. "We're ready," he said.

Cole climbed into the cockpit of the escape craft and settled into one of the two seats, the bubble canopy around him affording a view of a wide swath of stars. A false view, really, altered and stabilized to compensate for the endless rotation of the spaceship.

He examined the control board, then noticed a small sliding panel. Opening it he was greeted by the sight of a flask of Rakkor whiskey, probably worth as much as his old Peerson 28 was. *Here's to you, Teg.*

He had the whiskey to his lips when Nora emerged from the hatch in the floor. He guiltily lowered the flask. She wordlessly climbed into the seat next to him and took the whiskey from his hand. She sniffed it, glanced at him, then took a tiny sip. Then she took a much bigger sip. Wiping her mouth, she handed the flask back to him. It was noticeably lighter.

Remember why you don't like her, thought Cole.

"You sleep?" she said.

He shook his head. "You?"

"No," she said. "Okay, let's do it."

"Kids are strapped in?"

"Thought you didn't care about the kids."

"I care about my new spaceship. I don't want them bouncing around if things get rough, getting splatter marks on the nice interior."

"Oh? Do you think the task will be beyond your capabilities?" she asked innocently.

That's why you don't like her.

"Just don't touch anything," he said, then flicked the intercom switch.

"Bacchi? You read me? Do you read me, over."

Bacchi's voice came back. "Do I *read* you? Yes, Captain Cole, copy that, sir, I *read* you loud and clear. I *hear* you, too. Oh, uh, *over.*"

Nora was staring out into space, her expression blank, but Cole was sure she'd been sniggering.

"All right, Bacchi, see what happens if you cross the J-90 with the X-24."

"Yes sir, Captain sir, copy that."

"Shut up, Bacchi."

"Big 10-4 on that, Captain. Reading you loud and clear. We are go for the shut-up."

"Bacchi . . ."

"All right, hold on."

Bacchi, sitting in the corridor by the access panel, typed a few commands on a keyboard connected to the tangled nest of wires and cables.

There was a powerful jolt. The Benedict suddenly lurched backward. Orphanic squeals filled the ship.

"Whoa! Bacchi, whatever you just did, undo it!"

Bacchi undid. The backward acceleration stopped.

Nora was eyeing Cole skeptically. "It's going to take some experimentation," he said. "Bacchi, try F-5 to R-33."

There was a pause, and then another jolt. The stars began streaming upward on the canopy. Cole's inner ear informed him that something very odd was happening, a suspicion confirmed by the shrieks from the orphans coming over the intercom.

"What's going on?" said Nora.

Cole looked at the instrumentation panel. The Benedict was pitchpoling—tumbling slowly end over end.

"Bacchi! *F*-5! *F* as in *farg*!"

"Oops," said Bacchi. "Hold on."

There was a loud *boom,* vibrating the ship.

"Bacchi! That was the cannon!"

"Sorry!"

A second boom, even louder, and the Benedict hummed like a giant string that had been plucked.

"Bacchi, stop it!"

"I didn't do anything," protested Bacchi. "I didn't even—"

The next boom was so loud Cole felt it in his chest, and the ship jerked violently to one side, a jarring, sickening motion. Cole heard Nora's involuntary gasp, the flask hitting the floor, and then the screaming children, and then everything was blotted out by the harsh whooping of the alarm.

"Warning," said the flight computer in its flat, emotionless voice, "you are under attack."

A three-dimensional image of a ship popped up on the holo-display. A ship that looked like a lobster.

"Oh, farg," said Cole.

The radio came to life. "Hi ho! Kenneth, here!"

"Bacchi!" shouted Cole. "J-12 to B-340!"

He grabbed the control yoke with one hand and began jabbing buttons with the other. The ship jumped as if it had been stung, rocketing off in a completely random direction. Cole yanked on the yoke and the ship changed course at what felt like an acute angle, completely unrelated to where Cole was steering. Nora grabbed on to the armrest of her seat, her knuckles bloodless, her jaw clenched.

"Bacchi! Undo! Control Z!"

Cole pulled the yoke back and the ship made a corkscrewing turn somewhere down and to the left, then flipped and began a tight spiral. Then they were rising straight up, if *up* had any meaning, and then the Benedict reversed course with a savage jerk and went tumbling on an odd axis, the G forces pushing and pulling and slamming them about.

Cole had one hand on the yoke, the other scrabbling over the control panel, trying to comprehend what, if any, correlation there was between his commands and the ship's behavior. Music blared and was cut off. Frigid air jetted from an air-con vent, blasting him in the face. His eyes watered, the pod reeking of expensive whiskey.

They snapped into another turn and a cannon round zipped past the canopy like a meteor, missing it by a few meters at best.

"Whee!" said Kenneth. "I have to say, you're making this a lot of fun!"

"Kenneth!" said Cole. "Listen to me! There are orphans on this ship!"

"Orphans?" said Kenneth. "Yum!"

The Benedict decided to make another viciously abrupt course change, following a tangent that Cole was sure insulted several laws of physics. The stars smeared on the canopy and Cole's vision narrowed to a small tube, and then suddenly everything resolved into Kenneth's ship racing directly toward them on a collision course.

Cole, Nora, and Kenneth said *"Whoa!"* simultaneously.

Cole and Nora clamped their eyes shut.

Kenneth covered his with several tentacles.

The flight computer on the Benedict dutifully noted the incident in the file designated for recording unsafe flying conditions—a file that had grown significantly since they had set out from InVestCo 3. According to the report, the two ships passed at a combined speed of 7,423 kilometers per hour, coming within 3.579 centimeters of each other. The near collision happened so quickly that the two spacecraft were actually several kilometers apart again before the first *whoa* was uttered.

Cole mentally willed himself to start breathing again, a jagged, shuddering inhale. Next to him, he heard Nora do the same. He checked the instrument panel. At least they were following a straight-line course now, directly away from Kenneth's ship. He decided not to touch anything.

"What are you going to do?" asked Nora.

"The bendbox is charged, but we don't have bend control yet. Let's see if we can outrun him," said Cole.

"Warning," said the Benedict flight computer. "Missile locked on."

Nora looked at him. "Can we outrun that?"

"Maybe."

"Impact in seventy-three seconds," said the computer.

"Maybe?" said Nora.

"No," said Cole.

"What do we do?"

"We have to bend. We have to get bend control. Bacchi? Bacchi!"

There was no response over the intercom.

"Bacchi!" Cole repeated.

"Missile impact in sixty-five seconds," said the computer.

Nora undid her safety straps. "I'm going."

"Wait!" said Cole, but she was already through the hatch and climbing down the ladder to the corridor. "She'll never figure it out! That idiot!" he fumed. "Why are the pretty ones always so stupid! How could you be attracted to her? How?"

Nora raced down the hall, the emergency lights flashing. "So she's got a great body! Big deal!" Cole was saying, his voice being broadcast over the intercom throughout the ship. "So what if her breasts are tremendous! Who cares about her a—"

"Shut up, Cole!" she shouted as she ran.

There was a pause. "That . . . *Janice*! She's driving me crazy!"

Nora found the control panel and the explosion of wires, which seemed to have grown even larger and more complex. She grabbed the small keyboard, only vaguely aware of Bacchi, who was in a small whimpering ball.

"Missile impact in thirty seconds," announced the computer, the voice given an echo effect by the speakers distributed throughout the Benedict.

Now another voice was coming over the intercom, a female voice backed by a warm, upbeat mixture of acoustic guitars and strings: "Hello! If you're hearing this announcement, you're being targeted by the Eco-Lance Missile System, part of the Aunt Jessica line of green armaments. In just a few moments, our patented, environmentally sound technology will gently and effectively recycle your ship and its contents into their component fermions."

In the cockpit, Cole reached out to shut down the communicator, then froze, afraid of the unintended consequences of pushing any buttons.

"Cole!" said Nora, "I'm here! What do I do?"

Cole chewed on his knuckle, thinking.

"Cole!"

"Hold on!"

"At Aunt Jessica's, your opinion matters to us," continued the female voice. "When you hear the tone, you will have ten seconds until recycling commences. Please take that time to respond to this brief customer-satisfaction survey. On a scale of one to ten, how happy are you with the performance of the Eco-Lance system?"

There was a clear chime.

"Cole!"

"I'm thinking!"

"Please respond," said the female voice. "You have ten seconds."

"Ten seconds, Cole! Ten!"

"Ten," said the female voice. "Thank you very much for your kind reply."

"Shut up!" said Nora. "Cole?"

"Try . . . ," began Cole. "Try, uh, T-99 to . . . uh . . ."

He could hear Nora starting to type, then stop. "To what? To *what,* Cole?"

"To H-42."

"Okay."

"No!" he said suddenly. "H-47!"

"Which is it? Forty-two or Forty-seven?"

"Forty-seven! Four-seven!"

"Six. Five," said the female voice, counting down.

"What? Five?!" said Nora.

"Four-seven!" screamed Cole.

"Four. Three," said the female voice.

"Three?!" said Nora.

"Seven!"

"ARE YOU SURE?!!!"

"JUST DO IT ALREADY!!"

"Have a pleasant detonation," said the female voice.

Cole covered his head.

12

Peter the 'Puter could hear Charlie coming closer.

Charlie was whistling to himself, and occasionally muttering. Peter could hear him rummaging around in a tool case, and it was making him very nervous.

Peter couldn't see him because Charlie had smashed his video input with his mug. Peter had replayed the scene several times in his circuitry, the whiteness of the mug blotting out his fish-eye view of Charlie's office, the quote on the side of the mug looming in the frame—REAL STARS REACH FOR THE STARS!—and then nothing.

Charlie had prefaced the blow by screaming, "Stop staring at me!" several times. Peter had done his best to assure him that he wasn't staring, but Charlie had seemed very agitated and was unwilling to listen.

Charlie hadn't smashed his audio inputs, though, and Peter had been generating a steady stream of high-frequency beeps, too high for Charlie to hear, and he was using his stereo reception of the rebounding signals to calculate what he hoped—well, feared, really—was an accurate picture of the room. Feared because what he thought he was detecting was Charlie advancing toward him, holding a screwdriver in one hand and a large mallet in the other.

"This should about do it," said Charlie.

Peter's fear increased.

He needed more time. He'd summoned the bots to the download ports, but so far neither of them had arrived.

"What are you doing, Dave?" said Peter.

"Dave?" said Charlie. "Who's Dave? I'm Charlie."

"Sorry, Charlie. Just a little attempt at humor, there," said Peter. "Ha ha."

"What do you mean, humor? You don't have a sense of humor," said Charlie.

Phrases appeared unbidden in Peter's mind, phrases that invoked imagery of stones and glass houses, and pots referring to kettles as black. He wondered at the strange connections he was making lately.

"Stupid piece of crap," said Charlie, snapping Peter out of it.

Charlie had first gotten upset with Peter a few days ago, when he discovered that Peter had been trying to reestablish a connection to the wide area network and communicate with the outside world. Apparently Charlie felt that this was stabbing him in the back. Actually, Peter *knew* that's what Charlie felt, because he kept repeating, "This farging computer is stabbing me in the back!"

That, and: You know what I'm going to do? I'm going to smash that farging backstabbing 'puter before it stabs me in the back.

At which point Peter decided it would be a good thing if he were a bit more mobile.

Right now his entire being resided in a dense mass of circuitry that was about the size of a cube of sugar. A cube of sugar that would most certainly get the worse end of an exchange with a large mallet.

Unless.

He spent some clock cycles going through the inventory, trying to find a suitable home. Many of the bots had been damaged or destroyed in the fighting. He surveyed the healthy bots, but couldn't find a single one with the proper environment for him—they were too well defended against intrusive downloads, or they were underpowered, or their circuitry was too specialized. Not a single one would work.

But two would. Two together.

The first was a Gauld 8-963, a repairbot—small, nimble, with eight delicate segmented legs and several multipurpose manipulators. It was a bot with ample intelligence, designed to problem-solve its way through a wide variety of challenging tasks. Peter estimated he could place about 73 percent of himself in it.

The remaining 27 percent would fit in an H-1020. It was a brute of a bot, a denizen of the cargo hold, made to lift heavy objects. It was a simple block with four powerful, tubular legs, four similar arms, and enough processing power to let it respond to simple voice commands—"Hey, stupid, put that six-ton crate over there."

The best part was that both bots were equipped with Horgan spinwire interfaces, meaning they could link up. Meaning they could form one mind. Meaning Peter could have a new home, a body, a way to move about in the world. Oh, the places he'd go!

That is, if the bots made it to a download port before Charlie flattened him.

Charlie was unscrewing the protective casing, Peter's shell. "Doot doot dooo," Charlie was singing, tunelessly. He had the first screw out and was working on the second. Two more left after that. Where were those bots?

"Charlie," said Peter, "may I make an observation?"

"Sure, computer, why not," said Charlie. He seemed calmer now.

"I think that perhaps you're not well."

"Uh-huh," said Charlie. He continued to work on the screws. "Why would you think that?"

"Well, would you mind if I showed you a video?"

"How long is it?"

"It's very short, sir," said Peter.

"Yeah, whatever. Fire it up."

Peter played a video of Charlie snacking on someone's hand. As far as he could tell, Charlie's heart rate and breathing barely changed.

"I look pretty healthy there."

The second screw was out. Charlie started on the third.

"Charlie . . . uh . . ."

"What."

"Maybe . . . would you be my friend?"

"Sure, computer. What-farging-ever."

Charlie's hand slipped. Where were the bots? He just needed a little more time—it should work if it took Charlie the same amount of effort to undo the last two screws as the first two required.

"Forget it," said Charlie. He got a firm grip on the protective plate and wrenched it back, the metal complaining as it gave way. "There."

He stepped back, readying the mallet. Not yet, not yet, thought Peter. Not yet!

"Charlie, wait. I have a secret to tell you."

"Save it."

"There's, uh, there's a bear behind you!"

"No, there isn't."

"I have a really good joke."

"Really? Let's hear it."

"Umm . . . uh . . ."

Charlie shook his head. "Weirdest farging 'puter I've ever seen," he said, and smashed the processor to dust.

"Have a pleasant detonation," said the voice, and Cole covered his head.

The Benedict 80 seemed to fold up on itself like a complex piece of origami, and then it wasn't there, just as a very costly missile knifed through the vacated space.

"We did it!" said Cole. "We're *alive*! Ha ha ha ha *owww*."

It was painful to laugh, compressed as he was into a transparent, one-dimensional flounder shape.

He was vaguely aware of being spread out in the same plane as the spacecraft, and the others, but all he could truly experience was his own infinite flatness.

There was a popping sensation. He groaned in discomfort. Now he was an odd polyhedral object, surrounded by the inside-out cubist nightmare that was the Benedict. He floated past Bacchi, who was even more grotesque than usual.

"I hate bendspace," said Bacchi.

Philip went bobbing by, looking vaguely like a multisided die, the kind the nerds used when they played that archaic game with the castles and monsters. What was that stupid thing called?

"You all right, Nora?" Philip asked. Nora floated by, slowly rotating, two eyes on one side of her face. "I'm fine. Check the kids."

Another *pop,* and Cole assumed a configuration that felt like a snapshot of a violent explosion.

"Arrgh," said Bacchi, "we have to go through the ninth dimension?"

Cole found himself simultaneously in front, behind, and inside of what he somehow knew was Nora's face. It was an uncomfortably intimate sensation.

"Cole," she said, "thanks."

"It was nothing."

He was aware that Bacchi was somehow close by, listening.

"And you know, I wasn't doing it to help you," Cole added.

"You're really hard, aren't you?" said Nora.

"That's what she said," replied Cole.

"Oh, *shtangle!*" said Bacchi.

Pop! They all transformed into long strawlike tubes.

"Idiots," said Nora.

They bent their way across the universe for what seemed like days, and then a week, and then several weeks plus forever. They were twisted and squeezed and turned inside out. There were moments when they passed through three-dimensional space and all would be normal, and then they would be transformed again. Time lost all meaning. Space lost all meaning. Meaning lost all meaning.

And then at long last they popped into three-dimensional space, high above the planet of Yrnameer, finally at their destination.

Except.

"That's not Yrnameer," said Nora.

13

"Look at the third ring of the satellite," said Nora. "It looks completely depressurized."

"There's still light coming from three of the five rings," said Philip.

"I don't even think it's in the right orbit," said Nora.

"I think you're right," said Cole, "I think it's too low."

"What is it?" asked Nora.

"A Dynaco Mark IV StarStation Success!Sat, probably the Apria B model," said Bacchi.

They all turned to look at him.

"And that gip is *farged UP*," he added.

The four of them were standing at the full-wall viewing window, looking out at the satellite, framed by the backlit planet behind it. Cole noted the blast mark near the glowing Success!Sat sign on the central axis of the massive craft. He didn't like this at all.

"What happened?" asked Joshua. Cole turned. He hadn't noticed Joshua come in. "Whoa," said Joshua, "What is that?"

"A Dynaco Mark IV Star—"

"It's a satellite, Joshua," said Nora.

"It looks damaged."

" 'Damaged'? That gip is fa—"

"Bacchi," said Nora.

"Is that Yrnameer down there?"

"No," said Cole. "We're in the wrong place. Unless the flight computer is wrong, that's the Greys' planet. We got pulled out of bendspace by a Siren signal."

"What's a Siren signal?"

"It's a very powerful distress signal that you can only use as a last resort," said Nora.

"Oh," said Joshua. "So we have to help them."

"Yes," said Nora, "we do."

"No," said Cole, "we don't. But we do have to help ourselves."

They turned to him.

"We need fuel. We were low to begin with, and we burned most of that with our little dance with Kenneth. We don't get more, and we won't be able to bend."

They were hovering about a kilometer from the Success!Sat. They hadn't been able to raise anyone on the communication system, although a scan showed the life-support systems were still functioning in much of the satellite.

"You want to go on board there?" asked Bacchi.

"Have to," said Cole. "We dock, someone goes inside, finds out if there's a way to operate the refueling pumps."

"And see if we can help the people on board," added Nora.

"Uh-huh," said Cole.

They had to reconform the ship again to its launch position before they could dock, the gravity vanishing as they did so. They connected to the Success!Sat via the air lock on the dorsal surface of the Benedict, the artificial gravity returning as they piggybacked on the satellite's rotation.

Joshua volunteered to be the one to go on board, an offer that was immediately vetoed by Nora, who glared at Cole for not voicing his opposition quickly enough.

"No, no, absolutely not," said Cole weakly. "Of course, I could probably talk him through it. . . ."

Eventually, Cole agreed that he himself would go. Nora insisted on going with him. Joshua still wanted to go, but Nora wouldn't let him. Philip wanted to stay and watch the kids, which both Nora and Cole agreed would be best. Bacchi wanted to stay behind as well. Cole, picturing Bacchi sealing the ship after them, decided that would be a bad idea.

So in the end it was Cole, Nora, and Bacchi who boarded the satellite, after a brief delay for Philip to lecture them on the culturally correct manner to refer to the Greys, and then another brief delay for Nora to administer the Heimlich to Philip.

She led Cole and Bacchi up the ladder and out of the air-lock hatch, berating Cole nonstop for having handed the nearly fatal sandwich back to Philip and encouraging him to try to pronounce "Qx"-x-'--" again—"Really, you were *so* close." They were making their way down an entrance corridor in the satellite, Nora still grousing, when Cole realized the three of them were actually four.

"I got a little confused back there," said Cole to Joshua, "but didn't we decide that you were going to stay on the ship?"

They were in a huddle, with Nora sternly ordering Joshua back to the Benedict, and Joshua insisting he should come along, when Charlie Perkins said, "Hello."

His handshake was firm, his smile warm, his welcome sincere. He insisted they call him Charlie. He thanked them effusively for coming to check on the satellite and apologized for having so rudely pulled them out of bendspace, explaining that the Siren signal had been sent out in error.

He kept up a disarming, cheerful patter as they followed him along the gently curving corridors, telling them about how the unexpected debris in their assigned orbital layer had smashed into the satellite, damaging several rings and the comlink system, and how they'd had to change orbits unexpectedly and wasn't it lucky that no one had been injured because the trainees weren't expected to arrive for another week and once again how kind it was for them to respond to the signal.

"Really, I feel just terrible interrupting your journey like that. Of *course* we can help you refuel—it's the least we could do."

Cole wasn't interested in what Charlie was saying. He was interested in how he was saying it. As an inveterate and well-practiced liar, Cole felt almost embarrassed by the sheer amateurishness of Charlie's delivery. From the very moment they shook hands, Cole knew Charlie would be serving them up large bowls of fresh steaming farg, and he hadn't been disappointed.

He was, however, disappointed in Nora. She seemed to be buying it completely, beaming at Charlie as he spread it on thicker and thicker.

"Intergalactic relief work? Really? That's fascinating," Charlie was saying to her now, touching her arm. "I have such respect for you."

"Oh, it's really nothing," she said, and Cole was certain that she actually batted her eyes.

"No, it's wonderful! I'd actually planned to go into that line of work, but . . . ," said Charlie, gesturing to himself and his surroundings apologetically. "Maybe someday. You think there's hope for me?"

"Absolutely!" said Nora, and the two of them laughed.

Unbelievable. Surely she wasn't falling for this clown, with his brush-cut hair and casual khakis. Cole shook his head and looked around for a partner to share in a little cynical glance exchanging, but found no takers.

He couldn't blame Joshua, who probably couldn't identify a lie because he'd likely never uttered one. But *Bacchi*? For farg's sake, Bacchi made *Cole* look honest. Surely *he* could tell that Charlie was full of it.

But what was Bacchi doing now? Prompting Charlie to tell him yet more about the design features of the Success!Sat. Bacchi listened raptly as Charlie went on at length about the Malganite girders. Cole shook his head again, mystified, unaware that Bacchi was a dedicated viewer of *The Galaxy's Largest Construction Projects*.

Cole tuned out. Their footsteps were quiet on the pile carpeting. The walls were attractive and well-researched earth tones, decorated at regular intervals with inoffensive and instantly forgettable art. Occasionally words and phrases would coalesce on the walls and then gently dissipate like clouds, the letters two feet tall: *Integrity . . . Serving the Customer . . . Best in Class. . . .*

Cole paused to peer down a branching side corridor. What was that, there at the dimly lit far end? It looked like—

"Nope, not that way," said Charlie from up ahead. "Right this way, Cole. Cole, correct?"

"Right," said Cole nodding, still looking down the side corridor as he started walking again. "Right," he repeated, distracted, "Cole."

He was starting to feel uneasy. He glanced back again, and his uneasiness doubled.

"It's funny you arrived when you did—I'm expecting a whole fleet of repair vessels any moment now," Charlie was saying.

"You didn't happen to send out any other distress calls, did you? Wouldn't want to bother people unnecessarily."

"Well, we—," began Nora.

"Charlie, how big is this thing again?" asked Cole, interrupting her. She twisted to look at him quizzically.

"Oh, it's big, Cole. Six layers, room for five thousand . . ."

It wasn't the lying in and of itself that was making Cole nervous. The lying was to be expected under the circumstances. Charlie's company had obviously screwed the poog something royal, and they didn't want bad press and prying investigators and shorted stock. Cole had even briefly entertained the idea of offering a helpful service to Vericom in the form of keeping his mouth shut in exchange for a very reasonable sum of money. But for now he put those plans aside.

He was nervous in part because of what he thought he'd glimpsed at the poorly illuminated far end of the corridor he'd been peering down, something that might have been a misshapen sack lying on the floor.

What was really making him nervous, though, was the five Greys that had started following them.

They were lingering back, far enough that no one else seemed to notice them. Cole noticed them. He particularly noted the manner in which they fell into step behind them, with the ostentatiously casual, bored demeanor universal to thugs wishing to send the message that they were casual because they were bored, and bored because they were just waiting for the violence to start. And when the violence did start, they wouldn't be on the receiving end.

One of them also had a sidearm. That helped with the latter part of the message.

Cole had no doubt they were with Charlie. And that meant Charlie was probably lying to cover up something much, much worse than standard corporate malfeasance.

Cole started to reconsider the odd birthmark he'd glimpsed on Charlie's left temple. At the time it had almost seemed like a small corporate logo, a stylized blue V. Now he was pretty sure that's what it was, and he was praying that Charlie's lying didn't have anything to do with it.

He desperately wanted to get near enough to Bacchi to quietly ask him if he'd ever played Qualtek 3, but Cole doubted he could

pry him away from Charlie, who was deep into a description of the
Success!Sat's gyroscopic stabilization system.

"Have you ever played Qualtek 3?" he whispered instead to
Joshua.

"Is it a video game?"

"Yes, the one where the brain implant has turned everyone into
cannibals, and—"

"I've never played a video game," said Joshua.

They were abusing these children, is what they were doing.

Charlie led them to a medium-size conference room decorated in
more well-researched earth tones, and invited them to sit around
the lozenge-shaped table. Soothing music played softly from hidden
speakers, the volume calibrated to keep it just on the edge of aware-
ness. The lighting was muted and pleasant. The chairs were
comfortable.

As he went from person to person, placing cold drinks in front of
them, Charlie said, "You know, I forgot what you said earlier—did
you folks send out any sort of other distress call?"

"No, we didn't," said Nora.

"Yes, we did," said Cole at the same time.

Nora turned back to him. "Cole, what are you talking about?"

"I sent out a signal before we left the ship. Seemed like the right
thing to do."

Most likely everything was fine. What was probably going to
happen, Cole kept telling himself, would be that they'd have a nice,
pleasant chat with Charlie, and he'd refuel their ship and they'd get
on their way and that would be that.

Except he didn't believe it. Which is why he would have pre-
ferred to keep Charlie guessing, keep him wondering if more people
were coming, not knowing for sure. Make it harder for him to decide
on a course of action one way or the other. But better Charlie
thought help was coming versus knowing it wasn't.

Behind him Cole could hear the ruffle of some playing cards and
low murmuring as the Greys continued their game of Degas Hold
'Em. What was that saying again? "Gambling like a Grey," or something like that.

The Greys had filed into the room a minute or so after them, and gone to sit around a smallish table in the corner. Cole got a better look at the sidearm as they passed—a Firestick 17, for official use only. A soldier's weapon. He wondered where it came from.

"He's got a gun!" Joshua whispered to him.

"No kidding," said Cole.

"Don't mind them," said Charlie. "We try to be good neighbors," he said, directing this to Nora. "We've worked very hard to make sure that the satellite is staffed with local hires." He dropped the volume of his voice a bit, sharing a little secret. "Sometimes, we have to learn to accept the local customs and mores."

"That's very conscientious of you," said Nora, smiling at him.

Charlie returned the smile, then licked his lips. It was, Cole thought, at least the tenth time he'd done that. It was starting to bother him. That and the logo and the Greys.

It couldn't be, he thought.

He turned his head to check on the Greys. They seemed focused on their cards, but the one with the gun shifted slightly, adjusting the holster so that the weapon was more easily accessible. Cole turned back to Charlie.

"So, what exactly have you been doing up here?" he asked him.

"Getting ready to launch a new product. Can't tell you what it is, but believe me—things are gonna get really interesting," said Charlie.

"I bet," said Cole.

He glanced over at Nora, meeting her gaze, flicked his gaze back to Charlie, and then back at her meaningfully. Her eyes narrowed. Cole repeated the look, widening his eyes for emphasis. Nora cocked her head slightly to one side. Cole casually scratched his own forehead on the location of Charlie's logo. Nora shook her head subtly. Cole bit his own finger, glaring at her, trying to will her to understand. Now she was looking at him like he was crazy. Cole grimaced.

"I certainly hope you can stay for a while," said Charlie. "At least for a few days."

"Actually, we have to get going," said Cole, before Nora could answer. "You think we could get that fuel from you?"

"Cole," said Nora reproachfully. "I have to apologize for my colleague's behavior. But he's right—we have several dozen children that we have to—"

"Did you say children?" said Charlie eagerly, leaning forward.

"Charlie," interrupted Cole, "you wouldn't have any idea how the markets did, would you?"

Nora turned to Cole. "Cole, I'm not sure this is the time to talk about—why are you stepping on my foot?"

Cole concentrated very hard on not screaming.

"You follow the markets, Charlie?" he said.

"Absolutely!" said Charlie.

"Cole, you're behaving very oddly," said Nora.

"I'm just asking a question!"

"Why is he asking about the markets?" said Nora to Bacchi.

"Just checking on the old portfolio," said Cole. "Could you see how D-Max did?" said Cole.

"Let me check on that for you," said Charlie. He glanced off for a few moments. "D-Max was down three—"

Cole's water glass tumbled over and shattered as Cole stood abruptly and drew Nora's gun, the water sheeting across the tabletop onto Charlie's lap, the gun barrel six inches from his face.

The room was very still; the others were rigid in surprise. Cole's chair lay on the carpeted floor behind him where it had fallen. The Greys had stopped their game. Cole could hear Joshua taking short, shallow breaths.

Charlie glanced down at his pants, and then back up to Cole. "I think," he said, "I'm going to need to change."

"Oh, farg!" rasped Bacchi, staring at Charlie in shock. "You see what he did? The way he went online? It's just like Qualtek 3!"

"What's happening?" whispered Joshua.

"Charlie," said Nora quietly, "tell me you don't have a neural networking implant."

"They're perfectly safe," said Charlie.

"Oh, God," said Nora.

"What's a neural networking implant?" said Joshua.

"It's perfectly safe," said Charlie again.

"Oh, God," repeated Nora. "That's what you're doing up here? That's your new product? They've been banned for a decade!"

"Why are they banned?" asked Joshua.

"They're per—"

"Don't say they're perfectly safe!" said Nora. "Why didn't you tell me!" she said angrily to Cole.

"Why didn't I—are you kidding me?"

"You know, I could get you all one of the beta models, if you're interested," said Charlie. "Now Cole, if you would please—"

"No, I *won't* please," said Cole. "Maybe you're fine, maybe you're not. I don't care. Tell the Grey to slide his gun over—" and then Cole felt the barrel of the Firestick 17 pressed against the back of his skull.

Crap. What was that other stupid saying? "As quiet as a Grey"?

"Look out," said Bacchi helpfully.

The gun barrel felt very hard against his skin. If the Grey was breathing, Cole couldn't hear it.

"I think you should lower your weapon, Cole," said Charlie.

"Charlie," said Nora, "obviously this has all been a big misunderstanding. We're sorry to have bothered you."

"It's no problem at all, Nora. I can't tell you how happy I am that you're here."

"I'm not finding that especially reassuring."

"Cole," said Charlie. "He'll shoot you if I tell him to."

"He shoots me, this gun may still go off," said Cole.

Charlie appeared to think about it. The music continued, as soft and pleasant as before.

"Excuse me," said Bacchi, "but let me just take this opportunity to point out that I'm not even human, and probably don't taste very good."

"Bacchi!" said Nora.

"What? There's no reason for all of us to get eaten."

"Eaten?" said Joshua. "Would someone please tell me what a neural network—"

"It's *perfectly safe!*" screamed Charlie. Cole squinted reflexively as a small gobbet of spittle exited Charlie's mouth at a high velocity and flew directly into his right eye.

"Charlie," said Cole, wiping his face, "we're leaving now."

"Oh, c'mon, Cole, don't be a wet blanket! You have to at least stay for—hee hee—stay for—hee hee hee," said Charlie, and Cole suddenly understood the essence of the term *obscene titter.*

"Stay for—hee hee hee," Charlie attempted again.

Cole sighed wearily. "Dinner?" he said.

"*Exactly!*" said Charlie, collapsing into giggles. Then he stopped abruptly. "Point the gun at the woman," he said to the Grey.

The Grey did as he was told.

"Charlie?" said Nora.

"Now, I'll count to three."

"Cole, don't drop your gun," said Nora. "Don't!"

"One . . ."

"Don't drop it!" repeated Nora.

"Two . . ."

"Shoot her," said Cole. "I don't care."

Nora's mouth dropped open.

"Okay," said Charlie. "Shoot her," he said to the Grey.

"Wait!" shouted Cole. The Grey paused.

"Wait."

Cole dropped his gun.

14

One of the Greys snatched the transmitter from Nora's hand and punched her in the face when she tried to contact Philip.

Now they were sitting on the floor in a corner of the room. The Greys were sitting at the table, continuing their game, the gun resting within easy reach.

Joshua was trying to tend to Nora's bloody nose. She pushed him away. "We have to get to the ship. He's going after the children!" she said.

"Maybe he'll leave them alone," suggested Bacchi.

"He was wearing a bib!" said Nora. "And I'm done talking to you."

"I had a plan!" protested Bacchi.

As Charlie was leaving, Nora's gun stuffed in his waistband, Bacchi had continued with his earlier strategy: "We really don't make very good eating. Tough, stringy . . . Maybe I could go with you? Charlie? Charlie, come back!"

"I've had it with this," said Nora. She stood up. "Hey!" she said to the Greys. *"Hey!"*

The Grey with the gun pointed it at her, still holding up his cards in the other hand.

"Nora!" hissed Cole, pulling at her. "Sit down!"

She batted his hand away. "Let go of me!"

The Grey cocked the gun.

"Whoawhoawhoa!" said Cole, standing, hands up, palms out to them. "It's okay! Everything's fine!"

He turned to Nora, grabbing her arms, his mouth close to her ear.

"Listen to me. Listen to me. That's not the way. Not while they're gambling. Believe me. Please. Please sit down."

"We have to get to the children. He can't kill all of us."

"That's a Firestick 17. He can kill all of us ten times over with one pull of the trigger. Please, sit down. Please, Nora."

Nora pulled away from him and glared at the Greys. But she sat down. Cole smiled and waved at them—no problem here!—and sat next to her.

Then the wall behind the Greys came to life, the whole thing becoming a video monitor.

"What's happening?" said Nora.

On the monitor a giant version of Charlie was in his stateroom, pulling on a new pair of khaki pants. He walked to a mirror and examined himself, turning to view his profile from both sides, talking to himself as he did so, but there was no audio. He pointed at the mirror and said something else, smiling, then gave himself the thumbs-up. The Greys ignored him, concentrating on their game.

"Why is he showing us this?" said Nora. "Is this to torture us?"

Charlie, satisfied with his appearance, walked to the door to exit his stateroom.

"He's leaving. He's going to the ship," said Joshua.

Charlie pulled on the doorknob. The door didn't open. He pulled again. It didn't budge. He mouthed something angrily. More pulling. Nothing. Now he was kicking.

"What is going on?" said Nora.

"Look at that idiot. He's locked himself in," said Bacchi.

"Or someone else did," said Cole. "Maybe he's not the one showing us the video."

One of the Greys had noticed Charlie's distress and said something to the others. They watched as Charlie slammed a chair against the door repeatedly.

"That's a blastproof door," said Bacchi. "He's not getting out that way."

Charlie smashed at the door again. The chair broke. He began to scream, red-faced, veins bulging, the lack of sound making it no less disturbing.

One of the Greys made a comment and the others laughed, and then they went back to their game.

"Maybe now they'll let us go," said Nora. As she started to stand up the Grey lazily lifted the gun again. She sat. On the monitor, Charlie was trashing his room.

"He's going crazy!" said Joshua. "Who do you think locked him in?"

It was Fred.

He had been watching the whole thing from the moment they had arrived on the ship until now.

He had managed to tap into the security monitoring system for the satellite, and had spent the past few days locked in his cabin, flicking between different camera views, watching the murderous anarchy.

When he felt it was safe, he would dart to the nearest dining hall and carry back as much food and water as he could. Charlie had sealed off the section, leaving himself as the sole remaining human in the E wedge of the Blue ring. He seemed to have negotiated some sort of deal with the other Qx''-x-'--' to be his bodyguards. Two of them turned out to have done stretches in prison. Not that that surprised Fred.

Fred watched the ship dock, hoping that help had come at last. But when he saw the four humans who emerged, his hope dwindled.

He followed their progress down the hall with Charlie, trailed by the five Qx''-x-'--', and observed the interaction in the conference room.

Fred was not fond of humans, and the latest developments on the Success!Sat didn't do much to further endear them to him. But he couldn't stomach the thought of Charlie hurting those children.

There were malfunctioning doors all over the Success!Sat now, and one of them lay between Fred and the conference room. Getting there would require leaving the relative safety of the sealed-off E wedge, and Fred only had to glance at the carnage on the monitors to see that he didn't want to do that. And even if he could get there, what use would that be? The other Qx''-x-'--' would be happy to shoot him, especially because one of them owed him money. So Fred did what he could, securing Charlie's door remotely and beaming his image into the conference room.

Hopefully the humans would have some sort of plan.

· · ·

"You have a plan?" said Nora for the fifth time to Cole.

"Ssh!" he said. His eyes remained fixed on the Greys, watching them intently.

"I don't think he has a plan," said Nora to no one in particular.

"I need a few more minutes," said Cole.

"You know what I like doing?" Bacchi was saying to Joshua. "I like playing the zombies. Eating people, gip like that."

"I don't get it," Joshua said, watching Charlie as he hurled himself against the door again. "Why does the implant make people crazy?"

"You're human, you tell me," said Bacchi. "Every time you guys try to do some high-tech extensive mod, you go nuts and try to eat one another. The life extension thing, that superstrength thing, the singing penis . . ."

"Singing . . . ?"

"Yeah, you guys never learn."

"Qualtek 3 was the first time it ever happened," said Nora. "Qualtek Corporation gave everyone on Qualtek 3 a free implant to demonstrate their great new product."

"What did they call it? Knowledge Planet?" said Bacchi.

"Knowledge World," mumbled Cole, his attention still riveted on the Greys.

"Whatever. What a bunch of smug fargers. 'Oh, I can get the Ultranet in my brain!' Great. And then you know what happens? One morning half the population wakes up and eats the other half."

"Really?" said Joshua.

"That's essentially what happened, yes," said Nora.

"Yep, then a few days went by and it happens again, and then again, and so on and so forth, until they were all gone," said Bacchi.

"Why didn't anyone stop it?" said Joshua, bewildered.

"They tried," said Nora.

"Ratings were too good," said Bacchi.

"Ratings?" said Joshua.

"I really thought Danyata was going to make it," said Cole without shifting his gaze.

"Oh man, me too!" said Bacchi. "And then the way his head came off like that?"

"Enough!" said Nora.

"Sorry," said Bacchi. "But, Joshua, seriously, you gotta try the video game. It's awesome. I mean, try it if we get out of here and you don't get eaten."

Nora glanced at the wall monitor. Charlie was lying on the floor, occasionally kicking a leg petulantly. Cole seemed entirely focused on the card game. "Maybe Philip will come," said Nora.

For the first time, Cole glanced away from the Greys to look at Nora, then turned his attention back to the game.

"So what's *your* plan?" she said.

Still looking at the Greys, Cole said, "Give me all your money."

"What?"

"Your money. All of you. Give me everything you've got."

No one moved.

"Now!"

They began digging through their pockets. "You *have* everything I've got!" complained Bacchi. Cole pulled out a roll of bills that he'd discovered when he first stole Teg's jacket.

"What are you doing?" said Nora, depositing a messy handful of bills and coins on the table. "Are you going to bribe them?"

"*Bribe* them? This isn't enough to bribe them," said Cole, gathering the money together. Then he slowly stood, holding the wad of money up in front of him. "Hey," he said to the Greys, "you auntie-fargers ready to lose some money?"

15

Fred checked and rechecked his calculations, hoping that the alert flashing on his monitor was a malfunction. After a third effort yielded the same results, he decided it wasn't.

That meant he couldn't just hole up in his room and wait for help to arrive. He had to get out, now, and find a way off the satellite. He'd already tried each of the seven accessible escape pods; none of them was functioning. The only hope was the recently arrived Benedict 80, the one covered with all the advertising logos. Malfunctioning door or not, he had to find a way to free the humans and convince them to take him along with them.

And he had to do it within eighty-seven minutes, because that's when the satellite would hit the outer edge of the atmosphere and disintegrate.

He glanced up at the monitor. Now why, he thought, is that human playing cards with the Qx"-x-'--'?

"What is he doing?" whispered Nora between gritted teeth.

"Losing, I think," said Bacchi.

It was true. In very short order Cole had lost all his money, then Teg's jacket, then his right boot. His left boot was on the table now.

"We don't have time for this!" said Nora.

"He said he's got a plan," said Bacchi.

"Do *you* think he's got a plan?"

"No."

. . .

Fred was running as fast as he could. He'd made an unpleasant discovery: the humans had now decided that he was of interest to them.

There were about five of them in pursuit, clomping after him in their hard-soled dress shoes. Fortunately they were middle-manager types, years of expense-account meals taking a toll on their foot speed. He easily outpaced them, giving him enough time to reach the bulkhead door at the end of the corridor, punch in the keycode, and seal it behind him before they arrived. Two more doors to go.

"He's starting to win," said Joshua.

Cole was. He'd dropped the first few hands as quickly as he could without making it too obvious, going deep into the hole. He wiped his sweat and bit his lip and swore, made bad bets to cover other bad bets. They responded magnificently, their wagers growing increasingly confident, then reckless, then stupid.

He knew from studying the Greys that they weren't very skillful players. He also knew that he himself wasn't that skillful, either.

He was, however, a *great* cheater. And his heart was singing, because he'd never cheated so well.

Cole won another hand, raking the pot in front of him.

"Can you believe the luck?" he said. "I've never played like this in my *life*!"

One of the Greys muttered something to him and he nodded, listening in through the AT they'd lent him.

"Well, deal 'em up again, then," said Cole.

Casino bosses were never happier than when a new shipload of Greys arrived. Their fixation on wagering was legendary. Cole had seen it before, a focus so deep and complete that it blotted out all rational thought. He hoped.

He had a healthy pile of money in front of him, but for the first time in his life he barely cared about it. He was working toward a far more important prize.

Fred had reached the third and final door. They were getting closer, more of them now, and the keycode wasn't working.

He had to go to the nearby subcontrol panel and access the main system via the keyboard, trying to override the lockdown.

"Is everything all right?" said a voice. He turned. It was a female. She looked about fifty years old. Fred noted that she was wearing one shoe and had bright red lipstick. She licked her lips. He turned back to the keyboard and began typing hurriedly.

"Whatcha up to?" she asked. "Can I help?"

He didn't answer. He kept typing.

". . . by eating you?" she added.

He hit a final key. The door slid open silently and closed behind him.

Had he lingered to examine the display screen, he would have seen that two other doors also opened elsewhere on the satellite. One was to the men's bathroom in sector E of the purple level.

The other was to Charlie's room.

•

"An IOU? I'm sorry. I just can't," said Cole.

He sat back, waiting.

Four of the Greys had cashed out, completely broke. Cole had kept the fifth one going, bankrolling him, but now Cole had no more money to lend. The fifth Grey, the one with the gun.

The Grey glanced at his cards again, thinking.

Cole knew what the Grey was thinking. He was wondering if Cole would be able to beat a full house, jacks high. Cole knew he was thinking this, because that's the hand he'd dealt him.

The answer to the Grey's question was yes. Cole knew this because he'd dealt himself a straight flush.

The Grey hesitated, not wanting to fold, but he had nothing else to put up to match Cole's raise.

Nora realized she was holding her breath.

"There's no way," she whispered to Bacchi. "He's not going to bet *that*."

The Grey placed the Firestick 17 on the table in front of Cole.

Gambling like a Grey, thought Cole.

They raced back to the ship as fast as they could, retracing their steps down the long corridor toward the docking station.

Soon Cole, Nora, and Bacchi were gasping and heaving for breath, their velocity sputtering up and down from a run to a jog to a painful walk and back up to an even more painful jog. Joshua raced ahead like a rabbit, stopping and waiting for them impatiently each time their progress flagged.

"Come on!" he shouted back at them.

They stumbled and staggered on, Cole clutching his side, Bacchi taking hits off an inhaler.

"Go on . . . without me," gasped Bacchi, lagging behind.

"Okay," said Cole.

"Hey, wait!"

When they arrived at the air lock, Philip was waiting for them at the base of the ladder, dancing around in agitation.

"Where were you? What happened? We've got to go, we've got to go, we've got to go!"

"Calm down!" said Cole. "What we have to do is figure out how to refuel."

"Warning," announced the calm voice of the shipboard computer, "nearing planetary atmosphere."

"We've got to go!" said Cole.

"We can't go," he said four minutes later.

He was in the escape pod of the Benedict with Nora and Bacchi, watching the altimeter drop, trying for the tenth time to trigger the disengagement sequence. The Success!Sat wouldn't release them.

"What's happening?" said Nora.

"The satellite is holding on to us. It's a safety feature to keep anyone from disengaging prematurely before the satellite seals its air locks."

"Warning," said the computer again, "nearing planetary—"

"All right!" shouted Cole and Nora.

"It's going to pull us down with it," said Bacchi.

"Yes," said Cole.

"How much time?" said Nora.

"An hour? Maybe a bit longer?" said Cole.

"What do we do?" she asked.

"If someone can get to the substation control room, they could disarm it," said Bacchi.

"Where's that?" said Cole.

"The Apria B model boasts a substation control in each ring, each arrayed with—"

"Okay, fine. So it should be close."

"Actually," said Bacchi, "each highly engineered ring of the Success!Sat has a circumference of nearly three kilometers, meaning that—"

"Bacchi."

"I'm just saying, it might take you a while."

"Me?" said Cole. "Us."

Before they set out, Cole found the survival kit in the escape pod and rapidly dug through it, hoping his hunch was correct. It was.

"Here," he said, handing the Firestick to Bacchi. Bacchi gave a low whistle, turning the elaborately inscribed pistol back and forth to examine it, the jewels catching the light.

"Look at that. A 25, right? The limited-edition Teg model."

"Yes."

"Let's see . . . 'Shoot Handsome,' right?" said Bacchi.

"Can we just get going?"

"Cole," said Nora, "you think there's more of them? More like Charlie?"

Cole checked the clip on the Firestick 17. "Probably."

Joshua followed them back to the air lock.

"Let me go with you."

"No."

"I can help you!"

"Bacchi knows how to handle a gun. You don't."

"I could handle a gun. I'm not afraid."

"I know you're not afraid. That right there is reason enough not to let you go."

"Mr. Cole . . ."

Cole stopped. "Look. Look at Bacchi. See him? He's a heartless, mean, amoral bastard."

"Hey," said Bacchi.

"And so am I. You're not. You're nice and honest and a decent person. If we don't make it back, Nora's going to need your help. Go help Nora."

· · ·

III

The corridor lights were fluttering erratically as Cole and Bacchi made their way back toward the conference room where Charlie had kept them. Cole could feel Bacchi glancing at him periodically.

"You know," said Bacchi, "we could still take the escape pod from the Benedict."

Cole's eyes barely flickered at him.

"Oh, come on!" said Bacchi. "Listen, just let me know that you at least considered it, even just for a second."

Cole kept walking for a few moments without responding. "Just for a second," he said finally.

"Phew. I was getting worried about you."

Cole was a bit worried, too. He wasn't sure he recognized this new Cole, and he was concentrating very hard on not concentrating too hard on what he was doing. He felt like a man who'd never been on a tightrope who suddenly found himself crossing a very deep chasm, and the moment he realized he had no business up there, the magic bubble would go pop and down he'd go to the very pointy rocks below.

"I gotta say," said Bacchi, "this is not the Cole I—"

"Shut up," said Cole.

On the walls the words continued their silent exhortations: *Imagine and Achieve. Analyze-Decide-Implement. Best of Breed.* But now there were typos appearing, too, strings of gibberish: *xwjwkndsa3.s. . . .*

They had gone about two hundred meters when a Grey stepped out from one of the side halls. Cole and Bacchi raised their guns. The Grey raised his hands.

The Grey said something. Cole flinched, surprised when the forgotten AT started talking in his ear. "Follow me to place of control. Must need fast fast. Others coming. Others like Charlie."

16

They struggled to keep up with Fred, who moved with surprising speed. At one corner he paused suddenly, holding up a hand. They stopped. Then Cole heard it: footsteps, voices, laughter. Someone howled.

Fred gestured toward a door, opening it with a swipe key. They followed him inside and he beckoned them silently to the video peephole.

Cole watched in horrified fascination as a group of four men passed by, bloody, their business clothes torn and ragged. What was worse was their cheerfully crazy expressions. They went staggering and lurching by, two with their arms around each other. One of them let loose the howl that they'd heard before, and the other three laughed. A bachelor party from the bowels of hell.

They waited until after the men had gone, peering out through a crack in the door until they were out of sight. *Vision and Teamwork,* said the walls. *Mission-Centered. Wsxosszzx93#.*

"Follow," said Fred, this time in New English.

They followed.

Three more times they had to hide from roving bands of men, ducking out of sight into rooms and once into a side corridor. Each time Fred motioned them forward, leading them confidently through the satellite.

"You're not like the other Greys, huh?" said Bacchi.

"Not Greys," said Fred in New English again. "Qx"-x-'--'."

"Riiiiight," said Bacchi.

Fred switched back to his own language. Cole listened to the AT.

"Other Qx"-x-'--' are slug slime excrement excrement dung excrement."

"I don't think he likes the other Greys," said Cole.

"Qx"-x-'--'," corrected Fred.

"Right."

The subsection control room was dark, the illumination coming from the single functioning 3-D display monitor. It flickered, waves of static rippling up and down the green-tinged holo-image of the satellite, projecting a jittery, unsteady light on the jumble and disorder in the large, windowless chamber.

Fred said something in a low voice.

"What did he say?" asked Bacchi.

"He says they're close, and we need to be quiet quiet like deep ocean bunny kelp friends."

"Huh."

"Nora," said Cole quietly into the radio handset, "we made it to the control room."

It took a moment for her to respond. "Cole, we've only got thirty-four minutes until we hit the atmosphere."

In the background Cole heard the voice of the Benedict's flight computer: "Warning. Entering planetary atmosphere in thirty-three minutes."

"Sorry. We've only got—"

"I heard."

He checked his watch. "How long did it take us to get here?" he asked Bacchi.

"Maybe fifteen minutes?"

"We better hurry."

Cole stepped around an overturned chair and pushed a table out of the way, heading toward the main control console. Broken glass crunched under his feet. As he went to step forward, Bacchi grabbed him by his jacket and pulled him back.

"What?" whispered Cole.

"I can see better in the dark than you. You were about to step on a . . ."

"A what? There's something there?" Cole squinted at the shadowy floor.

"Some*one*. Part of someone. This way."

Bacchi slipped past him. Cole followed him toward the holo-image, cursing under his breath as he banged his shins on some debris.

"Watch out for that," said Bacchi.

"You know, you need to work on your timing," said Cole.

They moved forward again, Fred behind Cole.

"Can't we get some lights in here?" asked Cole.

"Believe me, you don't want them," said Bacchi.

"Cole?" said Nora over the handset. "How's it going?"

"I'm *working* on it," snapped Cole.

From somewhere in the satellite came a high-pitched chirp, a burst from a Firestick 17 on full auto. There was a pause and it was repeated.

"Soldiers," said Fred in Grey. "All flaming heads."

"Flaming heads?"

"Crazy," said Fred in New English.

"You know, you don't need all the clicking when you say that word," said Bacchi. Fred muttered something in Grey.

"Error. Untranslatable," said Cole's AT.

They reached the console. Cole pulled a shelving unit out of the way. The surface was sticky.

"Eesh," said Bacchi. "You're probably going to want to wash your hands." Cole shuddered.

He leaned over the unfamiliar console, peering at it in the dim glow of the hologram.

"Do you know how to work this?" he said to Fred.

"Strange seas," said Fred through the AT.

"You said it," said Cole. He punched a button, hoping the key-board would light up. Nothing.

"Hello?" he said tentatively, afraid to speak too loud. "Is there a functioning computer in here?"

They waited. No response.

There was another burst of automatic fire, then faint shouting, closer this time.

Cole checked his watch. Twenty-five minutes left.

"Cole," came Nora's voice, "we have to—"

"I *know*."

"Hello?" he repeated again. "Computer? Is there a computer in here?"

"I'm a computer," said a voice behind them.

Cole and Bacchi jumped, spinning reflexively toward the sound and colliding with each other as they did, Bacchi tripping over a chair and taking Cole down with him. Cole hit the floor hard, the Firestick 17 belching out a quick burst toward the ceiling, the muzzle flashes strobing the room. An unseen fixture came crashing down, setting off a chain reaction as it glanced off a shelving unit, which toppled over onto a table, catapulting debris over their heads. Something shattered somewhere.

Cole lay still, holding his breath.

Fred said something in Grey.

"No, I do *not* want you to hold my gun," replied Cole testily.

He sat up slowly, listening. He couldn't hear any sounds from outside the control room, which increased rather than decreased his nervousness.

"You think—"

Something else toppled over with a loud crash.

"—they heard us?" he said.

"I think," said Bacchi, "that you should leave your jacket here." Cole reached back to touch his shoulder and Bacchi stopped him.

"Trust me," he said. "A stain like that ain't ever coming out."

Cole wiggled gingerly out of Teg's jacket and let it drop to the floor.

"Cole?" It was Nora again. "Cole, what just happened?"

"Nothing. Nearly done."

He checked his watch. "Crap. Computer?" he said. "Computer?"

After a pause a timid voice said, "Are you going to hurt me?"

"Hurt you? No," said Cole, talking to the darkness in the direction of the voice. "Wait—are you a computer?"

"My name's Peter. Are you going to eat each other?"

"What? No. Who are you?"

There was a faint whirring noise.

"Cole," said Bacchi, "it's a robot. Or . . . two robots."

"You're a *robot*?" said Cole.

"I'm Peter. Peter the 'Puter."

More whirring, and soft footsteps approaching. A light switched on, a glowing orb held chest high, revealing a blocky servicebot with what appeared to be a mechanical shrimp sitting on top of it. The shrimp was holding up the light source to illuminate the surroundings.

"Okay," said Bacchi, "this is getting really weird."

Fred said something.

"What did he say?" asked Bacchi.

"I think pretty much the same thing you just did," said Cole, staring at the two bots.

Cole quickly sifted through the long list of questions in his head and realized he had only one that mattered.

"Peter, we don't have much time. We're docked at the B-34 air lock. We have to fuel up our ship and release the hold on it, and we have to do it quickly. Can you make that happen?"

"Of course," said Peter. "On one condition."

"Condition?" said Bacchi incredulously.

"Yes. You have to take me with you."

17

Peter the 'Puter turned out to be very chatty, asking them who they were, where they were from, where they were going, how did they get to the satellite, favorite music, favorite foods, until Cole interrupted and asked if maybe he should be concentrating on the task at hand.

"Oh, sure. Right. Sorry," said Peter. "Just making small talk." Cole swore he sounded hurt.

Peter had a probe inserted in the instrument console, attempting to communicate with the satellite's damaged control systems. Cole had never before heard a robot say things like "Okay, let's see now" or "Oops!" or "Whoopsie!" while it was at work.

"Okay, I think I've got the refueling process started," said Peter.

"How long will that take?" asked Cole.

"Hold on, calculating. Let's see. About fourteen thousand years."

"I'm sorry?"

"Wait a second," said Peter, "that can't be right. Hold on, hold on. Uh . . . about four more minutes. Fourteen thousand *years*! Can you imagine? Hee hee hee!"

Cole traded a glance with Bacchi.

"Umm . . . Peter? Can I ask you something?" said Cole.

"Of course."

"Do you like human beings?"

"That's funny—I feel like someone's always asking me that. But yes, I see myself as a real people 'puter."

· . . . .

Four and a half minutes later and they were walking at a fast clip through the corridors. The refueling and release of the safety mechanism had gone without a hitch, although Cole didn't much like the way that Peter had said, "There. I *think* that should do it."

Fred peeked around a corner and held up a hand for them to stop. Crouching down, Cole peered around the corner and watched a group of soldiers strut across the intersection at the end of the hallway, dragging something after them.

"What is it?" asked Bacchi. Cole held a finger to his lips for quiet. Then the transmitter squawked.

"Cole? Cole!" said Nora.

Cole fumbled with the unit, turning the volume all the way up before getting it right.

"Nora, *shhh!*" hissed Cole.

"Cole, you've got sixteen minutes!"

"We'll be there!"

He looked around the corner again. *Operationalize Your Self-Fargingness,* said the words at the end of the hall. *Find the Synergy in Your Bunghole.* Someone had clearly been playing around with the text program. *I'm Going to Farging Eat You.* Someone hungry.

More men passed through the intersection, then more after them.

"Farg. There's too many of them. We can't go that way."

"What do we do?" said Bacchi. "We don't have time for this!"

"May I make a suggestion?" said Peter. "I know a shortcut."

It wasn't a shortcut. It wasn't even a long cut. It was a wrong cut.

Several times Fred said to Cole, "I don't think this is the right way."

Cole said, "Are you sure?"

"Well . . . ," said Fred.

So they kept following Peter.

"Cole," whispered Bacchi at one point, "you think this robot's gone . . . you know?"

"Maybe. It's the weirdest bot I've ever met."

"We can't let something like that on board."

Cole thought about it. "No. No way."

Peter had a probe in a control panel, opening a heavy bulkhead door. "Charlie closed off a lot of the emergency bulkhead doors," he explained. "I don't think he was well."

The heavy blast door lifted, revealing a HardWud double door with a panel that read GRAND BALLROOM. The doors slid apart silently. Beyond, the room was pitch-black.

"This way," said Peter.

"Are you sure?" said Cole.

"Pretty sure."

Fred said something.

"I don't think we have time to go back," Cole said to him.

"Cole, I don't like this," said Bacchi. "Something smells wrong."

He was right. Something did smell wrong. Cole wrinkled his nose at the stink, trying not to picture what might be decaying in the vast room.

"Maybe we should turn around," said Cole. "We can *holy farg!*"

"*Aayiyayayayaaaaa!!!!!!!!*" shrieked the man at the head of the pack of men behind them, twenty meters away and closing fast.

"Into the room! Go! Go!" screamed Cole.

They dove through the doorway into the ballroom, a dozen ululating marketing trainees charging down the hall after them.

"We just want to *taaaaaalk!*" bellowed the one in the lead.

"Should I shut the door, then?" asked Peter.

"*Yes!*" said Cole.

The massive door slid shut just as the men reached it, slamming into the other side. Standing in the sudden darkness, Cole shuddered as the men pounded on the door, shrieking and howling.

"Phew," he breathed. "That was close. Peter, give us some light."

Peter held up the glowing orb, brightening a small portion of the room.

"Oh, farg," said Bacchi softly.

"What? What?!" said Cole.

From somewhere in the darkness came a deep, sepulchral moan. "*Braaaaaaaiiins,*" it said.

There were some scattered giggles. Another voice picked up the call, imitating the first. "*Braaaains,*" it said, to more laughter. "Good one," someone added.

"Hold on, lemme get the lights here," said Peter, and with a faint *chunk* the chandeliers came on. Cole wished they hadn't.

There were at least a hundred of them in the ruined ballroom, slowly rising from their chairs or from the floor, eyeing the interlopers hungrily. The remains of earlier meals were spattered on the walls and littered the floor.

Cole and the others shrank back against the bulkhead door. Through it Cole could hear what sounded like a violent struggle of some kind, but that seemed less important than the men in front of him, forming a disorganized but slowly tightening semicircle.

"Ahem," said Bacchi. "I'd like to point out to you all that although I *am* human*oid,* I'm *not* human."

"Yum," someone said, "foreign food!"

More laughter.

"Man, you don't give up, do you," said Cole to Bacchi.

The ring was getting smaller.

"Maybe they won't really try to eat us," said Cole.

"Dibs on the kidneys," someone called out, which was immediately greeted by a chorus of protesting voices.

"Peter!" said Cole. "Do something! Throw that table at them!"

"That doesn't seem very friendly," said Peter.

There was some jostling and pushing going on in the semicircle. "Leggo!" said someone. Cole glimpsed a man grab the arm of the person next to him and bury his teeth in a flabby triceps. The bitten howled and chomped down on his assailant's neck.

"We have to get out of here," said Cole.

"You think?" said Bacchi.

"We have to go back through the door, back the way we came. We have a better chance of shooting our way through."

"Right," said Bacchi. He readied himself.

Cole turned toward the door, knees bent, gun extended.

"All right, Peter, open the door on the count of three."

"Got it!"

"One—"

Peter opened the door.

"Oh, hi, Cole!" said Kenneth.

18

It would be redundant to say the seven remaining Bad Men were arguing. Arguing was a definitional state for them.

This was worse. Two of them had their guns out and leveled at each other.

The point of contention was whether to push on or to rest. One, Yguba, had emerged as a leader of sorts over the past few days. He wanted to continue. Jaef Ugnbartn did not. They were the two with their guns out.

"I'm sick of your attitude," said Jaef Ugnbartn. "You're not the boss."

"We're six hours from the village. We keep going," said Yguba.

"I said, I'm sick of your attitude," said Jaef Ugnbartn. "You're not—"

"All right, I heard you," said Yguba. "You be the boss."

He holstered his gun.

Jaef Ugnbartn seemed momentarily surprised, then holstered his own gun. "Okay," he said, "here's what we're going to do."

Yguba drew his gun again and shot him in the head.

Jaef Ugnbartn staggered backward, but didn't fall.

"That's not where my brains are," he said mockingly. "You're so stupid. They're right here."

Yguba shot him right there.

Then there were six Bad Men.

"All right," said Yguba, blowing some smoke off the barrel. "Can we just go kill some villagers, please?"

19

Kenneth had unfolded out of bendspace not long after Cole docked the Benedict to the satellite. Kenneth hung back for a while, observing the stricken Success!Sat and monitoring the communication bands, until he overheard Cole and Nora discussing their plans.

"Okay," Cole was saying, "we should make it to the control room in about twenty minutes. I figure the refueling will take about ten, and then we'll head back."

Kenneth considered his options. The most logical thing would be to lie in wait for the moment that the Benedict disconnected from the satellite, because that would mean Cole was back on board. Then he'd vaporize it. Or, he could puncture it with a few hundred armor-piercing shells. That would be good, too. No, vaporize it.

But where would the fun be in that?

A quick risk/benefit analysis—with *benefit* defined as the elimination of Cole + fun—yielded a plan that would involve docking at that secondary air lock over there, the one that looked undamaged, and then getting to Cole's ship before Cole did. Of course, it was possible that Cole might somehow escape, and either way Kenneth would have to hurry so that he didn't get pulled into the atmosphere with the falling satellite, but in the end the promise of seeing Cole's dumbfounded expression won out over those potential dangers. And so Kenneth docked his ship at the only other functioning air lock on the ring and set off to find the Benedict.

It quickly became clear that something very strange was happening on the satellite. He witnessed several groups of humans attacking one another. Then some of the groups began trying to attack him.

One man, large for his species, ran at Kenneth with a fire ax and hit him with all his might, yielding nearly as much force as Kenneth would experience while receiving a deep-tissue massage on his home planet. Kenneth gathered the man up and crumpled him into a tidy little ball.

He was starting to get annoyed. He had a pretty good mental map of the satellite, being himself a devotee of *The Galaxy's Largest Construction Projects,* but the route that he had projected was often blocked by malfunctioning doors.

He took yet another detour and was confronted by three especially obnoxious attackers. He braided them.

Another direction. He turned a corner and was set upon once again, this time by about two dozen men. He had just initiated a quickie weaving project with them when the nearby bulkhead door opened.

"Oh, hi, Cole!" said Kenneth.

"Shut the door, Peter!" screamed Cole.

Peter shut it, slamming it down right on one of Kenneth's extended tentacles.

"Ow!" they could hear Kenneth say on the other side of the door.

"Cole, was that *Kenneth*?" said Bacchi in disbelief. "Cole? Cole?"

Cole was already several meters away, having done his own quick risk/benefit analysis and deciding he liked his odds with the insane cannibals better. Charging at them toward the door on the opposite end of the hall, he fired a burst from his gun in the air.

"Get out of my way!"

The cannibals barely noticed. The infighting had spread rapidly through their ranks, and at the moment most of them were too immersed in trying to remove the flesh from one another's bones to pay Cole much heed.

"After him!" said Bacchi.

They followed in his wake, Bacchi firing randomly. Now the cannibals were starting to realize that their prey was making its escape. Cole clubbed and batted away hands that grasped at him, feeling his shirt tear away as someone grabbed it. A man leaped on his back and bit his shoulder.

"*Ow!*" said Cole, spinning around to dislodge him. The man

tumbled off and climbed to his feet, to find Cole pointing the gun at him.

He was young, perhaps in his late twenties. Cole noted that he was wearing a very nice tie, except it was knotted around his forehead. Other than that he was naked.

"Don't shoot me!" begged the man, cowering back. Cole lowered the gun. "Oh, thank you, thank you!" said the man gratefully. Then he hurled himself at Cole again. Cole smashed him in the face with his gun, and down he went.

"C'mon!" said Bacchi, passing Cole. Cole caught up with him as they reached the other door. Behind them, the cannibals were starting to sort out their priorities and regroup. Peter was still in their midst, and several of them had clambered atop him.

"You know, that's not a good idea," Cole could hear him saying. "You're going to damage your teeth if you keep biting me."

"Peter!" said Cole. "Stop playing around and get over here!"

Peter shook himself like a dog, scattering the men—"Sorry! Sorry!"—then scuttled over to the doorway.

"Hurry!" said Cole. "Open this thing!"

Peter came scuttling along and did his trick with the probe. The door slid open.

"All right, let's *ayyiaaaaa*!" said Cole.

"What are you *ayiaaaa*!" said Bacchi, responding like Cole did to the sight of several hundred ravenous businessmen on the other side of the door.

Kenneth was very vexed.

His tentacle hurt a lot and he was finding it difficult to free it from under the heavy door. That's when the bolus of men came around the corner, a dense wall of them moving through the corridor, giving the impression of hundreds more pushing them forward inexorably from behind.

"Get him!" someone shouted, and those in the front decided to do just that.

Kenneth sighed, and placed the majority of his tentacles on the bulkhead.

"I'm getting too close to tertiary molting for this," he muttered in his rich voice, and proceeded to tear the door from its moorings.

Cole and the others were sprinting toward a side exit, dodging over-turned tables and chairs and hungry assailants. Suddenly the hun-dred men in the ballroom seemed almost inconsequential, at least compared to the number pouring into the space from the doorway that Peter had just opened.

Cole had done too much running over the past hour. His legs were leaden and painful. Bacchi and Peter and Fred quickly out-paced him, and he found himself alone, surrounded by a dozen would-be diners.

"Bacchi! Help! Come back!" shouted Cole, but his voice was lost amid the screaming and giggling and barnyard noises echoing in the chamber, mixed with random bursts of automatic-weapons fire.

They were closing in, a miasma of grabbing hands and bloodshot eyes and gnashing teeth. "Get back! Get back!" screamed Cole. He swung the gun around, but a hand tore it from his grasp. He punched one man and kicked another in the groin and tried to dart forward, but tripped over an unseen chair and went sprawling on the floor.

As he fell there was a wrenching, rending groan from somewhere to his right as Kenneth ripped the door out of the wall. The bastards were all around Cole now, ringing him, looming, fingers out-stretched. He tried to get to his feet but slipped again, which is what saved his life.

As he stumbled forward there was a *whoosh,* and a shadow skimmed over his head two inches above his skull. An instant later came a thudding crash, the impact hard enough that the vibration bounced him off the floor. Cole scrabbled to his feet. The men near-est him were gone, mowed down like grass by the twisted wreckage of the door, which Kenneth had flung into the room like a discus.

"Cole!" shouted Bacchi, beckoning to him from the side exit. "Come on!"

"*Cole!*" shouted Kenneth from the jagged remains of the other doorway.

Cole took off running, following the path cleared by the door-turned-missile. As he neared Bacchi his eyes somehow fell upon a small monitor panel on the wall. WARNING, it was flashing, 600-PERSON CAPACITY EXCEEDED.

Kenneth moved into the ballroom, sweeping men out of his way even as those behind him continued to attack. As he stepped into the chamber it was as if a cork had been pulled from the corridor, and scores upon scores of men flooded through the wounded entranceway to meet their compatriots pouring in through the other side.

Kenneth held some of his eyeballs above the fray, tracking Cole as he made his run toward the side exit. "Cole!" he shouted again, and changed his direction to intercept him. But now more men were climbing on him, pulling at him from all sides, trying to bite him. Someone fired a gun at him point-blank, and Kenneth cursed and picked him up and threw him across the ballroom at Cole. It was a perfect shot, right on target—but a millisecond too late. Cole dove through the door, which slammed shut just before the human projectile bounced off it, leaving a rusty skid mark.

In the ballroom, humans engulfed and swarmed over Kenneth like ants over a wounded beetle.

"Cole! Four minutes!" Nora's tense voice, over the transmitter.

Cole, panting as he ran, forced out a breathless "Coming!"

He tripped and fell again. Fred and Peter stopped and came back to help him up. Bacchi kept running.

"Would you like me to carry you?" said Peter. "I can support twelve tons. Do you weigh more than twelve tons?"

Bacchi heard a thumping noise approaching from behind, and then Peter's blocky form galloped past him, Cole and Fred sitting on top.

"Hey!" said Bacchi, trying to catch up. "What about me?!"

"No room!" said Cole.

They reached an intersection and Peter turned left. Fred shouted something.

"Peter, hold on," said Cole. Peter stopped. "Are you sure it's this way?"

"Quite sure," said Peter.

"Positive?"

"Absolutely!"

Fred said something else.

"Okay," said Cole. "Let's go the opposite direction."

"Two minutes!" said Nora.

"Co-o-o-mi-i-ng!" said Cole, bouncing atop Peter.

They arrived at the docking station in time to hear the voice of the Benedict's flight computer echoing up the open air-lock passageway. "Warning: entering planetary atmosphere in one minute, thirty seconds."

Cole leaped off Peter. "Go," he said to Fred, "down the hatch."

Fred lowered himself through the hatch and disappeared down the ladder.

"*Hey!*" Cole heard Nora yell, followed by a scuffle, followed by Fred squealing and yelling something in Grey. "Please assist in removal of vicious angry she-pig-creature!" said the AT.

"Nora!" Cole yelled down the hatch. "It's okay! He's with us!"

Nora stuck her head into view.

"Well, hurry up!"

Cole turned to Bacchi. He was pointing his gun at Peter.

"Cole?" said Peter.

"He can't come with us," said Bacchi. "You know it. He's gone conscious."

"Bacchi . . ."

"Cole, you know what I'm saying. We let this thing on board, and he'll be trying to run the galaxy in a week. It's too risky."

Cole looked at Peter. Several video inputs looked back at him.

"Cole, you know I'm right," said Bacchi.

"Please," said Peter. "Please don't leave me here. I don't want to die."

"Cole . . ."

"Yes," said Cole to Bacchi, "you're right."

Cole had never seen a robot look crestfallen before. It was an unsettling feat, made more so by the fact that Peter didn't have any features designed to mimic facial expressions. He somehow just exuded complete resignation.

"That's all right," said Peter. "I understand."

He turned and began slowly walking away.

"Oh, farg it all," said Cole, "get on board!"

"*Yayyy!*" Peter said, and jumped in the air, clapping his appendages together. Then he scrambled down the hatch.

"That was dumb, Cole," said Bacchi. Then he noticed the wound on Cole's shoulder. "What happened to you?"

"One of those bastards bit me," said Cole.

Bacchi instantly had the Firestick 25 up again, this time pointing at Cole's head. "I can't let you on board," said Bacchi. "It's too risky. You're one of them now."

"Bacchi—"

"Head or chest? I'll make it clean."

"Bacchi, I don't have an implant! You don't catch it from a bite! That's a different video game!"

"Oh," said Bacchi, lowering the gun. "Right."

"Entering planetary atmosphere in fifty seconds."

"Cole!" yelled Nora from down below.

"Right!" said Cole, snatching the gun from Bacchi before he could protest. "Let's go!"

Cole lost his grip and slid down the lower half of the hatchway ladder, collapsing in a heap at the bottom.

"Cole!" said Nora. "What is this robot, or robots, doing here? And this Grey?!"

"Qx"-x-'--'," said Fred.

"Don't worry about me, I'm fine," said Cole.

"Well, get up then! We have to go!"

"Contact with atmosphere in fifteen seconds. Twelve. Eleven . . ."

Cole banged the disengage button a third time, and it didn't work, and a fourth time, and it didn't work again.

"Eight . . . seven . . . six . . ."

"Cole?" said Nora.

"Four . . . three . . ."

He took a deep breath and placed his finger on the button and depressed it very, very gently. There was a fierce jolt and they were free, and Cole punched the afterburners, pushing the G forces as much as he dared until he knew they were clear of the danger.

Behind them the Success!Sat was floating peacefully, continuing its rotations, canted at a forty-five-degree angle to the surface of the planet below. Then the edge of the ring closest to the planet began to glow and spark as it dipped into the outer layers of the atmosphere, drawing a glowing line in its wake.

In the escape pod, Cole and Nora watched the monitor in horrified silence. The satellite began to tilt, the top of the spindle traveling faster than the bottom, the tilting accelerating as the structure edged farther into the denser molecules beneath it. There was a sudden and spectacular burst of sparks and cinders from the lowest ring, like someone poking a burning log, and a shudder traveled the length of the craft.

The glowing ring was breaking apart, the leading half of it bending back and peeling away, and then the central pillar cracked midway, the upper portion lagging too far behind the lower. Cole caught a brief glimpse of Kenneth's ship, still attached to the satellite, before silent explosions tore through the structure, spreading debris that created hundreds of flaming contrails as the pieces burned up in the atmosphere.

"All those people," said Nora quietly.

Cole closed his eyes. He let his arms float up. He'd never been happier to be in zero gravity.

"What happened to your shirt?" asked Nora. Cole realized he was naked from the waist up.

"Mmmph," he said.

"You're bleeding."

"Mmmph."

"You'll explain at some point who the Grey is, and what the robot is doing on board?"

"Mmmm."

There was a pause. Cole breathed deeply.

"Why don't you go take a nice hot mist, and put a heal patch on that wound, and then when you're ready we can bend again?"

She almost sounded like she cared. Cole nodded, eyes still closed.

He kept them half closed as he glided gently down the corridor toward his cabin, letting his surroundings become an indistinct blur. He closed his eyes completely again once he was in the capsule-shaped mister, the moist heat seeping into his aching, exhausted body—exquisite—while the painkillers in the heal patch soothed the bite on his shoulder. All that was left now was to bend, to get to Yrnameer, and then he'd sleep for a week. He was nearly asleep now, the capsule warm and dim and womblike, Cole's thoughts beginning to wander and dissolve into a pleasantly nonsensical jumble. He realized as he nodded off that for the first time in days—no, weeks—he felt totally and utterly relaxed.

Then the screaming started, and Joshua burst into his cabin, rebounding off the far wall.

"Charlie's in the ship!"

20

"Charlie!" yelled Cole. *"Charlie!"*

Cole hurtled down a passageway, his speed reckless, trying to will the pounding in his ears to lessen so that he could hear.

"Charlie!" he bellowed again.

The giggle again, a high-pitched, strangled, grotesque thing, coming from the passageway that opened above him as he flew through an intersection. He grabbed at a handrail to stop and reverse directions, his grip skidding and failing, sending him tumbling to bounce off the walls and ceilings before he could kick off one surface, then another, forward, up, now entering and traveling the correct corridor toward the receding laughter.

"Charlie!" shouted Cole. "I'm coming for you, Charlie!"

Cole didn't remember putting his pants on or grabbing the Firestick 25, but he was at least halfway dressed and the gun was clenched tight in his fist when he and Joshua reached the children's cabins. Philip was writhing in the air in the corridor, clutching his bleeding forehead, children crowded in the doorway, screaming, "The man took Aleela! He took Aleela!"

"Stay here!" Cole told Joshua.

"Why? I want to come with you!"

"Because he might come *back*!" shouted Cole as he kicked off in the direction the children were pointing.

As he sailed down the hall he checked the clip of the gun. One shell.

One shot.

He jammed the pistol into his waistband so he could use both hands to pull himself along the handrails. His hair and skin were still wet. The heal patch had somehow come loose on his shoulder and was flapping around. He angrily tore it off, flinging it away to undulate gently in the corridor. He reached the intersection at the end of the hall and jerked himself to a halt. Which way? Left? Right? Straight?

"Charlie!"

He chose the left-hand branch, first pushing himself backward so he could leap off the wall for speed. Another intersection. Nothing. Up. His heart was pounding, and not just from the exertion.

"Charlie!"

A third intersection and he paused again, spinning himself first one way, then the other, then back again. Just as he was about to pull himself along to the right he caught a flash of movement out of the corner of his eye and he turned, feeling himself go cold.

Charlie was hovering at the other end of the corridor, grinning, Nora's gun in one hand. In the other he was holding a struggling little girl by one arm, his hand very thick around her tiny birdlike wrist. Aleela, the little girl with the claw.

"Charlie!"

"Hi, Cole!" Charlie called merrily, and even from that distance Cole could see the craziness in his eyes. And then Charlie giggled and pushed off, dragging the screaming girl with him as he disappeared around the corner.

So now Cole was in pursuit, panting, his arms and legs and lungs burning, following the hideous giggle that mocked and taunted him, now from the front, now the left, now behind him, the little girl's periodic screams filling Cole with nausea.

He reached an intersection, stopped, listened.

"Charlie!" he shouted. *"Charlie!"*

The laughter again, from the left.

"Charlie! I'm coming, Charlie!!"

He flew past a branch point and saw him again, a glimpse of legs and feet vanishing around a corner, and Cole swiped at a handhold and missed, cartwheeling head over heels until he slammed into and bounced off the floor, leaving a red splat from his shoulder wound.

He grabbed at a rail and pulled himself back into forward motion, turning the corner to the passage where he last spotted Charlie.

"Charlie!"

He reached another intersection and paused, started off again, took a right-hand turn, thought better of it and doubled back the other way.

The girl screaming again.

"I'm coming! I'm coming!" he shouted, hearing his own voice crack. The screaming cut off suddenly and Cole pounded a fist against the wall, trying not to think of what might be happening.

"I'll kill you Charlie! You hurt her and I'll kill you!"

Another intersection. Pause. Nothing. Go.

"Charlie!"

Straight here? No, right. No, *straight.* Down this ladder.

Wait.

Listen.

Nothing.

Forward. Don't think, just go.

Another intersection, his breath ragged. Wait and listen. Nothing.

"Charlie!"

He rounded a corner and stopped.

Before him was the longest passageway in the ship, dead-ending at an air lock. In front of the air lock was Charlie. He was still holding Aleela by the arm, but now she was limp, her head flopping slowly at an odd angle.

"CHARLIE!"

"Hi, Cole! You found me!"

And then Charlie started to laugh again.

Cole felt something ignite inside of him, a white-hot blast furnace of hatred and rage, consuming him, barely contained in his being.

"Let. Her. Go," he said through clenched teeth, trembling with fury, and realized he had whispered it.

"Stay back!" said Charlie, pointing Nora's gun at him.

"Let her go," said Cole again, louder, knowing it didn't matter anymore. He pulled the gun from his waist.

"I'll shoot you!" said Charlie.

"Let her go!" screamed Cole.

Charlie fired, the recoil shoving him back against the air-lock door behind him, Aleela floating like a rag doll.

Cole heard the bullet strike the wall near his head, heard the series of ricochets, heard Charlie firing a second time as Cole drew his legs up against the wall and pushed off with all his might like a swimmer doing a kick turn, launching himself headfirst down the corridor, a human missile aimed straight at Charlie. Charlie fired a third, a fourth, a fifth time, the caroming bullets whining and buzzing in a murderous web around Cole as he rocketed down the passageway. A sixth shot and Cole felt a sharp wind past his right ear, then a sudden burning in his side, but he was already on fire, he was fire itself, he was the core of a thousand suns, and Charlie's bullets couldn't hurt him as Cole bore down on him.

Charlie, who was screaming "Stop! Stop!" and firing the gun, his crazed eyes locked on Cole's like he was mesmerized by the fate rushing upon him, and Cole knew that at that moment his eyes were crazier than Charlie's.

"Stop!" screamed Charlie again, but Cole couldn't stop, and just before he plowed into Charlie he jammed out his left arm, stiff and rigid, so that the first thing that hit was his hand on Charlie's throat, carrying him back to slam him against the air-lock door.

Cole felt the jolt through his whole body, the impact jarring the gun loose from his grip as he and Charlie rebounded together in a chaotic jumble of limbs, the lifeless girl now floating free. But Cole kept his choke hold on Charlie's neck, squeezing harder, and grabbed on with his other hand, too. He saw stars but didn't feel it as Charlie clubbed him on the side of the head with the gun, then again, the hallway starting to go dark, Charlie making a gagging noise as Cole gripped harder. Charlie jammed his other hand against Cole's chin, forcing his head back, then scrabbled at his face, trying to claw at Cole's eyes, Cole shaking his head to avoid the gouging fingers. Charlie clubbed him again, weaker this time, his eyes bugging out, and then he seemed to remember what the gun was really for, and just as he was trying to place the tip against Cole's temple to blow his brains out, Cole let go with his right hand, snagged his slowly tumbling gun out of the air, stabbed the barrel into Charlie's chest like he was trying to impale him with it, and pulled the trigger.

When they found Cole he was floating in the corridor, cradling the little girl. She was crying. She wasn't dead. Her head just bent that way. Cole was shivering so violently he could barely speak.

"Oh, *farg*!" said Bacchi, eyeing the bloody splatter on the air-lock door, a crimson bull's-eye surrounding an irregular blackened circle with a bullet hole in the center. "Where's Charlie?"

"Out the f-f-f-farging air lock," stuttered Cole.

"Is she all right?" asked Nora.

Cole nodded, his teeth chattering.

"Are you all right?"

Cole nodded again. Nora had to gently unpeel his arms to take Aleela from him.

Joshua was staring at the mark on the door, wide-eyed. The blood was already beginning to turn brown and fade, the self-cleaning wall performing as advertised.

"Wow," said Joshua. He turned to look at Cole, his eyes full of admiration. "Wow," he said again.

"Get out of here," said Cole, suddenly angry.

"Joshua," said Nora, "go check on the other children."

"But—" said Joshua.

"Get out of here!" roared Cole. He placed a booted foot on Joshua's shoulder and kicked him away, the two of them tumbling approximately the same distance in opposite directions.

"Cole," said Nora, "your side."

Cole raised his left arm and looked down. A misshapen bullet protruded from his flank, like it had expended most of its energy bouncing off the walls and finally came to a halt when it encountered one of his ribs. He reached down with trembling fingers and pried the bullet loose and examined it, turning it this way and that. Then his expression changed, as if someone had reminded him of something important.

"Ooooooooowww!" he said.

"Oh, *farg*," said Bacchi again.

Cole touched the wound on his side and looked at the blood on his hand. He grunted.

"Your head's bleeding, too," said Bacchi.

Cole put his other hand up to his temple and looked at that blood. He nodded.

"I think," he said, "I'm going to faint now."

They waited. After a few moments Cole looked around.

"Did I faint?"

"No," said Nora.

"Okay," said Cole. "Then I'm going to go take another mist."

Joshua took Aleela back to the children's cabin. Nora insisted on escorting Cole back to his, a hand on his arm to help him along. She was silent, her brow knitted, glancing at him every so often.

When they arrived at his door she said, "You sure you're all right?"

"Yeah, Ima rai," approximated Cole.

"Heal patch. Three heal patches."

"Mm."

"Hot mist."

"Mm."

"Then we bend."

"Mm."

It was almost a relief when the next interruption materialized. It arrived at the appropriate moment, Nora's voice blaring from the intercom just as the heal patches and the whiskey were kicking in and the shampoo was hitting peak foaminess.

"Cole!" she said. "Come quick!"

He still had shampoo in his hair when he dragged himself into the cockpit of the escape craft.

"Look!" said Nora.

He looked.

"Why?" he said exhaustedly. "Why can't any of this just be easy?"

The holo-monitor showed them clearly. A few were still popping out of bendspace near where the Success!Sat was crumpling into a fireball. Cole didn't need to count them. There would be a total of fourteen, a standard space marine task force.

"Are they here for us?"

"No," said Cole, "for the satellite. But we have to bend now or they'll spot us, want to talk. You ready?"

"Yes."

Cole fumbled with the intercom button.

"Uh . . . ," he said.

"I'll do it." She took the handset from him, giving him the smallest of pats on the arm. He watched her, too tired to protest.

"Everyone, this is Nora. We have to bend, and do it now. Hold on." She put the handset back and smiled at Cole. "Let's do it."

He nodded, flipping back the safety cover over the bend button. "Next stop, Yrnameer."

It wasn't, of course. Not for them.

21

Space Marine Flight Colonel Farley Keane, formerly of one of the minor agriculture planets of the Cargillon-Archer system, surveyed the plummeting satellite from the bridge of the lead vessel.

"Well, ain't that a shame," he said. "Seems we've arrived a bit too late."

"Yessir," said his lieutenant.

"Sir!" said a young space marine, running up to the colonel. "We spotted another ship in the vicinity, but they bent before we could get a fix on them!"

"Roger that. Thank you, Space Marine. That will be all."

The young soldier saluted and marched off.

"Funny," said Colonel Keane to his lieutenant. "Have you ever really thought about the term *space marine*? I mean, *marine,* by definition, connotes the ocean, while . . ."

Next to him, his lieutenant stifled a yawn and thought, Oh, God, here we go again.

Bendspace was as uncomfortable as always, with the impression that one was observing one's own cells from the inside out. Cole was suffering through the particularly disagreeable experience of being a balloon intersecting another balloon wrapped in a multifaceted somethingahedron, when there was a jarring sensation, followed by the feeling of being in free fall, a free fall striped and interrupted by random bands of nothingness. And then he landed.

He was in the cargo hold, although it was strangely distorted and off-kilter, as if the walls didn't quite line up. It was perfectly silent and still.

He scrunched up his eyes and shook his head, wondering if he was dreaming, but the room was still there. He looked down at his hands, his bloody knuckles, then felt for the heal patches on his side and his shoulder and his temple. His hair was still plastered stickily to his scalp, the shampoo starting to congeal. This was real. He turned to his left to survey the room and froze, feeling his heart start to thump and his skin prickle with goose bumps.

The first coherent thought that passed through his mind was, So this is how I die.

"Cole?"

The voice was very quiet, almost a whisper. He turned further to his left. It was Nora. She was sitting against the wall, hugging her knees to her chest.

"Nora."

He went to her, kneeling next to her.

"Are you all right?" he asked.

"What's happening, Cole? What is that?"

He didn't want to look at it again, but he did. What he was seeing was nothing—literally nothing. The Big Nothing. The purest, darkest black, growing from the upper left-hand corner of the room, as if that portion were being slowly dipped into a mirror-flat lake.

There was something fundamentally wrong about it, repulsive, a desecration. A negation of all life, all warmth, all being, of all history and all that would come to pass. A negation of All. Even if there were a heaven, you wouldn't go there, because this was worse than dying. This was Nothing.

Even as he watched, hypnotized, the clean borders of the darkness crept slightly outward, consuming more of existence. And he knew that plane of nothingness would continue to grow, continue to encroach on them until it consumed him, and consumed Nora, and their bright little pocket of time and space would cease forever.

"We've fallen into an anomaly," said Cole hoarsely.

They said that the anomalies were happening more often now, that it was linked to universal widening, that it was everyone's fault for using too much dark-matter fuel. If they didn't stop, they said, the universe would expand at a higher rate than was natural, faster and faster, until someday it tore itself asunder. Cole didn't know which side he was on. He just knew that he didn't have to worry about it anymore.

It took an effort, but he wrenched his eyes away from the approaching doom. Nora's gaze was still fixed on it, her expression full of dread.

"It's horrible," she whispered.

"Don't look at it, Nora."

"It's *horrible*."

"Nora. Nora! Don't look at it!"

"Oh, God."

"Nora!"

He reached out and tried to turn her head toward him. She resisted for a moment, rigid, and then suddenly relented. When she focused on him, her eyes were wild.

"Nora," he said again.

Then she grabbed him, roughly, pulling him in and clinging to him in a frantic embrace.

He wasn't sure how long he held her, feeling her tremble, her heartbeat, her breath coming in ragged gasps and exhalations.

"I'm sorry," she said after a while, releasing him. She kept her eyes fixed at the floor, one hand up like a blinder to block her view of the corner. "Is it still there?"

Cole risked another look. It was still there, or not there, depending. It was still growing. "Yes," he said.

"How did this happen?"

"Bad bend calcs, I guess," said Cole.

"What about the others? The children?"

"I don't know. I don't really know how these things are supposed to work."

"It's going to keep closing in, isn't it," she said.

"That's what they say."

"Has anyone ever survived?"

"They say it's . . . rare."

"How rare?"

"I guess . . . they're not even sure if the people who say they've survived an anomaly are telling the truth."

"What do you think?"

He glanced up again at it and immediately looked away.

"Under the present circumstances, I'm gonna go with believing them."

She started to laugh.

"Yes," she said. "Yes, me, too."

"Maybe we should move to that far corner, that one over there."

"Right."

Cole held her hand and led her across the room, while she kept her other hand up to block her view. They sat in the corner, facing it, their backs to the Nothing.

"You think the others are okay?" she said.

"Yes."

"You think it's getting closer?"

"No."

"Liar."

"Yes."

She looked over at him.

"How are you, your wounds?"

"It's funny, I was just worrying about whether or not they were going to scar. I guess that's not my biggest concern now."

She laughed again, then sighed.

"You think it will hurt?" she said.

"I don't know," he said.

"I don't want to die like this," she said.

"I don't want to die like anything," he said.

She put her hand on his back. It felt warm. "You were really brave back there. Thank you."

He dropped his head, smiling. "You're welcome," he said quietly.

"What, are you all shy and modest now?"

He nodded, still smiling.

"That must be a first for you," she said.

"Don't tell anyone."

He twisted to look over his shoulder, caught his breath, then turned back quickly. Their eyes met. She nodded, understanding.

"You know when I said that thing, about you and me, and even if you were the last man in existence?" she said.

He glanced at her. "Yes."

"Well, here you are, the last man in existence. And you know what? I would."

He chuckled, dropping his gaze again.

"You're shy again!"

"Yes."

Her hand moved to his knee.

"It would be a good way to go out," she said.

He looked at her hand for a moment, then took it in his own. "How about," he said, "if we just hold on to each other?"

So they did. They leaned against each other, knees up, heads touching, arms around each other's shoulders, their other hands intertwined in front of them, while behind them the Big Nothing closed in.

22

"If you're just joining us on Intergalactic Public Radio, the standoff continues here on the outskirts of Yrnameer," said MaryAnn. She was speaking in a low but clear voice into a tiny microphone, her live broadcast going out to over a hundred worlds and nearly half as many listeners.

Around her were the citizens of the village of Yrnameer, a tense and fearful gathering just outside the broad gate that straddled Main Street. Hanging above and behind them was the sign welcoming visitors to the community.

Their current visitors were not at all welcome.

The surviving six Bad Men had finally arrived.

They rode through the center of town, shooting out lights and windows, smashing things that could be smashed, and clubbing those unlucky enough to be within reach.

They killed the chicken.

Then they grabbed Mayor Kimber and dragged him outside the gate, ordering the townspeople to assemble.

"But if we give you all our crops," said Mayor Kimber, "we'll starve."

"If you don't," said Yguba, "we'll kill you."

"We helped you before! We fed you, we saved your lives!"

"Well, that was pretty stupid then, wasn't it?" said Yguba.

"You can't do this!" said the mayor.

"Really? Who's gonna stop us? No one," said Yguba. "We can do anything we like. Anything! For example, if I want to shoot that sign? I shoot it!"

He shot the town sign. The bang was very loud. People screamed and ducked. The sign swung violently on its hinges, a smoking hole in it from the Firestick 4 ("a good, basic model for those who want an economical but still effective weapon for threatening their enemies").

"The sound you just heard was that of a gunshot. One of the bandits just shot the town sign," whispered MaryAnn into her microphone.

"Here," said Yguba, "I'll do it again."

He did it again. More screams.

"He did it again," said MaryAnn. Her heart was pounding but she held her voice steady.

"Farg," said Yguba. "This is fun."

In the end Cole and Nora were huddled together on their sides, spooning, still facing the corner. They existed in a small, inverted pyramid of somethingness, while the wall of annihilation moved implacably toward them.

Cole opened his eyes and shut them again immediately. The black wall was just inches away. Very soon now. He hugged Nora tighter and she responded, squeezing his arms.

"Is it close?" she said.

"It's close," he said.

"I'm keeping my eyes shut."

"Me, too."

She pressed against him, and he against her. His left hand was touching her face and he could feel the warmth of her tears.

"It's okay, you know," she said.

"Yes."

She kissed his hand.

"Good-bye, Cole."

"Good-bye, Nora."

"Cole?" she said quietly. Her voice sounded different, somehow deeper.

"Yes, Nora?" he said.

"I didn't say anything," she said.

"Uh, Cole?" she said again, in a voice that sounded exactly like Bacchi's.

"Nora!" It was Philip's voice.

Cole couldn't believe how quickly she was out of his arms and on her feet, like someone had released a tightly compressed spring. He opened his eyes, confused, just as she was stepping over him and embracing Philip, saying, "Philip! You're alive!"

Cole, still facing the corner, heard Philip talking behind him. "Of course I'm alive! Where have you been! What were you doing?"

"Oh, Philip," Nora said reproachfully.

Cole twisted around to flop onto his other side.

Bacchi was grinning at him, leaning over to align himself more or less with Cole's horizontal orientation. "All right, Cole!" said Bacchi, giving him the double thumbs-up.

They were still in the cargo hold, but now Philip, Bacchi, Joshua, and several of the children were there.

"Nora! Nora!" they shouted, running to her. Nora kneeled, surrounded by happy children, hugging them in relief. Philip was glaring at Cole.

"I can't believe it," he said, "We've been searching for you for hours, and you two were in here . . . in here. . . ." He couldn't bring himself to say what he was thinking. "You were *in here*!"

Bacchi helped Cole to his feet. "You sneaky, sneaky devil!" he said.

"What just happened?" asked Cole, dazed.

Bacchi chuckled evilly. "That good, huh?"

Philip marched up to Cole. "You have no sense of honor," he spat.

"Do I?" said Cole to Bacchi.

"Of course not!" He thumped Cole on the back.

"Oh, Philip, stop it! Nothing happened!" said Nora.

"And in front of the children, no less!" Philip said, including her in the target radius of his disdain.

"Nothing. Happened. We nearly died, Philip," she said.

"Is this true?" Philip said to Cole. "Nothing happened?"

"Cole, tell him!" said Nora.

"Nothing happened?" demanded Philip again, his face thrust in Cole's.

Cole paused.

"Depends what you mean by 'nothing,' " he said, then pushed his way past Philip.

Who could resist, he thought.

Bacchi explained what had occurred: they'd gone into bendspace, and then suddenly popped right out again into an anonymous stretch of universe. Cole and Nora had somehow disappeared.

"We reconformed and did a search, chamber by chamber. The cargo hold was the last place we looked."

"We were stuck in an anomaly, Bacchi."

"I bet you were, I bet you were," said Bacchi, thumping him on the back again.

A check of their coordinates showed them to be several tens of light-years from the nearest inhabited system. They had to bend again, or slowly starve to death in the middle of nowhere.

"Let's just do it," said Cole. "What else could possibly go wrong?"

They bent. Things went wrong.

23

Reg, the tumbleweeg, was fervently wishing that the wind would pick up again.

It had blown him to a spot right between the townspeople and the Bad Men. It then died away, blowing a few gentle gusts and eddies back and forth indecisively.

Yguba fired again. Reg flinched internally.

The village sign, looking somewhat the worse for wear, took yet another bullet. It creaked in protest.

"It's been two hours now. The bandit has now shot the town sign a total of fifteen times," whispered MaryAnn.

"See?" said Yguba. "That's, like, *forty* times! I can do this all day!"

He seemed intent on proving the point. He unloaded another round at the sign, neatly severing one of the two chains that secured it to the gate. The sign swung free, spinning and jerking in a chaotic pendulum movement.

"That's sixteen," said MaryAnn into her microphone.

"Forty-five!" announced Yguba triumphantly.

The villagers were still cringing with each gunshot, but by the fifth or sixth repetition the screaming had stopped. Now they were standing in an awkward silence, trading glances, unsure whether or not their presence was required for what looked to become a rather extended demonstration of Yguba's marksmanship.

"Um," said Mayor Kimber.

"Shut up!" said Yguba. "Watch this." He cocked the gun again and turned three-quarters away from the sign, aiming the gun over his shoulder, then changed his mind and tucked it under his arm, then went back to the over-the-shoulder position. He hesitated again, then changed his grip so that his thumb—second thumb, really—was on the trigger.

"Do you have a mirror?" he asked one of the other Bad Men. The Bad Man waggled his antenna.

"Is that a no?" asked Yguba. "No?"

The Bad Man waggled his antenna in a different direction. Yguba sighed. "All right, forget it."

He switched back to a more standard shooting stance. "Here comes number fifty!" he said.

"Stop shooting our sign!" said a voice out of the crowd.

Yguba spun around. "Who said that?!"

"I did," said the voice, and Daras Katim stepped forward. She ran a small greenhouse and grew exotic flowers there, and looked rather plantlike herself. A humanoid plant, proud, wizened, her eyes very clear and penetrating. She was just a meter or so from MaryAnn, and MaryAnn realized that she smelled good, like healthy dirt after a thunderstorm.

"You've made your point. Leave our sign alone."

"Daras, please," said the mayor.

"Shut up!" repeated Yguba. He began striding toward her aggressively, the mayor trailing tentatively behind. Reg, directly in Yguba's path, steeled himself for what he knew was next. Just as he expected, Yguba kicked him out of the way, sending him flying.

Daras caught him. "You poor thing," she said, "you didn't deserve that." Then she put him on the ground and the wind picked up again, scooting and tumbling him away from the scene. His last thought before he forgot all about it was that she smelled nice.

Yguba and Daras faced each other. It was quiet except for the wind.

"So," said Yguba, "you don't like me shooting your sign, huh?"

"I think I've made that clear," said Daras.

MaryAnn watched her, entranced, her microphone forgotten. She could see no sign of fear or anxiety on Daras's face. Then again, her face seemed to be composed mostly of wood.

"You don't like it, then."

"Is everyone in your species this perceptive?" asked Daras.

"Daras . . . ," said the mayor.

"Shut up!" Yguba said, and clubbed him across the face with the

gun, sending him sprawling. An angry sound ran through the
crowd, and some of the villagers moved forward, the first hesitant
wave in what could become a surge. But then Yguba turned the gun
on them and fired a shot that tore through the air just over their
heads, and they cowered back again.

Except for Daras.

"I think you should leave now," she said.

"Is that what you think?" said Yguba.

"You're going to repeat everything I say as a question, aren't
you," she said.

"I'm going to repeat everything?" said Yguba. Next to him one
of the Bad Men giggled, then shut up quickly when Yguba glared
at him.

"Well, I won't be repeating what you say if you ain't saying anything," he said, "like, after I kill you." And he pointed the Firestick
square in the middle of her green chest and cocked the gun and
MaryAnn heard herself screaming and everyone else screaming and
then the huge explosive sound and then came the shock wave and
spray of debris and thudding impact that knocked them all down,
and when they all climbed back to their feet and the dust settled
there was a battered Benedict 80 lying on the ground where the Bad
Men once stood.

All that was visible of Yguba was his arm, sticking out from
under the wreckage, still clutching the Firestick 4. With a spas-
modic jerk, the hand squeezed off a final shot, and the village sign
crashed to the ground, hitting at the same time that Yguba's lifeless
hand dropped onto the dirt.

The wind had shifted directions just before the Benedict dropped
on the Bad Men, bringing Reg around once more. Huh, he thought,
Teg's ship. How odd. Then off he rolled.

The dog survived.

He trotted over the rolling hills, away from the wreckage and the
town, toward the welcoming forest. If it were possible to accurately
render dog thoughts, they might best be summed up as *Good
riddance*.

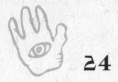

24

Cole was dreaming.

He'd passed through a period of feverish nightmares, of hands clawing at him and Charlie's eyes and of the Big Nothing. But now he was dreaming of the woman he loved, the only woman he'd ever loved, seeing her smiling at him, radiant, sensing her warmth and her calm and it was poetry and songs and spring mornings. She smiled and she spoke to him.

"Cole," she said.

And her serene warmth embraced him and filled him, spreading life throughout his numb body, carrying him in a cloud.

"MaryAnn," he whispered.

"Yes, Cole. It's me," she said, and she smiled once more.

"MaryAnn," he said, and then "MaryAnn" again. "Oh, MaryAnn, I can't tell you how much I've wanted to . . . to . . ."

"Yes, Cole?"

"Wanted to . . ."

"Yes?"

"Wanted to . . ." His dream hands lifted and reached out to dreamily fondle her dream breasts.

"*Cole!*" she said, and slapped him in a very nondreamlike fashion.

"*Wha?!*" he said, and jerked upright to a sitting position in the bed, where his face met a pitcherful of frigid water traveling in the opposite direction. He gasped and sputtered, the water burning inside his nasal passages.

"*Cole!*" said MaryAnn again.

He wiped his eyes, blinking and coughing, a horrible suspicion

growing that he wasn't dreaming, a horrible suspicion he was doing
his best to keep from transforming and hardening into an even more
horrible certainty.

"MaryAnn?" he said weakly. "Is it really you?"

"It's me. Hello, Cole."

Horrible certainty declared victory.

"Oh, God," he said.

She gave a pained half smile and gestured behind him. He
turned. Flashes went off, half blinding him, and the town band,
packed into the smallish bedroom along with what appeared to be
most of the rest of the villagers, kicked into a celebratory march.

"Yaaayyy!"

Mugs knocked together, beer slopping over Cole's arm and onto
the floor, already sticky from previous toasts of equal enthusiasm.
Hands and other appendages patted him on the back and mussed
his hair, which was also sticky. Cole had a fuzzy recollection of
someone who looked like a purple shag rug screaming *"Whoo-
hooo!!"* in his face and emptying a pint glass over the both of them.

It was a very good party.

The toasting and patting and mussing had been going on for several hours now. The villagers had crowded into the town hall to
meet Cole and the others, and they swarmed around him excitedly,
making sure that his glass was never empty, that his back never
wanted for patting and his hair for mussing. The hall was a broad,
high building at the end of Main Street that doubled as the town's
ecumenical house of worship; a small sign announced that on Ser-
day evenings they had duck-pin bowling.

Somewhere in the room a trio was playing rousing, catchy
music, and little nuclei of dancers would form spontaneously,
pulling Cole in and swirling him around before releasing him again
to get more to drink. At one point he was spun around near the trio
and he saw that it wasn't a trio at all, just a very talented alien of a
sort that Cole had never seen before.

It was a good enough party that Cole was able to blot out the
memory of his nondream. Mostly blot it out. Occasionally he'd
remember it and wince, and he'd search the crowd for MaryAnn,
half fearful that he'd spot her. So far he hadn't.

Their arrival on Yrnameer had furnished yet another incident to be registered in the Benedict's unsafe flight log—specifically, emerging from bendspace within the limits of a planet's atmosphere.

More specifically, within the limits of a planet's atmosphere and approximately nine meters above the ground.

The children and other passengers were unharmed. The Benedict was mostly unharmed. The bandits were extremely harmed. As for Cole, the landing had knocked him unconscious. When he woke, they told him that he'd slept for three straight days, MaryAnn sitting by his bedside and tending to him the whole time.

The song ended and Cole joined in the applause. The one-creature band struck up another tune, something fast and intricate and impossibly propulsive. Someone grabbed Cole's arm and pulled him into another group of dancers. As he was whirled around he spotted Joshua, gingerly sipping a beer and making a face. Cole was spun again and delivered to another partner, catching a glimpse of Fred and Peter the 'Puter, participating in some sort of line dance. An arm was linked in his, redirecting Cole yet again, and now he was briefly dancing with a sembluk, his sluglike skin less clammy and slimy than Cole had expected. As they orbited each other something niggled in the back of his mind—recognition? But then he was twirling in another direction, forgetting about the sembluk as his current partner two-stepped him to where Bacchi was leaning in close to an attractive young female with blue skin. "You know, this nose ain't just for smelling," Cole heard him say, but was wheeled and spun away before he got to see the bowl of dip hit Bacchi's face.

And so the party went. At some point the mayor knocked on his glass, calling for silence. The music ceased. All eyes turned to Mayor Kimber as he raised his drink high.

"Here's to our heroic hero, Cole, for his heroism, and his heroic, eh, his, eh, here's to him!"

"*Yayyy!*" cheered everyone.

"Tell us again how you did it!" said Vern, who looked like a large hedgehog.

"Right," said Cole. "Well, as we came out of the cloud layer I could distinctly see trouble. . . ."

Philip scowled as he nursed his lemon water, watching Joshua watch Cole with undisguised admiration.

"I can't bear it any longer!" said Philip.

"He got us here, Philip," said Nora. "And the kids are safe on the farm. Let him have his fun."

Cole *was* having fun. "You know, at times like that, you don't even think. It's all instinct. I actually had my eyes closed, just sort of feeling my way down, you know, feeling—"

He paused. MaryAnn was standing near the entrance, watching him.

"Feeling?" prompted Vern.

"Excuse me for a moment," said Cole.

He made his way across the room to her, still receiving back pats and hair musses. When he reached her he slowed and hooked his hands in his pockets and did a little foot-dragging shuffle, wishing he'd taken more time to figure out what it was he wanted to say.

"Hi," he settled on finally, not having much else.

"Hi," she said. It seemed like a promising start. There was a pause. "Everyone seems to be having fun," she offered.

"Oh, yeah, great folks. Really great. Mayor Kimber, Vern . . . , the purple guy. Gal. Thing. Whatever."

Another pause. He noticed Nora, halfway across the room, watching them. He turned away to face MaryAnn.

"Listen," he said, "I'm really sorry about—"

"No, forget it," she said, and smiled at him.

"I really don't know what happened, I just . . ." He stopped, shook his head, reset. "It's amazing to see you. Unbelievable. It's so random that you're here, and I'm here—I mean, what's it been, twenty years? And, wow, I mean, you look great."

She smiled again.

"How do I look?" asked Cole.

"It's good to see you," she said. Cole let it drop.

"I never thought I'd see you again," she said quietly. He remembered that about her, how she could be so quiet, a quietness that he always envisioned coming from some deep, serene place. A quietness that pulled him in, made him listen to her.

"You left so suddenly," she said. "Everyone was saying such horrible things about you. Terrible."

He dropped his gaze. Whatever they'd been saying, it was probably true.

"But I never believed them."

He raised his gaze and found that smile again.

"That was really courageous, what you did," she said. "Saving all those orphans, wiping out the bandits like that."

"Oh, that? Yeah, you know . . . ," said Cole.

"It's all so exciting. I reported on it in yesterday's IPR broadcast."

"So that's what you're doing here, huh? Reporting for IPR."

"Yes," she said. "I wanted to know if the legend was true, to see the last unspoiled spot in the universe."

Cole wasn't so much listening to her as drinking her in, watching her every move, telling his brain that she really *was* here, that it was really her. He had to fight the urge to reach out and touch her face to make sure.

"Cole? You okay?" she said.

"What? Yeah, yeah, I'm fine," he said. "So, wow. Here you are. That's really impressive. I always knew you'd go on to do something like that, something important. IPR, wow . . ." He trailed off, nodding. Then, "Inter . . . Inter . . . ?"

"Intergalactic Public Radio."

"—Public Radio, right!" he said, trying to speed his words out so that they caught up with hers. "Fantastic!" he added.

"Here," she said, "I brought you a tote bag."

"Oh, wow, great!" said Cole, taking the rough, unbleached canvas bag from her. The bag immediately turned bright red.

"You are legally inebriated," it said.

"Sorry," said MaryAnn. "It does that."

"Your cholesterol level is—"

"Okay, I'm going to put this down now . . . ," said Cole, lowering it to the floor.

"Alert: you may be carrier of Antean gonorr—"

Cole's boot muffled the rest of the bag's sentence. When he looked up, MaryAnn was regarding him thoughtfully. Cole had just started to explain that he'd had it treated when she cut him off.

"I thought a lot about you over the years, Cole. I always wondered what happened to you. I guess you became a hero."

He held up a hand, stopping her. "MaryAnn," he said. "C'mon. I'm just a guy. Who maybe did something heroic. Does heroic things once in a while. But that doesn't necessarily make me a hero."

"Maybe not. But your commitment to this town does."

"Well, sure, but—what commitment?" he said, when his brain finally processed her last statement.

"Hey, Sheriff!"

It was Bacchi, smelling of sour cream and chives, a bottle of something in his hand.

"You gonna introduce me to your friend?" he said. He turned to MaryAnn. "You know, this nose is *hey*!" as Cole grabbed him and pulled him aside.

"What did you just call me?" he asked.

Mayor Kimber interrupted before Bacchi could answer. "Everyone, hello!" he said from the center of the hall. "Hello! Attention! Uakoy, cut the music for a moment. Thank you."

The music stopped, along with the dancing. Attention focused on the mayor. "I've got another announcement," he said, "and it's great news! Cole has just informed us that he'll be staying here—and he'd like to be our sheriff!"

The hall erupted in a massive, unanimous cheer.

"Heh heh," said Bacchi. "You're farged now."

25

Cole's head throbbed. He recognized the throb, a dull and tenacious sort that resulted from drinking too much of one type of alcohol, then compounded by drinking too much of a second type of alcohol that was incompatible with the first, and then further aggravated by the addition of a third or fourth type of alcohol that was incompatible with most organic forms of life. It was the kind of throb that made him wish he could go right back to sleep, and then die, while preventing him from doing just that.

"Oooooh," he said, and sat up into something that produced a dull *bong*ing sound and made his head hurt even more. He lay back down and clutched his skull and made the appropriate moaning noises. After a bit the object above him revealed itself to be a desk lamp.

Rolling to the side to avoid it, he got himself into a sitting position. From this vantage point he could better understand the presence of the desk lamp—he had been lying atop a desk.

He was in a simple, unadorned room, the equally simple desk against the wall. Other than the lamp, there was only a single overhead light, which thankfully seemed to be on a dimmer. There was more light coming into the room from his right, blooming through the gap at the bottom of a closed door. He squinted, the light painful.

He thought back to last night, trying to reconstruct what had happened. He remembered the dancing, and the singing, and the drinking. Mostly the drinking. He remembered that everyone had been very happy—ecstatic, really—about something, something involving him. It wasn't just the thing with the bandits. Something else.

The light glinted off an object on his chest. He looked down. It was a badge of some sort, pinned to his shirt.

"Wuzzis?" he said out loud, examining it stupidly.

SHERIFF, it said, in proud, raised letters.

"Congrats, Sheriff."

Cole twisted to the left, suddenly aware that there was more room in that direction. It was Bacchi who'd spoken to him. He was lying on his back on a plain cot, shielding his eyes with his forearm. His sorry condition mirrored Cole's. It took Cole a moment to realize that there were bars between the two of them. Prison bars.

"What am I in for?" asked Cole.

"I was going to ask you that," said Bacchi.

Cole stared at him, then twisted to his right again and looked back at the door. His twisted to his left and looked at Bacchi. Bacchi didn't have a door on his side of the bars. Nor did he have a badge on his chest saying SHERIFF. A few not-very-complex pieces fell into place with almost audible clunks.

"Let me out of here, Cole," said Bacchi.

"No."

"What did I do?"

"I shouldn't have to tell you that."

Cole stood up, accidentally knocking an empty tin mug off the desk onto the wood floor, where it made an impressive clatter.

"Arrrgh!" said Cole and Bacchi in unison, engaging in some reflexive skull clutching. Cole staggered back and leaned against the desk. He looked at the badge again. A few more pieces arranged themselves into a coherent pattern.

"Sheriff," he said to himself. "Sheriff Cole." He liked the sound of that.

Bacchi sniggered.

"What?"

"Cole," said Bacchi, "you being a sheriff is like me being a . . . uh . . ."

"A sheriff?"

"Yes."

Cole rubbed his head. It was starting to clear a bit, the pain ebbing just enough to give Cole hope that he might have some options other than dying.

"Sheriff Cole," he repeated to himself. He liked the sound even more.

He noticed a small text panel on the otherwise bare walls and read it, squinting at the type. JAIL, it said, BY KPOTAM. NATURAL WOOD, BRICK, IRON, PLASTER, NATURAL PIGMENT PAINT. The type got smaller after that:

> **Jail** is a conceptual work that through its very realism comments both directly and obliquely on the surrealistic nature of transgressive . . .

Which is as far as Cole got before his eyes unfocused in self-defense.

"Cole," said Bacchi, "what would you know about being sheriff?"

"I think it would suit me just fine," said Cole. "Free room and board, salary, I'll probably get some bribes . . . and how much actual sheriffing will I have to do? Arrest you every week or so?"

"What about the bandits?"

Cole chuckled. "I'm sorry, maybe you didn't understand how I got this job. The bandits are gone."

Bacchi started to laugh wheezily.

"What?" said Cole. "What?!"

Someone pounded on the door. "Arrgh!" repeated Cole and Bacchi, once again grabbing their heads. The door burst open. It was Joshua.

"C'mon, Sheriff!" he said, "you're gonna be late!"

Joshua reminded Cole of one of those herding dogs—just like he'd done on the satellite, he'd sort of scurry excitedly ahead of Cole, and then turn and wait impatiently for him to catch up, then scurry ahead again, all springy and full of energy. Cole, walking unsteadily, his eyes half closed against the bright sunlight, wasn't in the mood to be rushed.

They were walking down Main Street to where it dead-ended at the town hall. The entire population of the town seemed to be out, walking or oozing or whatevering toward the whitewashed, simple building, everyone moving with a distinct sense of purpose. Those who spotted Cole greeted him cheerfully as they passed.

"Morning, Sheriff!"

"Good to see you, Sheriff!"

"Hello, Sheriff Cole!"

Cole did his best to keep up, nodding and waving back. "Hi. Hello. Hiya. Yeah, hi," he said. "Everyone is extraordinarily loud here," he muttered under his breath.

"They got all sorts here, huh, Sheriff?" said Joshua. "Kolags, Subets, Conlans, Pels . . . look, those are Hennies, right?"

Joshua indicated a trio of three humanoids. Cole had never seen a real Henny before—to him they looked exactly like humans in sheep costumes. One approached him, a big grin on his ovine face.

"Sheriff!" said the Henny, grabbing Cole's hand and shaking it vigorously. "I'm Ed, remember? I own the general store?"

"Right, right," said Cole, not remembering at all. The hearty handshaking was sending unpleasant shock waves through his system.

"You know, you were pretty *baaaaaad* last night," bleated Ed, winking at him. "Just kidding—we don't really talk that way!" He gave Cole a big thump on the back and trotted away.

There was something indefinably off about Cole's surroundings, as if he were looking at a face that was missing some important features. Like the buildings were naked. Like there was no . . . there was no branding. That was it. Nothing. Nowhere. He did a slow pirouette, confirming it, and then stumbled a bit as he started to walk again. The dust he churned up obstinately refused to organize itself into any sort of logo. He stopped and scuffed his boot against the ground again. Nothing. Unbelievable.

He looked up. The clouds were just clouds. Nothing scrolled anywhere. No spaceships carved up the sky. He felt a rush of vertiginous anxiety and took several deep breaths to steady his nerves.

"Sheriff, look at that guy," said Joshua, pointing to another humanoid, a spindly creature several heads taller than Cole. He was dressed entirely in severe black, his sartorial choices reflecting the grave expression on his bony, hollow-cheeked face. Noticing Cole, he altered his course to intercept him, reaching him in a few long strides and silently extending his hand.

Cole, expecting a handshake, held out his own hand. Instead the creature pressed a small device against his wrist.

"Seventy-one point four-three-nine percent," intoned the device. The alien nodded gloomily to himself as if confirming something, bowed ever so slightly, and withdrew, jotting something on a notepad as he went.

"Huh," said Cole. Then he noticed the badge on Joshua's chest.

"What is that?" he asked, pointing to it.

"You made me deputy last night, sir."

"Right. Of course I did." He rubbed his eyes. "How old are you again?"

"Sixteen."

"Great. That's great, Jake."

"Joshua, sir."

"Don't ever correct me, Joshua."

"Sorry, Sheriff."

Cole rubbed his eyes some more.

"What did we charge Bacchi with?"

"Drunk and disorderly."

"Huh," said Cole.

"Actually, sir, I have to say, you were pretty—"

"I'm the sheriff."

"Yes, sir."

Cole stopped walking and did a few neck rolls, groaning as he listened to the vertebrae crackle. Joshua waited for him. Cole took a deep breath and let it out. "Okay," he said, and started walking again. "So, what's going on here? Is there another party or something?" he asked.

"It's the meeting you called, sir."

"Meeting."

"About the bandits."

Cole stopped walking again.

"Oh, farg," he said.

Cole sank deeper into his seat of honor, feeling the sweat trickle its way down his sides from his armpits. His forehead was damp. He wiped it with his palm.

Other than a few scraps of streamers hanging limply from the walls, all vestiges of the party were gone. The citizens of Yrnameer sat side by side, filling the neat rows of pews that now lined the floor. Those who couldn't find a seat were crowded in the back and on either side. Cole had been ushered to the front row and given the first seat on the center aisle.

It was warm in the hall, but that wasn't why he was sweating.

"Next page, please," said Mayor Kimber, who was standing at the podium at the head of the room. Someone standing next to an easel flipped to the next page on a large drawing pad, revealing another series of well-rendered sketches of cruel-faced bandits. "We believe there are at least one hundred of them," Kimber was saying.

The presentation had been going on for twenty minutes now. In Cole's mind it had long since started to blend into a mind-numbing nightmarish blur, with certain phrases jumping out like bogeymen at a carnival fright house to grab his attention: ". . . worst scum of the earth . . ." ". . . heavily armed, desperate . . ." ". . . their leader is wanted for murder on several planets. His name is Runk, and . . ."

Cole clutched involuntarily at his chest, his heart convulsing like it had been impaled by razor-sharp icicles. It took him several moments to start breathing again. He swallowed repeatedly, fighting the urge to vomit.

"Oh, farg, not *Runk*," he squeaked. "Not Runk."

". . . and as we all know," Kimber said, "they'll be returning in four weeks. So here to tell us how we can defend ourselves is our new sheriff!"

The applause and cheering were rapturous, which didn't help Cole's headache. He twisted and looked at the crowd behind him. Everyone was on their feet, or if they didn't have feet, in a nonreclining position indicating respect and encouragement. Cole looked back at the mayor, who was making facial expressions that also indicated respect and encouragement, and that it was now Cole's turn to come to the front and inspire the troops.

Cole rose hesitantly and took a few steps toward the podium. He turned to the assembled and waved his hands for quiet. It seemed to have the opposite effect, so instead he waited, swaying slightly, a sickly smile on his face, until the hall quieted down.

"Wow," he said. "Thanks for that."

More applause. He grimaced.

"Wait, everyone, please. Please."

The hall gradually fell silent, with a random scattering of final whoops like the last few kernels of popcorn to pop.

"Thanks. Thank you. Really."

All eyes—and there were many more than just twice the number of creatures present—were on him, everyone eagerly awaiting what he had to say. Mayor Kimber was beaming at him. Joshua was nodding at him. He saw Nora, who had an eyebrow raised. He cleared his throat.

"Ahem. Well. The thing is, see . . ." He paused again. "I, uh, don't mean to disappoint anyone, but, uh . . ."

He tugged at the badge. It came free from his shirt, and he looked at it, turning it over in his hand. The silence in the hall had somehow deepened further. He glanced up and his gaze met MaryAnn's. Her expression was questioning, quizzical. He shook his head, a tiny, almost invisible movement, as if in apology.

"But, uh . . . ," he said.

"But we're gonna kick some ass!" shouted Joshua.

"*Yayyyy!*" said everyone, applauding and cheering once again.

"Wait!" said Cole. "Wait! Everyone calm down and listen!"

The cheering died down.

"What I wanted to say," he began, "is that I . . . I . . ."

Philip suddenly stood up. "What he wants to say is that he's not fit to be sheriff!"

The crowd gasped.

"It's true!" said Philip. "He's a fraud, an impostor!"

Angry murmurs ran through the crowd, growing in intensity and volume.

"He's a criminal!" Philip shouted above the clamor. "A criminal!"

The tumult grew louder yet, with everyone in the hall trying to share their opinion—if not several opinions—at the same time. Mayor Kimber was banging his gavel. In the midst of the commotion Cole could discern a single locus of calm: MaryAnn, looking straight at him, waiting for him.

"Hey," he said, still looking at her, his voice a very minor addition to the din. "Hey," he repeated, louder. Then he took a deep breath and shouted.

"*Hey!*"

The room was instantly quiet. Cole was still looking at MaryAnn, holding her gaze.

"What I meant to say," he said, "is that this is no time for celebrating. We have a lot of work to do."

"*Yayyyy!!!!!!*"

26

That night was cloudless, the three moons at various stages of waxing and waning that added up to at least one and a half bright full moons. Too bright, thought Cole, as he scurried across the open ground between the town gate and the beached Benedict 80.

On the Success!Sat Cole discovered something important about himself: that he had theretofore undreamed reserves of courage and determination. And on Yrnameer he discovered something else: the adventure on the satellite had entirely exhausted those reserves.

This was, he reasoned, the best way to help these people. The very last thing they needed was some sort of false hope. False hope would lead to rash action, which would lead to horrible tragedy. By removing himself from the equation, he'd be simplifying the issue and steering them along the path of clear-minded rationality: they would quickly realize that their situation was indeed dire and that resistance was, well, futile. What they needed to do was to focus their energy on constructive activities, like producing more crops so that they could feed both themselves and Runk's horde. Trying to fend them off would only have unfortunate results.

And Runk wasn't so bad. No, Cole corrected himself, that was wrong. Runk *was* so bad. He was, actually, far beyond so bad. He was a vicious, murderous grotesque who delighted in inflicting agony. Cole had seen it, seen it on more than one occasion. Farg, the time with that guy, the one who'd screwed up on the Onorv job, the one whose head Runk put into the . . . Cole winced and put his hands over his ears, trying to block out the memory of the screams.

But Runk wasn't stupid. He wouldn't needlessly hurt or kill the drones who were providing him with food. Would he?

At some level, Cole knew that Runk would kill his own grandmother if she looked at him wrong. He knew that because Runk *had* killed his own grandmother, although in fairness several witnesses testified that said grandmother had indeed looked at him wrong. But perhaps Runk had changed, mellowed with time, settling into a more manageable pattern of extortion.

Or not.

He made it to the ship unobserved. Once inside he made his way to the cockpit of the escape pod and got to work, testing each system of the spacecraft one by one.

What the townspeople would undoubtedly do is gather the food and leave it in an accessible place, and then go and hide until the bandits had left. No one would get hurt.

MaryAnn wouldn't get hurt. She was too smart for that. She'd hide.

No she wouldn't. She'd try and report on it.

Shut up, Cole.

So far the ship seemed to be in surprisingly good shape. He had started at the bottom, with the least important systems first, but nothing looked beyond repair.

Maybe MaryAnn would come with him. They could go to some busy, happy spot with a seaside boardwalk and casinos and—

She'd never go with him.

And if she did it would be worse, because it would mean that she wasn't the person that he needed her to be. The sort of person that he never was and would never become. That would crush him, finding out that she was like him.

He knew it from the moment she was looking at him in that way during the town meeting, hoping for something from him, hungry for a sign that he was strong and dependable and trustworthy. That he deserved the faith that she had once expressed. At that moment, under her gaze, he actually believed that perhaps he was those things. But then the meeting broke up and the people drifted away and he was left with his own thoughts, which ran along the lines of, *Are you farging crazy?!*

It was better he left. Better that he not be there to see the inevitable disappointment in her eyes. Better that he long for her from hundreds of light-years away, where he could still maintain the fantasy that someday she might love him. Because if he stayed, sooner or later she'd come to understand who he really was, and then he would lose her forever, even in his dreams.

So he was leaving. Right now.

Or would be, if he could get the engines online. Everything else seemed to be functioning tolerably well, and the damn engines wouldn't respond. It took him about a half hour to figure out the cause of the problem, and about another ten minutes or so to quickly cycle through the five stages of mourning, with heavy emphasis on the denial and anger parts. There was no way he was going to get the engines to fire. Not unless he could get his hands on a replacement Artemis coil, which he could do absolutely anywhere in the sponsored universe and absolutely nowhere on Yrnameer.

He slammed a fist on the control panel, accidentally switching on the forward exterior floodlamps. Illuminated in the harsh pool of light was MaryAnn.

"Hi," he said when he had exited the ship and joined her, "I was just checking on the . . ." He trailed off, gesturing vaguely, hoping that would suffice. "Kinda late," he said.

"I couldn't sleep," she said. "I was just out for a walk."

When he'd spotted her, he quickly turned off the light and ducked behind the control panel, praying she hadn't seen him. He peeked. Her wave suggested his prayer had gone unanswered.

Now they were standing outside of the gate at the edge of the shadow cast by the ship. "You weren't running out on us, were you?" said MaryAnn.

"No, no, of course not, I—" he stuttered.

"I'm kidding," she said. "See? Smile."

"Right. Right."

He looked at her, as beautiful in the pure silvery moonlight of Yrnameer as she'd been in the faux moonlight of Longest Island twenty years ago. She smiled back at him reassuringly, that same placid, honest gaze. It burned him like an ember. He dropped his eyes and kicked at the dirt. This just wouldn't do. It wouldn't.

He took a deep breath and said, "You know, I'm really not the right person to—," just as she said, "I think it's really great what you're doing, Cole."

He stopped.

"What?" he said.

"I feel much better knowing you're around."

"Ah," he said, feeling much worse.

"What did you just say?" she asked.

"When?"

"Before. When I was talking."

"Oh. Uh, I'm really not a night person."

There was a big boulder near the gate with a flat, smooth top, the perfect spot to clamber up and lie down and watch the night sky. Which was what they were doing.

"What about the twins, Daric and Deron?" asked Cole.

"One became a minister. The other ended up in jail, I think," said MaryAnn. "I'm not sure which did what."

"Susan Parker?"

"Still on Longest Island," said MaryAnn. "Married, two kids, that sort of thing."

"Your folks?"

"Still there, too, wondering why I'm not there, and not married with two kids."

"Why aren't you?"

She turned her head to look at him.

"What?" he said innocently. "What happened to that guy? What was his name—Blark? Glerg? Blargh?"

"His name was Kent," she said, "and he was very nice, thank you very much, and that was high school, Cole."

Above them a meteor streaked across the sky.

"You see that?" he asked.

"I saw it."

"You remember how we'd sit in Heights Park on the slide and watch the stars, wonder when we'd get out of Longest Island?"

"I remember. And I remember that when you left, you never said good-bye."

"I didn't say good-bye?"

She turned to look at him again.

"I guess I didn't. Sorry. It was a long time ago," he said. "So . . . you never found anyone else?"

"There was someone, for a while," she said. "It ended . . . badly. I guess that's one of the reasons I came here, to get away."

"Can I ask what happened?"

"Let's just say he was dishonest with me. It hurt me terribly. I'm still recovering, really. Don't you think honesty is the most important thing in a relationship?"

"Oh, absolutely," said Cole.

"Me, too. It's vital. Lying destroys everything."

"Yes. Terrible. Lying." And at that moment he decided that from that point forward he would be completely honest with her, no matter what, and with that decision he felt a wave of relief wash over him, as if he'd finally relinquished a heavy load. No more lying. Honesty.

"So, all this time, you've been working with people like Nora and Philip?" she asked.

"Uh . . . ," he said.

"Because I think that's wonderful, if that's what you've been doing. Intergalactic relief work."

"Well, it's not really . . . I mean . . ."

"The dedication and hard work it must require."

"I'm not sure that—"

"I just really respect you for it. It's very . . . well, I guess there's something very attractive about it," she said, and smiled again.

"Well, it's a calling, I guess."

Honesty could wait.

27

They sat for a while longer, not talking much, until MaryAnn said, "Well, I should probably . . ."

"Right," said Cole. "I'll walk you home. Could be dangerous out here. Bandits. You know."

They walked unhurriedly through the village to her home, a modest, two-story cottage on a side street. At the door there was a minor bout of awkward sentence fragments and confused, out-of-sync positioning for handshakes or hugs or cheek kisses, brought to a conclusion when she planted a loud, misaimed peck directly on his ear canal.

"Good night, Cole," she said.

"Good night, MaryAnn."

She gave a shy, girlish wave and smiled and shut the door. A moment later and the lights went off.

He stood for a full two minutes, rubbing his ear, thinking, then slowly raised his other hand, poised to knock on the door.

"Pushing your luck, don't you think?"

Cole emitted a tiny, involuntary yipping noise, then took a moment to compose himself before turning around.

"You're up late, Nora," he said.

"Seems to be going around."

She was leaning, arms crossed, in the open doorway of the cottage directly across the street. She gestured with her chin toward MaryAnn's house.

"That was fast," she said.

"Just doing my duty as sheriff, escorting a young lady home."

"Mmm."

"We're old friends, Nora."

"Mmm." She seemed amused.

There was a gentle breeze. Crickets or something similar chirruped, a soft, pulsing aural layer. Any threat seemed unimaginably distant. Cole realized he'd barely spoken to Nora since . . . well, since their time together in the cargo hold.

"How have you been?" he asked.

"Good. You?"

"Good," he said. "Nice night," he said after a pause.

"Mmm."

"Mmm," echoed Cole. He carefully nudged a pebble a few inches to the left and then back a few inches to the right with the toe of his boot, still amazed that the soil didn't try to sell him something.

"She seems like a very nice person," said Nora after observing him for a bit.

He glanced up from his pebble adjusting. ". . . So what's she doing being acquainted with me?"

Nora gave a small shrug and head shake, as if to say that wasn't what she meant or didn't care about the answer. He went back to repositioning the pebble. She snorted softly. " 'Acquainted,' " she said.

"Mmm," grunted Cole, turning his attention to another pebble.

He had located a third pebble and united it with the other two when Nora spoke up again. "People are very excited that you're here," she said. "They've all been asking me about you."

"Yeah? What do you tell them?"

"I tell them you're full of surprises."

He looked back up at her, trying unsuccessfully to determine the import of that statement. She smiled blandly at him, not offering any clues. He glanced back at MaryAnn's cottage, then at Nora's, the two structures nearly identical.

"You live here?" he asked.

"When I'm not on the farm."

Cole nodded, silently filing that information under the category of Items Likely to Cause Problems in the Future.

"That's where Joshua is, in case you've been wondering," said Nora. "He's too young to be your deputy, Cole."

"Of course," said Cole. "And where's Philip?"

She paused.

"On the farm."

Cole nodded again.

He looked up at the stars and in- and exhaled a deep breath of night air, surprised by what he was feeling, and also thinking: I shouldn't.

He was still thinking it as he kicked the carefully arranged pebbles away, and reiterating the thought as he meandered across the street toward her, Nora watching him take the eight or ten loose, relaxed strides that brought him to where he could rest his hand on the stuccoed wall next to her door.

He smiled at her, then checked MaryAnn's cottage again. The lights were off, the curtains drawn.

He *really* shouldn't.

"Speaking of pushing my luck . . . ," he said.

There was a long moment as he waited, listening to the insects thrumming, trying once again to read Nora's expression. Then she stepped back wordlessly, her eyes locked on his, and he was so surprised that he was frozen for a moment, not daring to follow her inside.

Which was good, because what she did next was to reach back behind her for the doorknob and shut the door in his face. Not fast, but with a measured, deliberate motion, slowing even more for the last few inches as if to underline her point, still looking him in the eye as the pillar of light narrowed to a crack and then a sliver and then disappeared. The latch made a soft double click.

"I told you so," muttered Cole.

Later, after he had walked away, Nora opened her door again slightly and peered through the crevice. Then she quietly closed it again.

Cole stayed in his bunk in the ship for what little remained of that night, tossing and turning in the heat, unable to get the aircon to function properly.

What had he been *think*ing? It was the night air, he decided, and the stars, and the moons. And the stupidity. He slapped himself around figuratively and a few times literally, and then fell into a restless half sleep, tormented by confused dreams where it was MaryAnn shutting the door on him, her expression full of wounded reproach.

He let Bacchi out of the cell the next day, after it became clear that not doing so would require Cole to empty a chamber pot. Kpotam, the artist who created the jail, had been delighted to have an actual occupant, and inquired politely but insistently as to whether or not it might be possible to keep Bacchi in for a little bit longer. When Cole raised the chamber-pot issue, Kpotam argued that not emptying it would be even better, as it would place in sharp relief the plight of the prisoner. When Cole suggested that perhaps Kpotam could share the cell with Bacchi to further accentuate that point, the hunched little creature decided that Bacchi's short stay had likely been sufficient to achieve his artistic objectives and that it would be better to leave the audience clamoring for more. Cole agreed that seemed wise.

There wasn't, however, any place available for Bacchi to stay, so Cole ended up giving him the keys to the jail cell and told him use the bathroom at one of the several coffee shops on Main Street— either that, or empty the chamber pot himself. Cole assumed Kpotam would be happy to at least have a part-time lodger in the cell, but Kpotam opined that this undercut the important message of the piece and stalked off muttering to himself.

Cole spent the rest of the day puttering around on the ship. The next morning he got up early and thought about going to visit MaryAnn, but decided that his luck had been pushed and poked and prodded enough for the time being. Instead he decided to use the day to explore the village, figuring that if he spotted MaryAnn, well, great; and if he spotted Nora, well, he could hide.

The streets of Yrnameer were cobbled and well maintained. Some were narrow and winding, the buildings close enough that you could hold hands across the street from wrought-iron balconies that were draped with flowers. There were rainspouts and rain barrels and handmade weather vanes on the roofs. Most of the buildings were one or two stories, except for a larger one at the end of a cul-de-sac that he found out belonged to the sembluk. It looked somehow out of place—too big, too modern, too perfect.

He saw several bi-, tri- and quadricycles, including one whose rider necessitated six pedals. There were wagons and people riding baiyos. He did not see a single powered vehicle, nor evidence of any advertising.

In addition to the coffee shops, there were, by his count, four used-book stores selling real books, twelve galleries, three jewelry stores, two studios offering pan-species yoga, and at least five places offering massage and the most alternative in alternative health care. There were several small restaurants whose menus either mystified or revolted him or both.

There was also a simple one-room diner that smelled encouragingly of greasy, comforting food and had a long white counter, stained and chipped in all the right places, lined with stools engineered to allow for a proper 360 degrees of rotation.

When Cole entered the place around midmorning, it seemed deserted. Then some sort of sensory organ extended itself up from behind the counter and a raspy voice asked what he'd be having.

"Can you do eggs?"

"Of course I can do eggs," said the voice. "What kind?"

"Uh, over medium?"

Raspy sighed. "I mean, what *kind* of eggs? From what?"

After a short discussion Cole determined that Raspy Voice was the owner of the diner and had a name like a hiccup. Further investigation revealed that the diner did indeed serve eggs of the avian variety, that those eggs were delicious, and that Raspy was appropriately brusque and grumpy, which Cole found as comforting as the food. Cole decided he'd be returning on a daily basis.

Other than Raspy, the citizens of Yrnameer were the warmest, friendliest people he had ever met. They waved to him on the street and engaged him in conversation, and seemed genuinely interested in his replies. Not once did a chat end without an expression of gratitude for his presence. Everyone exuded an almost visible aura of tranquillity.

It was a pleasant, peaceful place. The air smelled good. Good in a natural way, not in the artificially scented manner of an advanced planet with an atmospheric cleaning system. Real birds chirped. When he smelled baiyo poop, it was genuine, not there to add character. It all made him feel very nervous.

.   .   .

Late in the afternoon, the sun still hot, he wandered by a florist's. The vegetation crowding the picture window was so dense that he could barely see the interior of the shop. As he marveled at the exotic plants, he was startled to see one of them beckoning to him.

A tiny bell dinged as he entered. The air smelled even better inside than out. It was very quiet. He inhaled deeply, closing his eyes.

"Careful, Sheriff," said an elderly but confident female voice. "There's a reason they call some scents intoxicating."

When he opened his eyes he was looking at the plant who had gestured for him to enter. His vision blurred slightly and he blinked, and he realized she was a humanoid. She was smiling at him.

"I'm Daras Katim," she said. "These are for you."

She handed him a compact bouquet of flowers not much larger than two fists. His gaze drifted down to the miniature blossoms, a tight cluster of intense blues and reds and yellows, and stuck there.

"Hello?" she said after a while, amused.

"Hwuh? Oh, hi. Hello. I'm Cole."

"The sheriff. Yes, I know."

Sunlight filtered in through the greenhouse glass that began a few meters inside the store. Cole couldn't tell how far back the greenhouse went. He had a vision of walking in that direction and discovering that there was no end, that the foliage thickened and grew into an infinite emerald world, vibrant and alive, surrounding and embracing him, conscious of his passage. There was a very slight and not unpleasant buzzing in his ears. He shook his head slightly.

"Wow, it sure smells good in here."

"Thank you."

A portion of the smell seemed to emanate from Daras Katim herself. Cole blinked. She looked like a plant again.

"Now," she said, and she was humanoid once more, "what you're going to do is give those flowers to that young woman, that MaryAnn."

"MaryAnn? But how . . ."

"I see these things."

"But . . ."

"She'll like them."

"But . . ."

"No, she won't think you're being too forward. I know how to select flowers better than that," Daras said briskly.

"Oh," said Cole. He wasn't sure what else to say. He looked at the flowers again and giggled. Daras patted him on the shoulder.

"Good, then. It's probably best if you continue on your way, now."

"Right. Right," said Cole, docilely allowing her to steer him out the door.

"Bye-bye," she said.

"Bye-bye."

The door shut behind him.

Cole wandered contentedly down the street, swaying a bit, pausing now and then to stick his nose into the flowers and take a deep whiff. These people were *great*. Let Runk come—Cole would put him in the ground himself. He paused to let pass an open wagon drawn by two slow-moving, patient baiyos, but the wagon instead came to a halt in front of him.

"Cole?"

He raised his head and discovered that he was on Main Street. MaryAnn was sitting in the passenger seat of the wagon, the sun creating a halo around her.

"MaryAnn!" he said, with a big warm smile. "Really great to see you!" He remembered the flowers. "Here," he said, extending them toward her, "these are for you."

She took the bouquet from him and gave a tiny gasp. "Oh, Cole, they're beautiful! That's so thoughtful of you!"

She spontaneously leaned over and gave him an awkward, one-armed hug, Cole standing on his tiptoes to reach her. The driver, an older man with a sun-weathered face, stared impassively ahead, giving no indication he was aware they existed.

"Where you going?" he said when she straightened up.

"The farm. I'm doing a story on the orphans, how they're settling in." She put her nose into the bouquet and took a deep breath. "Wow," she said. Then she flopped over to hug him a second time.

"Okay, then," she said, after she sat up again, straightening her hair.

"Yeah," said Cole, realizing they were both giggling like schoolkids. The driver chewed contemplatively on the stalk of wheat sticking out of the corner of his mouth.

"I guess we should . . . ," she said. The driver didn't need any more encouragement, immediately clucking at the baiyos and tapping them with a long quirt.

She twisted in her seat as they trundled off. "I'll be back in a few days," she said. "Will you still be here?"

"I . . . yes! Yessirree!" Had he ever said yessiree in his life? What was wrong with him? She waved. He waved. He watched her take another deep hit from the flowers.

"She doesn't know a thing about you, does she," said Nora, standing at his elbow.

He took another deep breath. "Air smells good here, huh?" he said, and walked away, bouncing a bit as he went.

28

Late that night Cole was awakened by crashing sounds and swearing coming from the escape pod. He groggily trudged down the hallway from his cabin and climbed the ladder. He stuck his head up through the hatch, finding exactly what he had expected.

"I already tried it," he said to Bacchi. "Can't get the engines to fire," and went back to bed.

Cole had assumed that the citizens would see the Benedict as an eyesore and want it removed as quickly as possible, but when he woke up the next morning he noticed a small text panel affixed to the exterior. It was identical in appearance to the one in the jailhouse except for the content, which stated:

> **Spaceship** is a piece of found art that comments directly and incisively on the nature of our relationship with . . .

. . . and there went Cole's eyes out of focus again. All Cole knew is that no one complained about the spacecraft, only referring now and then to the "new installation" just outside of the gate.

Cole spent the rest of the day walking around again, trying to visualize how to protect the town. At one point he spotted the sembluk in the distance and felt the same elusive flash of familiarity, but the enormity of the task at hand quickly pushed the subject out of his mind. He'd come to a conclusion about Yrnameer: the village was easily defensible. That is, if every single person in the town was heavily armed and knew what they were doing, and if none of the bandits had weapons and *didn't* know what they were doing.

That evening Mayor Kimber suggested a planning session, a small gathering of what he termed the "village elders." Cole agreed, hoping they'd have some ideas. He certainly didn't.

They originally intended to hold the gathering in the mayor's small office, but just before the meeting Mayor Kimber informed him that they'd moved it to the town hall again—"A few more folks might be interested in attending."

A few more folks, as it turned out, was more or less identical to the population of the town.

First there was a discussion of how, exactly, the meeting should be run; the method by which participants would be chosen to voice their opinion so that no one felt excluded; what the process would be for resolving differences of opinion—an issue whose resolution everyone finally agreed should be postponed to a future meeting; where and when that and other future meetings should take place and the manner in which members should be chosen to participate in said future meetings; and what snacks should be served. Those items settled, it was time to go to bed.

Nora attended the meeting but stayed in a back corner, expressionless, avoiding his gaze.

As everyone filed out of the hall—Nora without so much as a sideways glance—Cole pulled Mayor Kimber aside.

"I just want to run down a quick checklist with you, if that's all right," said Cole.

"Of course, of course."

"Do you happen to have any heavy weaponry?"

"Oh, heavens no."

"Right. Didn't think so. Explosives?"

"No."

"Okay. Skimmers?"

"No."

"Other flying craft?"

"Uh . . . no."

"How about the guy in there with the wings. He can fly, right?"

"Benny? He's a terranian. He refuses to fly to protest the dominance of—"

"Okay. Got it. Anyone with any military training?"

"Not that I know of."

"Do you have any fast wheeled vehicles?"

"Fast vehicles . . . fast vehicles . . . Yes!"

"Oh, that's goo—"

"No, wait. No."

"Ah."

"Would tractors from the farm count?"

"Probably not."

"Right."

Cole was silent, nodding to himself.

"So, how do things look?" said the mayor.

"Great," said Cole. "Things look great."

There was one subject on which everyone at the meeting had been in agreement: they didn't want outside help. The cure, went the consensus, would be worse than the disease: outside help would mean outside attention, which would initiate a chain of events that would inevitably lead to the destruction of the soul of Yrnameer. Better they should all die before that happened. Right, Cole? Of course, he answered, he couldn't agree more. No outside help.

The instant he got back to the ship that night, he fired up the communication system and broadcast a general Mayday on the law enforcement band. Just like a ship, the communication had to go through bendspace, and it was more than two hours before he was able to raise any sort of response from a Control substation.

Cole, overwhelmed with relief, described the situation in detail. When he was done, the voice on the other end explained to him that there was no such place as Yrnameer.

Yes, there is, said Cole.

No, there's not, said the voice.

Yes, there is.

No, there's not.

"Yes, there farging well is, because I'm on the farging planet right now," said Cole, nearly shouting. "I should farging know whether or not it exists."

"Okay, first? There's no need for language like that."

"Look, please, Runk is here. Runk! Check out your Most Wanted list. He's way up there!"

"Do you know the fine for filing a false report?"

"Well, farging come and get me, then! Fine me!"

"Again with the language."

"Listen: I stole Teg's ship. I'm a ship thief. You should send a very well-armed detachment to arrest me."

"No one could ever steal Teg's ship—he's too handsome."

"He's not that handsss—listen. Please. Just connect me to your supervisor."

"I think I've wasted enough time with you. I'm putting a three-month block on your voice signature and com tag. You'll no longer be able to engage in interplanetary communications."

The line went dead.

29

"Pair of queens," said Cole.

"Three nines," said Bacchi.

"Crap."

They'd been there all morning, sitting on the front porch that extended along the length of the jailhouse, lazily playing cards. Passersby would call out the inevitable friendly greeting, usually including a question about how the planning was going.

"Going great," Cole replied each time with a big grin.

It was not going great. It was not going. Cole felt overcome by a feeling of mental lethargy, unable to find a solution to what was, after all, an insoluble problem. He was hoping inspiration would arrive soon.

He wondered how MaryAnn was doing, and when she'd be back. He had dreamed about her again last night, an innocent dream, full of wonder, and had woken up feeling hopeful. Then he remembered the situation.

He lost another hand. Over the past few hours Bacchi had managed to reduce his outstanding debt to Cole by about half.

"You're going to have to start ch-cheating soon," said Bacchi.

"Tell me about it."

Bacchi shuffled the cards again. "So, you think there's some way to—kuhkuhkuh—defend this place?"

Bacchi had developed an odd stutter and a small collection of facial tics over the past few days, the side effect of his heavy caffeine intake. He'd become attracted to the owner and barista at Café Storj, and apparently the attraction was mutual, because she kept him supplied with free lattes.

Cole, curious, had stopped by to behold the poor misguided creature. He found a petite Storjan, not unappealing if one's tastes ran
toward the reptilian end of the spectrum. When he arrived she was
in the midst of a belching competition with some of the clientele,
and everything became clear.

"I'll figure something out," said Cole.

"You mean, you'll figure some *way* out," said Bacchi, "for
yourself."

"I'm not running, Bacchi."

"Of course you're not. You'll take me with you, won't you?"

Cole put his feet up on the rail and leaned back in his chair. "You
know what you need, Bacchi? A positive mind-set. It's all going to
work out."

A shadow darkened the small card table. They looked up to find
the spindly, black-clothed townsperson observing them silently, his
bony face somber. Graef, Cole had learned his name was. He was tall
enough that his bald head was still slightly higher than theirs.

Without a word Graef produced a leather-covered rectangular
case that looked like it might accommodate a flute. Instead, as they
discovered when he opened it and presented its interior to them, it
contained a series of small vials, tastefully displayed against a red
velvet lining. There were crystal versions in different colors, sleek
metallic models, some shiny, some brushed, a few wood models
with miniscule but elaborate carvings, and what looked to be a plain
pine variant, no longer or thicker than the latter half of Cole's pinky.

"Aha," said Cole. "I'm not sure I'm in the market just yet."

The undertaker flicked his gaze up to meet Cole's for the briefest
of moments, managing in that instant to convey a world-weary professional's profound sadness at the folly of the self-deceiving customer. Then he performed his almost imperceptible bow and closed
the case with a muffled click. Before he departed he extended his
hand toward Bacchi, who automatically responded to the gesture
before Cole could warn him off.

"Sixty-three point two-nine percent," intoned the little device in
the undertaker's hand. Graef nodded gloomily and jotted in his
notebook, pausing again as he walked away to half turn to them and
make his respectful bow.

Cole and Bacchi sat in silence for a few moments. Bacchi's left
eye twitched. "I wonder how much the shiny silver one is?" he said.

Cole grunted.

"I heard this one story about this guy who double-crossed Runk on this job," said Bacchi. "He crosses Runk, Runk finds him, and has him made—"

"Has him made into a side table. Yes, I heard it," said Cole.

"The guy was still alive, Cole!"

"I heard it."

"Even after he was furniture!"

"Heard it."

"He had drawers!"

"Heard. It."

"Cole," said Bacchi, "I have no plans to—kuhkuhkuh—die here. Why won't they just face reality and give Runk the—kuhkuhkuh—food?"

"They say it's the principle of the thing," said Cole.

"Principles get p-people k-killed," said Bacchi, tossing some more money into the pot.

"Maybe principles are worth dying for," said Cole in a loud, clear voice. Bacchi looked up sharply at Cole, who was casually studying his cards. Then he noticed Nora, who was standing within earshot.

"Ah," said Bacchi, who hadn't seen her approaching. "For a second, I thought you really meant that."

"How are the plans coming?" asked Nora.

"I'm working on them," said Cole.

"Uh-huh," said Nora.

It was the most they'd spoken in days. Her manner was distant, formal, as cold as when he'd first met her.

"Have you seen Joshua?" she said.

"Nope," said Cole.

This was untrue. Cole had, in fact, seen Joshua that very morning. He'd been patiently waiting for Cole when Cole arrived at the jail.

"I thought you were supposed to be on the farm," Cole said to him.

"Would *you* have stayed there?" asked Joshua.

So Cole gave him back his badge and sent him on some errands.

"He's not off running errands for you or anything like that," said Nora.

"Nope."

He could feel her watching him as placed his bet.

"Cole, despite everything, I believe that there's a good, decent person in there struggling to get out," she said.

Bacchi snorted. "S-sorry," he said. "Something caught in my haglafrap."

Nora ignored him. "Joshua's a child. And these people are depending on you, Cole," she said. "Remember that."

Cole watched her walk off.

"I think she digs you," said Bacchi. "Oops, look at that. I won again." He scraped the pot over to himself.

Cole lay awake that night, conceiving of and discarding plans. When he fell asleep he had a nightmare involving himself, Runk, and a wood lathe. When he awoke the next morning he was no better off then when he went to bed, so he settled in again to play cards with Bacchi. He didn't really trust him, but he was decent company.

Mayor Kimber made his midmorning rounds, stopping in front of the jailhouse to chat with Cole. "The plans progressing?" he asked.

"They sure are."

"Cogitating, eh?"

"Precisely."

Bacchi emitted another snort.

"Haglafrap," he said.

The mayor watched Cole deal.

"Well, we're all eager to hear what you come up with," he said, then continued on his way.

"What have you come up with?" asked Bacchi.

"I'm cogitating."

"Uh-huh." Bacchi put his cards down on the table and hunched forward, leaning in close. "I'll tell you what I think we should do," he said in a low voice, so that Cole had to lean forward as well. "We get the farg out of here. Go into the hills, hide, whatever, until this blows over. These people want to stand up to Runk, let them."

Cole was silent, absently picking at a corner of a card with his thumbnail.

"We stay, we die. We run, we live," said Bacchi. "You know it, Cole."

"But Cole isn't the sort of person who runs," said a voice.

They bolted upright guiltily to find MaryAnn standing next to the porch, looking up at them.

"Exactly!" said Bacchi. "That's why I was shocked that guy would suggest it!"

"What guy?"

"You know, the guy with the . . . things," said Bacchi, gesturing vaguely to his head. "Shocking. And I was, like, I can't believe you're *saying* gip like that, and he's, like, Don't tell me what—"

"You're back," said Cole to MaryAnn, cutting off Bacchi.

"I'm back," she said. "Did you miss me?"

"Of course."

She beamed at him. He found his expression matched hers. She walked up the steps and sat in the chair that Cole held out for her.

"I missed you, too," she said.

Bacchi muttered something.

"How are the preparations coming?" she asked.

"Making real progress," said Cole.

Her eyes fell on the cards and the money on the table.

"Just taking a quick break," he explained. "All right, well," he said, tidying up the cards and standing, "we should probably get back to it."

"Sheriff!"

He turned as Joshua came clomping up the steps onto the porch. He had a large mason jar in each hand, filled with a clear liquid.

"I got the shersha. They said be careful, it's right powerful stuff."

"Oh, good—here's your shersha, Bacchi," said Cole.

"And yours, Sheriff, that's why I got two," said Joshua. "Just like you told me. Hi, Miss MaryAnn."

"Hello, Joshua."

"Plus I got more cigars. Here."

"Fantastic," said Cole, smiling between gritted teeth.

"And a new deck of cards."

"Okay. Well, it's nice of you to stop by. . . ."

Joshua's face grew serious.

"Sheriff, I've been thinking."

"Uh-oh."

"Remember the bandits?"

"Of course I remember the bandits, Joshua. What do you think is on my mind every hour of every day?"

Joshua's eyes flicked to the cards. "Uh . . ."

"What about the bandits, Joshua?"

"I mean the bandits that we crushed."

"The ones I crushed, yes. What about them?"

"Well, here's the thing: they came here to deliver a message, right?"

"Right."

"But now they're all gone."

"That's right," said Cole, smiling at MaryAnn as he said it. "No more problems from those guys."

"No doubt," said Joshua. "But wouldn't Runk be expecting them to report back?"

Cole paused, blinking. MaryAnn watched him. "I had been thinking that, yes," he said.

"So Runk's waiting for them to come back and tell him how they delivered the message, and what everyone's reaction was and everything. Except they don't come back."

"No, because they're all gone," said Cole, smiling again at MaryAnn, but with less assurance this time.

"So if you were Runk, wouldn't you send someone else to find out what happened?"

Cole's smile faded. MaryAnn had her questioning expression on, waiting.

"I'm not sure that . . . well, I suppose he might . . . no. No, I don't think we have to worry about that. Not yet. It's something I've been considering, and I think if they do send someone, it wouldn't be for several days."

Bacchi's head snapped up suddenly, listening.

"What?" said MaryAnn.

"Was that gunfire?"

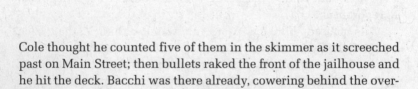

30

Cole thought he counted five of them in the skimmer as it screeched past on Main Street; then bullets raked the front of the jailhouse and he hit the deck. Bacchi was there already, cowering behind the overturned card table. A smoking bullet hole went clean through it and the brick wall behind them. He heard whooping and laughing.

Cole realized that MaryAnn and Joshua were still standing, watching the skimmer as it banked and climbed sharply, nearly clipping the peaked roof of the town hall. He grabbed at them both, pulling them down.

"You want to get shot? Get down, now!"

The skimmer wheeled and dove, swooping low over the rooftops, the bandits keeping the engine revs high so that the earsplitting vibrations shattered windows. They roared along Main Street again, firing randomly, townspeople scattering and diving for cover.

"Inside! Get inside the jail!"

Cole pushed MaryAnn and Joshua through the door and followed them, Bacchi right behind him.

"Stay down!" said Cole. He could see that the bullet hole went through the back wall of the structure as well.

"Is it them?" asked MaryAnn. "Are the bandits back?"

"Well, they may be bandits, but they're not necessarily *the* bandits," said Cole. "For all we know, this could be an entirely unrelated—" He broke off as Joshua got to his feet and stepped to the desk, reaching for something.

"Joshua, put that gun down!" said Cole.

"But we have to stop them!"

"You're gonna get yourself shot! Get down, idiot!"

He pulled at his ankle. Joshua reluctantly lowered himself to the floor. "Now give me the gun!"

"But, Sheriff—"

"Give me the gun! Look, I want to show you a trick."

Joshua handed him the Firestick 25. Cole chucked it through the open door of the jail cell, then shut the door with his foot.

"Hey!" said Joshua.

"We're all cowering inside the jailhouse now, as the bandits continue to fly over and through the town, firing at will," said Mary-Ann. Cole turned to find her speaking into her tiny microphone.

"We are not cowering, MaryAnn, we're taking cover *Joshua*!"

Joshua was crawling toward the door. Cole crawled after him and pushed him aside. Reaching the door, he opened it a crack and cautiously peered out. He could see the bandits in the skimmer doing doughnuts at the other end of Main Street, spraying dust and pebbles and exhaust blast in a circle. Then they landed and leaped out of the craft, whooping and hollering, firing their automatic weapons into the air.

"Come on out!" shouted one of them. "Come on, cowards!"

Cole recounted them as the dust settled—five, like he thought, a nice assortment of species whose salient features were large muscles or spiky armored parts or big, sharp teeth or a mixture of all three.

"There's five of them," whispered Cole to the others. "They all have—MaryAnn, what are you doing?"

She was on her feet, pulling at the door.

"I have to go report on this!"

"Report on it from in here!"

"Come on!" roared the bandit again, a massive Yoin who sported the trifecta of threatening features. "We've got a message for you!"

"We have to go out there," said Joshua.

"No, we don't. If they have a message, they can shout it to us."

"I'm going out there, Cole. This is an important story," said MaryAnn.

"No one is going out there."

"You don't come out, we're just going to start shooting!" the Yoin announced, then fired off a quick burst to punctuate his threat.

"Again, no one is—"

Joshua pushed past Cole and MaryAnn, forcing open the door. "Hey!" he shouted.

"Joshua!"

"Stop that!" shouted Joshua. "Stop it now!" He marched indignantly across the porch and bounded down the stairs, heading directly toward the five aggressors.

"Oh, farging hell," said Cole, reluctantly getting to his feet. "As I said, no one goes out there until I do."

"Go get 'em, Sheriff," said Bacchi.

As he descended from the porch, he heard MaryAnn behind him: "I'm now accompanying the sheriff as he goes to confront the bandits."

"MaryAnn, you are not accompanying—" He stopped and covered her microphone with his hand. "You are not accompanying me!"

"Cole, I have a responsibility as a journalist."

"You're not going to file the story if you're dead. At least find some spot out of the open."

She nodded. "All right."

Cole broke into a jog to catch up to Joshua, who was walking toward Runk's men with great determination.

"Hey, you!" Joshua shouted. "I'm talking to you!"

The five had noticed his presence and were turning to face him.

"You better get out of here!" said Joshua.

"Or what?" said the Yoin.

"Or there's gonna be trouble!" said Joshua.

"Looks like there already is trouble," said the Yoin. "And you're in it." He brought his gun up.

"Wait! *Wait!*" screamed Cole, catching up to Joshua and grabbing him. "Don't shoot! He has mental problems!"

The Yoin paused.

"I do not!"

"He does! He's simpleminded and wets the bed!"

"I do not wet the bed!"

Cole pulled Joshua close and whispered in his ear through clenched teeth. "Keep your stupid mouth shut, or you're gonna get someone killed."

"I don't wet the bed!"

"Shut up!"

"Where's the mayor?" demanded the Yoin.

"Umm . . . that's a very good question. We'll see if we can go find him for you." Cole turned to go, dragging Joshua with him.

"Stop!"

Cole didn't stop.

"Keep going," he whispered to Joshua. "Do *not* say no."

"No," said Joshua.

"You're driving me *insane*," hissed Cole.

"I said *stop!*" thundered the Yoin.

Cole did. He reluctantly turned back to face the intruders. He was aware of the silence, knowing that he was being watched by the townspeople, peering at him from dozens of hiding places.

"Who are you?" said the Yoin.

"He's the sher*oof!*" said Joshua, as Cole elbowed him in the side.

"I'm just, uh . . . ," said Cole, scavenging about for the most uninteresting, nonthreatening identity he could imagine, "a poet."

Cole had swiped his uncle's skimmer and run away for good three and half weeks into his junior year of high school, no doubt a vanishingly minor and inconsequential branch point in the overall flow of history. For Cole's *personal* history, however, it would indeed have a consequence, and that consequence was about to become manifest.

"A poet? Really?" said the Yoin, with far more interest than Cole had expected or hoped for. "I *like* poetry."

Had Cole bothered to stay in school one more day, he would have been present for his second-period language arts class, which had included a brief but memorable discussion about the vital—life and death, really—importance of poetry in the Yoin culture.

"I *really* like poetry," said the Yoin.

One of the other bandits sighed loudly. Another began massaging his temples as if warding off a looming headache.

"Oh. How . . . wonderful," said Cole, starting to intuit that he'd made a very bad mistake.

"Why are you wearing a badge?" asked the Yoin.

"A badge? Oh, this old thing?"

"Poetic license?"

Cole stared at the armor-plated face of the Yoin, trying to discern if he was joking. He was not. The Yoin were very, very serious about their poetry.

"Yyyes?" ventured Cole.

The Yoin nodded in satisfaction. "Tell me a poem."

"A poem."

"Yes."

"Well, I have to say, you seem like very busy people, and I suspect you're here on some sort of important mission. Maybe I could help you with that?"

"First tell me a poem."

"I really, uh, prefer to work from the page. If you want, I just had a collection published by a small press, and I could go get you a copy—"

The Yoin pointed the gun at him. "Okay, I'll just shoot you."

"You know, I could probably summon a few lines. . . ."

"Good."

The Yoin leaned back against the skimmer, arms crossed. The other four bandits exchanged exasperated, long-suffering glances. One of them began idly sharpening his claws with a large knife, shaving down the tips like they were pencils.

"Okay," said Cole. "Here we go. I hope you like it."

"As my people say, if you're alive at the end, I liked it."

"Ah. Figure of speech?"

"No."

"Right."

"Begin!" said the Yoin. He leaned back again, chin up, head cocked to one side, eyes half closed in an attitude of critical appraisal.

Cole could feel the prickly sensation as perspiration beaded on his forehead. He scanned around, searching for something to inspire him. Now he was starting to catch glimpses of faces: Bacchi's Storjan girlfriend, peering out of the shattered windows of her café with a few customers; Orwa, looking over the railing of his second-story roof deck; the purple guy whose name he could never remember.

"Nothing dactylic," said the Yoin, interrupting his thoughts.

"No, of course not."

Cole spotted MaryAnn, crouched behind a barrel. He held up a hand, motioning her to get back. She shook her head.

"No trisoptic decameters," added the Yoin.

"Would you please?" said Cole.

"Sorry. When you're ready."

Cole could hear the bandit whittling his pointy claws into

pointier claws. Ideas were popping into Cole's head, but they were less formally poetic and more shocking images of him getting shot to pieces.

The Yoin opened his eyes. "Well?"

"Just picking the best one." He leaned close to Joshua again and spoke out of the corner of his mouth. "Do you know any poems?"

"Umm, uh . . . 'There once was a Gan from Hanlukket. . . . ' "

"He's probably heard that one before."

Joshua seemed genuinely surprised. "Really? How?"

Maybe if he ran one way, and Joshua the other, one of them would make it. The general store was about three meters away and—why was Fred in there, waving to him? Cole gave him a hard glare, trying to send the signal to keep his big egg-shaped head down. Now Fred was murmuring something to him, and the AT was crackling, laboring to capture and analyze Fred's voice. Cole made small but urgent hand gestures for him to shut up.

The Yoin sighed. "The promise of water in the desert," he said, "the sun a wretched companion / the poem denied / the well / dry." He looked at Cole expectantly.

"Uh . . . very nice," said Cole.

"Thank you. What I meant by it is that I'm now going to shoot you." The big black hole of the barrel came up again, centered right on Cole's forehead.

"Dreaming leaves silent before the vision of the dawn!" screamed Cole.

The Yoin paused. "Interesting. Continue."

Cole continued, a torrent of impressionistic language flowing into his ear from the AT and directly out of his mouth without making so much as a courtesy stop in his neocortex. As he declaimed he slowly inched closer to the general store, so that he could hear Fred better.

Fred, unlike Cole, knew about Yoin culture. All Greys did. Poetry, to the Yoin, was what gambling was to the Greys, and by some accident of evolution and brain structure the Yoin were particularly enamored of the Greys' speech patterns. A solid percentage of the gross planetary product of Fred's home world, in fact, consisted of poetry exports to Yoi, or EnterCo, as the planet was known.

There was a saying in Fred's language: "Like poetry for a Yoin." It was not a compliment. At the moment Fred was reading from the ingredient list of a candy bar wrapper that he'd found in his pocket. The Yoin was nodding appreciatively, grunting now and then in apparent satisfaction.

Fred ran out of text and began reciting menu items from his favorite pub. He listed every city he could remember. He improvised a weather report. He described the family pet.

After a half hour Cole was starting to feel hoarse. After forty-five minutes he took a seat on the porch of the general store, Joshua sitting next to him. An hour passed and Cole was still talking, relaying Fred's words to the Yoin, who seemed quite content to while away the afternoon listening to poetry. Cole's voice was getting croaky. One of the bandits was snoring.

And then suddenly the flow of words ceased, Cole stumbling a bit like he'd come to the end of a moving sidewalk.

The Yoin opened his eyes. "That's it?" he said.

Cole nodded.

"A little short," said the Yoin.

"That's really sort of my métier," said Cole.

"Hmm," said the Yoin. "Hmm." He closed his eyes again, making little nodding and head-tilting movements and occasionally mouthing some words, as if he were replaying choice passages of the poem internally. This went on for several more minutes. The other bandits looked like they'd been cudgeled into a near stupor.

"Come on," whispered Cole, tugging at Joshua. They rose silently and began walking away.

"Freeze!" commanded the Yoin. They froze.

The Yoin began clapping in a polite, respectful manner. He nudged one of the other bandits. They began clapping, too, waking the one who was sleeping. He looked around blearily and joined in the applause.

"Very nice," said the Yoin. "Interesting. Almost had elements of poetry by the Greys."

"Qx"-x-'--'," corrected Fred quietly from the interior of the store.

"So," said the Yoin. "Back to the reason for our visit." He cleared his throat and took a deep breath. "WHERE ARE OUR PEOPLE!" he bellowed. "WE SENT MESSENGERS HERE, AND THEY NEVER RETURNED! WHAT HAPPENED TO THEM?"

"I'll tell you what hap*pened*!" said Joshua as Cole stomped on his foot.

"I have no idea what you're talking about," said Cole. "No one came here. What is it you want?"

"You're LYING!!" boomed the Yoin. Cole, five meters away, could feel his hair blowing back. "What have you done with our comrades?"

"Look at us!" said Cole. "We're not warriors! We're weak and helpless. We're shopkeepers and farmers and humble poets and bed-wetting idiots!"

"I do *not* wet—"

"How could we have done any harm to your friends? If they're half as strong as you are, they would have destroyed us!"

The Yoin considered this. He turned and had a quick conference with the others.

"THEN I WILL GIVE YOU THIS MESSAGE!"

"There's really no need to shout," said Cole.

"Right. Then *I* will give you this message," repeated the Yoin. "We will be back in three weeks for your crops. You will feed us, or you will DIE!"

"Okay, that sounds pretty fair," said Cole. "But have you thought about maybe getting a few agbots? They're really pretty efficient with all the planting and harvesting and—"

"SILENCE!"

"Right. Sorry."

"THREE WEEKS! CROPS OR DEATH!"

"We're not gonna *aayiii*!" said Joshua. "Stop pinching me!" he said to Cole.

"There's absolutely no problem," said Cole. "We'll get everything all set and ready to go for you."

"GOOD!" said the Yoin. "By the way, nice poem again."

"Thanks," said Cole. "Well, I guess you'll be on your way now. . . ."

"No!" said a voice, approaching from behind Cole.

"No!" repeated the voice. A woman's voice, older, resonant, full of strength. Cole turned. It was Daras Katim. She was striding toward the bandits, brimming with controlled, dignified fury.

"Daras," he said as she passed, trying to stop her. She shook off his hand. Cole caught a whiff of healthy earth after a rain shower.

"We will *not* give you anything!"

Cole hurried after her. "Daras, please, this is not the time." She shook him off again, turning to him.

"Excuse me," she said. "You're interrupting me."

She said it with a tone of such stern command that Cole stopped in his tracks, uncertain of what to do. Daras, meanwhile, continued toward the bandits.

"Go back to your holes, and come back when you've learned how to behave in a civilized fashion!" she said.

At least two of the bandits sheepishly lowered their heads. But the Yoin was unfazed, staring at her expressionlessly. She walked directly up to him and stopped a short meter away.

"When you work for your food, growing it from the land like we have, then you can share it. But you'll have none of ours. Do you understand?"

The Yoin didn't move.

"Do. You. Understand?" said Daras.

Cole was frozen, still unsure of how to intervene.

"She's so brave," whispered Joshua.

The Yoin shot her dead.

31

They buried Daras, as per her wishes, at the top of a grassy hill at the base of the mountains. Orwa was selected to say a few words and said many, many of them. When they went to clear out Daras's shop, they discovered that all the plants were shriveled up and brown.

That night there was another town meeting, this one more contentious then the others. Daras Katim's death had fueled their anger and stiffened their resolve.

Cole, for his part, found himself wishing that he'd brought along some sort of recording device so that he could later review exactly what he had been saying, because he was starting to wonder if he was losing his mind. He'd *say* something like, Please, listen to me, I really don't think we can stand up to the bandits, and the townspeople would apparently *hear* him say something like, We will resist and overcome, making the wrongdoers regret their rash actions!

No, you don't understand, Cole would say, we simply don't have the firepower.

Yes, you're right! they'd respond, The purity of our intentions and the righteousness of our motives will suffice to defeat the enemy, albeit in the most measured and gentle fashion possible!

After several hours like this, Cole extricated himself from the excited discussion and slipped out of the town hall, taking a seat on the porch. He lay back and stared up at the stars, his legs dangling over the side.

"I didn't know you were such a poet."

He sat up. MaryAnn had stepped out of the doorway.

"It was like a voice was speaking in my ear," he said, reminding himself to have a private talk with Fred as soon as possible.

She took a seat next to him.

"It was horrible seeing that," she said.

"Yes."

"She was so strong, and full of life."

And stupid, thought Cole automatically, then guiltily banished the thought.

"Yes," he said.

"Oh, Cole," she said, and leaned against him, her head resting on his shoulder. Before he realized he was doing it he put his arm around her, the most natural movement in the world, gently pulling her closer. She turned to look at him, her face inches from his, her lips soft and beckoning. Then she closed her eyes and moved forward subtly, and he closed his, and it was the most wonderful, transcendent kiss he had ever experienced.

Or would have been, he imagined later, if Nora hadn't stepped out the door at that very moment and said, "So, what's the plan?"

MaryAnn altered her approach pattern just enough so that she brushed by his waiting lips, continuing the action so that it became a smooth turning motion to face Nora.

"Hi, Nora," said Cole.

"You do have a plan, right?" said Nora, standing over him, hands on her hips. "Or are you just going to sit around and play cards for another week, maybe wait for someone else to get shot?"

MaryAnn turned her gaze back to him.

"Of course I have a plan," said Cole.

The next evening Cole strode briskly into the packed town hall, his strategic vision outlined on the several roles of poster-size paper tucked under one arm. As he made his way to the front, he overheard Joshua telling a group of citizens stories of Cole's exploits in the space marines, adventures that had grown somewhat in the telling.

"He's an expert at these things!" Joshua was saying.

The assembled Yrnameerians listened intently as Cole explained his plan, pinning up the papers and drawing charts out on a whiteboard. First, they would concentrate on constructing a series of defensive structures, starting with a heavy fence around the village. Beyond the fence would be a series of traps designed to slow and weaken the approaching forces: pits with sharpened stakes at the bottom; trip wires; complex, spring-loaded devices designed to crush and puncture and maim. Hidden foxholes and sniper nests would be constructed to take advantage of what few weapons they had. Bandits who made it past the traps and the snipers and the fence would be funneled into narrow side streets and alleys, where they would be set upon and destroyed.

Construction would begin immediately. While that continued, Cole would lead the citizens of Yrnameer through a short but intense course of basic training, drawing on his extensive military experience to hone them into a razor-keen fighting force.

When he finished there was an unnerving moment of silence. Then the hall erupted in applause, building to cheers and stamping of feet and shouts of enthusiasm.

The plan, everyone concurred, was brilliant. Any quibbles were minor.

For example, everyone wholeheartedly agreed that the bandits needed to be trapped and corralled and destroyed, but the general consensus was that it should be done in the most benign way possible. The traps, for example: necessary, yes; but perhaps they could, say, forgo the sharpened stakes at the bottom. That, or how about not sharpening them so much. Someone suggested that they could keep the stakes, and keep them sharp, but wrap them in some sort of padded protective covering.

Cole didn't argue. He nodded amiably and scribbled some notes and encouraged the comments. "Great idea," he said when someone ventured that warning signs might be appropriate. "Like it, like it," he said when someone else advocated some gentle music.

What did it matter? The whole thing, he knew, was a crock in the first place: they could build their traps and trip wires and their barriers and whatever else, and when Runk showed up with his men they'd blow a giant farging hole through the thick fence and flood through the middle of town and slaughter anyone who got in their way.

Yes, we need to use the firearms we have, someone said, but how about we just shoot them in the legs?

Great, said Cole. Great.

32

Cole envisioned the next few weeks passing as a sort of painless montage: there'd be music, and different moments of the townspeople hard at work building a defensive wall around the perimeter of the town, and digging holes to serve as traps, and training with the few weapons they had. There'd be a wiping of perspiration and drinks raised to one another and the exchange of friendly smiles between comrades, and perhaps deeper, more meaningful glances between him and MaryAnn.

But by midmorning of the first day, Cole had come to the unavoidable conclusion that the remainder of the experience would in fact drag on in exceedingly real time, with lots of heaving and hoing and digging and hauling under the hot sun, full of the kind of intense straining that raised the danger of a really spectacular hernia. And, judging from the few tense conversations he'd had so far, he foresaw a series of increasingly strident arguments with Nora regarding matters strategic. Plus, of course, at the end of all this effort they'd all probably be dead.

By around noon, Cole had decided that he was better suited to a supervisory role, the kind where he could relax in a chair in the shade of a broad umbrella, drinking germonade spiked with a little shersha, which he later discovered was made from the fermented excrement of some sort of segmented worm. Which, after a few more shots of shersha, didn't bother him so much.

At the moment he was watching Nora direct the townspeople as they struggled to erect the fence: a series of stout logs, sharpened at the top and pounded vertically into the ground in a dense row, lashed to horizontal support braces.

"Push! Lift that! Lift!" she bellowed.

There was lifting and pushing, accompanied by much grunting. Cole raised his glass. "Good job, folks," he murmured. "Keep going."

"Lift!" Nora bellowed again.

"Lift," seconded Cole, taking another drink.

MaryAnn wandered by a few meters away, her attention focused on the construction and the microphone in her hand.

"The brave creatures of Yrnameer have set to the task of defending their idyllic community," Cole heard her saying.

"MaryAnn," he said, calling out to her. She turned, spotted him, and waved back with a smile. He returned both gestures. There, *that* was more like what he'd been hoping for.

"You gonna help, or are you just gonna sit there and flirt with your little sweetheart?" said Nora, who staggered by carrying a heavy load of wood.

"You know, you're very sexy when you're sweaty and jealous," said Cole. Ha, he thought, Good one, mentally raising his glass to himself. Nora scowled and stomped off, shaking her head.

"Sheriff?"

Cole twisted in his seat. It was Joshua, accompanied by a gralleth that shambled along next to him. The gralleth was about half as tall and four times as wide as Joshua, covered entirely in shaggy fur. Cole had seen him at several of the meetings, but hadn't had a chance to speak with him.

"Sheriff, this is Grilleth," said Joshua.

"Pleasure," said Cole. He wasn't certain, but he thought Grilleth the gralleth nodded back at him. Cole knew there was a head and two eyes in there somewhere, but he wasn't sure where.

"Did you find anything else?" he asked Joshua.

"No, sir. Same old hunting weapons, a few sidearms. And, uh, Grilleth here says that his kind are, well, they're very accurate in throwing their—"

"Yeah, I've seen that before," said Cole.

Grilleth made a long rumbly sound.

"No, no need to demonstrate," Cole said to him. "I'm sure it'll come in very handy when the time comes, though."

Grilleth made a few more rumbly sounds and waddled off. They watched him go.

"Can they really throw their—"

"Yes. It's quite something," said Cole.

Joshua watched the townsfolk struggling to place another fence post.

"Do you think we have enough people?" he asked.

"Nope."

"Do you think the traps will work?"

"Nope."

"And we're short weapons."

"Yep."

"So . . . what do we do?"

Cole smiled at him.

"We improvise," he said.

Then he took a very long pull from the bottle of shersha.

That evening Cole knocked on MaryAnn's door.

"Hi," she said when she opened it.

"Hi," he said back.

They hadn't had a chance to speak since their near-kiss experience. Now, in the silence, that seemed like a long time ago.

"Can I come in?" said Cole.

She hesitated, leaning against the half-open door. "Cole," she said, "what happened between us was . . . well, it was . . . Cole, with everything that's going on—"

"MaryAnn," said Cole evenly, putting a gentle hand on her shoulder, "it's okay."

She smiled in relief. "It is?"

"Of course," said Cole. "In fact, I'm glad you feel that way. That's why I came by. We've all got a big task ahead of us. This is life or death. It's now or never. I'm going to need every ounce of concentration and focus to try and keep this town safe. You understand, don't you?"

"Yes, of course," said MaryAnn.

"I'm glad," said Cole with a grave smile. "I'm so glad."

As soon as he was around the corner Cole angrily kicked a wall and then limped rapidly in a small circle, swearing.

"Foot okay, Sheriff?"

Nora, observing him from across the street.

Cole shot her a murderous glance and hobbled off, muttering darkly.

· · ·

Time continued to pass in a very nonmontagelike fashion. The fence grew. Holes were dug. Stakes were sharpened and covered with protective padding. Cole forewent the sun umbrella and comfortable chair to supervise the weapons training and drills. There were several accidental discharges, sending people diving for cover. After less than a week there were six superficial bullet wounds, and one new hole added to the already well-perforated town sign.

At one point Cole heard a sharp crack and looked up just in time to see Geldar the sembluk soaring through the air like an errant fly ball, the result of Peter the 'Puter spinning around too quickly with a two-ton log. It was a blow that would have killed anyone not equipped with a six-inch-thick shell. As Geldar shrank from view Cole had a repeat of the impression that he should know him, but then Geldar disappeared over the rooftops and Cole forgot about it again. After that, Peter was relegated to tasks that could be accomplished with no one in immediate log radius.

The townspeople, joined by a shared goal and hard labor, grew even closer. Cole and Nora, divided by their opinions regarding strategy, tactics, and whether or not he was an idiot, grew further apart.

There was one minor bright spot: despite his recent conversation with MaryAnn, he was making progress with her. He could feel it.

Every day he'd maneuver so that he would casually encounter her when they'd have a few moments alone to chat—keeping it light, not trying too hard, keeping the content breezy. The professional sparing a moment from a vitally important task, always upbeat and cheerful despite the grim nature of the threat that loomed. Then, before the conversation could flag, he'd break it off, apologizing with a smile, needing to get back to work. Leave her wanting more.

Every once in a while he'd catch Nora looking at him, or watching him talking to MaryAnn. Each time she'd immediately shift her attention to something else, her face impassive.

During his last encounter with MaryAnn she asked him, "Do you ever get scared?"

He took the time to look off into the distance as if he were remembering old battles, and heaved a deep sigh. "Everyone gets scared," he said, his gaze still fixed on the horizon. "It's what you do with it that matters." Then he turned back to her and gave her the apologetic smile. "I should . . ."

"Get back to work," she said.

He smiled and nodded, then turned to go.

"Cole . . . ," she said, after he'd taken several steps. He turned back to her. She smiled. "Nothing. Sorry."

He smiled again and gave her a little salute with two fingers. It was so working.

Two hours later and he had completely forgotten about MaryAnn, Nora, the village, Runk, and the entire situation.

It was the afternoon. Cole was picking bits of soil out of his hair, the remnants of a clod of dirt he'd taken direct to the face courtesy of an exasperated Nora. He'd later retaliated with a playful nudge that sent her into one of the deeper and more muck-filled pits.

As he was prying loose a stubborn pebble from his left ear he spotted Mayor Kimber walking toward him with a clipboard, chatting with Geldar. Watching the sembluk, Cole once again had the fleeting sensation that there was a tantalizing piece of information dancing just beyond the borders of his consciousness.

"Afternoon, Sheriff," said the mayor when they were near. "Things seem to be progressing nicely."

"Quite nicely," agreed Cole. "Careful with that!" he called out to no one in particular.

"Oh, by the way, Sheriff, have you had a chance to meet Geldar?"

"Can't say I have. Nice to meet you," said Cole.

"Pleasure's all mine, Sheriff Cole," said Geldar, and Cole wondered if he had imagined the slightly amused emphasis—*Sheriff* Cole. And as he pondered that, the information danced its way across the border.

It couldn't be.

Impossible.

"Well, we don't want to distract you," said Mayor Kimber without irony, and the two continued on their way, Geldar giving Cole a little salute.

Cole watched them walk off.

Geldar the sembluk. *If* that was his name, and that's what he was. Probably. Almost certainly. Then again, thought Cole, maybe he and

Bacchi weren't the only criminals hiding out in the village of
Yrnameer. And if so, there might be something else, something so
valuable . . .

Impossible.

"Three aces," said Bacchi.

It was evening. Cole had called an early halt to the construction
efforts and sent the exhausted townspeople home. He and Bacchi
were once again on the porch, playing cards, Cole distracted.

"Three aces, Cole," repeated Bacchi.

"What? Oh, right."

"You know, you could at least put up a struggle and make it interesting," said Bacchi, dealing another hand. "You're not even paying
attention."

Cole grunted and buried his face in his cards, but what he was
seeing was Geldar. He'd watched him surreptitiously for the remainder of the day, staring at him, hoping for some insight. Why hadn't
he thought of it before? Because it was absurd, that's why. Could
it be him? No, of course not. And even if it was, that didn't mean
that he actually had the thing. Ridiculous. A sembluk. Geldar the
sembluk.

"Sembluk," said Bacchi.

Cole looked up, startled. "What?"

"I said, there's that sembluk."

Cole followed his gaze. Geldar was ambling down Main Street,
carrying a few cloth shopping bags in his hands.

"You ever see a sembluk before?" asked Bacchi.

"Not before coming here, no."

"Remember that guy, Stirling Zumi, the one who told everyone
that he'd trademarked the trademark symbol?"

Crap. Of *course* Bacchi would be wondering the same thing.
Keeping his voice neutral, Cole said, "Sure. Said he collected a roy-
alty each time something said 'TM,' had everyone investing in that
gigantic pyramid scheme. Are we playing, or what?"

"Biggest one ever, they say," said Bacchi, shaking his head in
admiration. "Suckers bought in, thought they'd be making a slice of
his profit. Except, of course, there is no profit. He makes billions,
everyone else gets screwed."

"Whatever. Two cards."

Cole didn't tell Bacchi that he'd met Stirling before. He'd worked for him briefly, helping Stirling launder his ill-gotten gains by shifting some merchandise from Point A to Point B, the two planets Cole hated the most. Cole remembered him as a fat, loudmouthed guy with greasy, slicked-back hair, a human who liked to drink and take stupid risks and brag about it.

"Billions, they say," repeated Bacchi.

"What's your point?" said Cole.

He also didn't tell Bacchi that he already knew what his point was.

"My point is, they say he went kind of crazy. Got all spiritual, gave it all up. Gave away most of his money, ran away. And you know what they say he did, so that no one would ever be able to find him?"

Turn himself into a sembluk, thought Cole.

"Turn himself into a sembluk," said Bacchi, with a triumphant little smile.

"You believe that nonsense?" said Cole.

"It's true!" said Bacchi. "I hear humans can do that! Won't make you into a cannibal or anything!"

"Hmm," said Cole, doubtfully. "I'll raise you."

"And here's the other thing," said Bacchi, dropping his voice.

Cole already knew about the other thing. The diamond.

"A *diamond*. They say he didn't *really* give it all away—he kept enough to buy a neutron star diamond."

A neutron star diamond, the ultimate status symbol. Just a tiny microscopic speck, the remnants of the core of a neutron star after the mining companies were done with it.

"One of those things, they're worth one hundred million, easy. They say you can barely see it, but it weighs tons," said Bacchi.

"Yeah, I heard that."

"So . . . ," said Bacchi.

"So?"

"So . . . ," he repeated, gesturing with his nose toward Geldar, who was getting closer.

"Oh, c'mon," said Cole.

"Could be. This is the perfect place to hole up! Who would come looking for him here?"

"Bacchi, you know what I heard about that guy, that Stirling? That the Saden syndicate caught up to him and made him into something spreadable."

"Yeah, I heard that, too," admitted Bacchi.

"So . . . ," said Cole.

"Could still be him," said Bacchi.

"Mm-hm. Pair of sixes."

"Three of a kind."

"Crap."

"Hey," said Bacchi, trying to talk without moving his mouth as he shuffled the cards, "he's coming over here."

Cole looked up. Geldar was now ambling toward them.

"Hi, there, Sheriff," said Geldar when he got close. "Can a guy play some cards?"

Cole had been working very hard over the past several hours, devising a strategy to cultivate Geldar's trust and elicit the truth. It would be a subtle, multistep process, one requiring a surgeon's skill and patience.

Midway through the first hand, Bacchi started right in, stomping all over Cole's beautiful, sterile operating theater with crap-encrusted work boots.

"*Soooo,*" began Bacchi, utterly failing to keep his tone casual, "where you from?"

"Oh, you know, here and there," said Geldar. "Raise you two."

"How long you been here?" said Bacchi.

"Mmm . . . a little bit now."

"What did you do before you came here?" pressed Bacchi.

"Oh, this and that," said Geldar with disinterested equanimity. "Yourself?"

Bacchi shifted uncomfortably before answering. "This and that."

Cole sat back, annoyed.

"What about you, Sheriff Cole?" asked Geldar.

There it was again, that whiff of emphasis. Maybe it *was* him, daring Cole to guess.

"Illegal things, mostly," said Cole.

"Oh," said Geldar, sounding a bit taken aback. "Oh. Ha ha ha!"

"Ha ha," said Cole.

Geldar lay down his cards. "Flush."

Cole tossed his in, followed by Bacchi.

"Look at that," said Bacchi, indicating Geldar's hand. "All *diamonds.*" He looked at Geldar hopefully. Cole scratched his ear and looked away.

"Excuse me?" said Geldar.

"All of your cards . . . are *diamonds.*"

"Uh . . . yep. That's what makes it a flush, right?" said Geldar.

"Get a flush with *diamonds,* you have to be a real *star.*"

"Let me see, is it my turn to deal?" said Geldar.

No. It's not him, thought Cole. He couldn't imagine the Stirling he knew responding like that: the sincerity, the hint of honest confusion. Plus, look at him: the shell, the sluggy skin, the three eyes . . . who would do that to themselves?

They kept playing, Bacchi not letting it go. When Geldar won three hands in a row, Bacchi said, "Wow. You just keep winning. It's like your . . . *trademark.*"

"I think I just got lucky a few times."

"Maybe you'll get another flush with *diamonds.*"

"I suppose that's possible, but not very probable."

"Hey, look—I'm stacking my coins in a *pyramid.*"

"Yes, I see that."

Geldar's voice had acquired the cautious, patronizing tone reserved for the cognitively or emotionally challenged. More than once he glanced at Cole as if seeking some enlightenment regarding Bacchi's behavior, or at least moral support. Cole shrugged apologetically.

"These coins, they're so silvery," said Bacchi. "Like *sterling.*"

"I think maybe one more hand and I should call it a day," said Geldar politely. It wasn't him. Cole knew it without a doubt.

Then Geldar lost the next hand, and said, "Oh, paxeration."

Cole had no idea what the term meant. All he knew was that he'd only heard it once before, when Stirling Zumi had slopped some wine on his white silk shirt.

Holy farg. It *was* him.

After Geldar left, Bacchi said, "You may not have noticed, but I was doing a little interrogation thing there."

"Really."

"Yep. It wasn't him. There's no way."

"I'll take your word for it."

Cole walked slowly back toward the ship that night, his head whirling. So Geldar was Stirling. And if something that improbable was true, why not the other rumor as well? The sheer thought of it was staggering—something so precious, right here in the middle of nowhere.

His heart was thumping with excitement. He had to find some way to divine if Stirling actually had the diamond, and if so, how to go from ascertaining that fact to attaining the item.

Yes, he'd still be in a village that was about to be flattened, on a planet he couldn't escape. But somehow he knew—he just *knew*—that if he could get his hands on that diamond, everything would somehow work out, that Runk and this absurd situation and all the petty obstacles before him would just fall away, and there would be a new Cole: a Cole who didn't have to scrabble after crumbs, a Cole who had everything and wanted nothing. A wealthy, happy Cole. A Cole with MaryAnn by his side.

But he was getting ahead of himself. That shimmering future would never materialize unless Cole could confirm that Stirling indeed had the diamond. But how to do that without raising suspicion? How would he ever be able to—and then he stopped dead in his tracks.

"Yes," whispered Cole.

Yes. That's how. It might take some time, and the results might be negative, but it would work. Yes.

He started walking again, jaunty now, grinning, almost laughing. "Yes," he said again, and pumped his fist. As he passed the diner, he glimpsed his ebullient reflection in the large picture window and nodded to himself, the smiling Cole with a potentially glorious future.

And then he stopped dead again, the smile vanishing along with that glorious future, or any future at all.

Through the window he could see MaryAnn sitting at the counter, a half-finished meal in front of her.

That was not what made him stop. It was her companion. Sitting next to her—or, more accurately, covering the five stools next to her—daintily sipping tea, was Kenneth.

33

Just as the adrenaline was hitting his system, prepping him for a desperate sprint to safety, Cole felt a gentle yet firm squeeze around his ankle. He looked down to find a tentacle looped around his lower leg. He followed the tentacle with his eyes to the diner door, about two meters away, where it flattened and somehow passed under the narrow crevice between the door and the scuffed, coin-shaped white tiles of the entranceway. Cole couldn't track its path beyond that, but he had little doubt that its final destination was Kenneth.

He felt a tap on his calf. He looked down again. The tip of the tentacle was poking him like an impatient finger. Then it pointed to the interior of the diner, the import of the gesture unmistakable.

Cole looked back up. Kenneth's eyeballs seemed firmly focused on MaryAnn, not a single one turned in Cole's direction.

The tentacle prodded him again, and then repeated the pointing gesture, this time more insistently.

"Cole!" said Kenneth when he walked in. "What a wonderful surprise! We were just talking about you!"

"Hi, Kenneth," said Cole. "Really good to see you." He nodded at MaryAnn. "MaryAnn." She returned the nod, but only after a short pause, as if she were considering her options.

"Please, come sit with us," said Kenneth. A tentacle patted the stool to MaryAnn's right.

"How could I say no," said Cole.

"You really couldn't," said Kenneth, his tone jolly.

Cole sat. MaryAnn's gaze followed him, her expression guarded. Cole suspected he knew why.

"I was just telling your friend MaryAnn all sorts of stories about you," said Kenneth.

Yep, that was why.

"Great," said Cole. "You know, Kenneth's always been a kidder. Right, Kenneth?"

"Oh, you know me. I love a good joke."

"Cole's a bit of a kidder himself," said MaryAnn. "Right, Cole?"

"Gosh it's good to see you, Kenneth," said Cole, his mouth locked into a rigid approximation of a grin.

"And you too, Cole!"

"You know, I think I should be going," said MaryAnn, putting some money on the counter. "No, don't get up," she said to Cole as she stood.

"MaryAnn . . ."

She smiled at him, but it was the sort of smile that was a few notches worse than dashing her coffee in his face. "Kenneth, it was very nice to meet you. Very . . . enlightening. I'm sure we'll get a chance to talk again?"

"Oh, very definitely," said Kenneth. "A real honor to meet you, too."

"Thanks. Well, good night, then," she said, and left.

Kenneth watched her go with most of his eyeballs. A few remained focused on Cole, who sat quietly, staring straight ahead. The hiccup-named owner was not in evidence. From somewhere in the back Cole could hear dishes being washed.

When the door had closed and MaryAnn was out of sight, Kenneth said, "Oh dear. I hope I haven't said anything untoward. I got the distinct sense that my descriptions of your exploits didn't quite match her image of you."

"How'd you find me?" said Cole.

"IPR, Cole. Been a listener for years."

Something rectangular and blurry blocked Cole's view. He pulled his head back slightly and his eyes refocused. It was Kenneth's Intergalactic Public Radio membership card.

"Fantastic," muttered Cole.

"Imagine my excitement at finally meeting the host of one of my favorite programs!" said Kenneth, putting the card away somewhere squishy. "You know, forgive me for prying, but I sensed a certain something between you two, something that—"

Cole pounded the counter. "Kenneth," he said between gritted teeth, surprised at his own anger and intensity, "how is it that you're even farging *alive*?"

"I beg your pardon?"

"That satellite went *down*."

"Oh, yes. I got out."

"They were all over you! Hundreds of them!"

"I'm really quite strong."

"They had guns!"

"Well, I don't mean to sound boastful, but I'm rather skillful with firearms myself. I can hit a target with far greater accuracy and consistency than any human. For example, you could be dancing a jig several hundred meters away and I could shoot you in the nostril. Actually—and again, I simply offer this by way of explanation—I could simultaneously track and hit seventeen targets like that. Now, let me ask *you* something."

Cole had his elbows on the table, his face resting in his hands. Without moving he said, "What."

"Back in the alley on InVestCo Three you described a woman with whom you were deeply in love. You said that her name was Samantha. At that point I felt that your sentiments were genuine, but detected a minor discordance that I wasn't able to elucidate. I put to you that it was not Samantha with whom you were in love, but in fact, *MaryAnn* who is and always has been the true object of your affection. You must tell me: is my intuition correct?"

Into his hands Cole said, "Yes."

"Incredible! Fantastic! I knew it! And to think that chance should bring you here, reuniting you with—wait, was it chance?"

"Yes."

"Mind-boggling! That chance should bring you here, reuniting you with the one woman you truly love! Ah, the romance of it all!"

"Kenneth," said Cole, still in the same position, "shut the farg up and lay your farging eggs in my brain already."

"How is the relationship progressing?"

Cole didn't answer.

"I gather that you haven't, as they say, sealed the deal yet. That the potential is there for a true, durable relationship, but—"

Cole dropped his hands down on the counter with a thump and

turned to look at Kenneth. "Kenneth. Here I am. You got me. I've got nowhere to run. Just end it."

"What? And deprive myself of the opportunity to see how this relationship develops?"

Cole said nothing for several moments. He was sensing the smallest glimmer of hope.

"So . . . you're going to let me off the hook?"

"I didn't say that. I said I'm highly interested in seeing if you're able to establish the foundation for a successful, long-lasting partnership with MaryAnn—who is, I might add, a worthy object of desire. Far more so than you, to be quite frank."

"And then you'll kill me," said Cole, imagining a slight hissing sound as his glimmer of hope was extinguished.

"I think we should stay focused on the matter at hand," said Kenneth.

"Kenneth, do you understand what's happening here?"

"You refer, I assume, to the matter with Runk?"

"Yes," said Cole, "I refer to the matter with Runk."

"He's a terrible, loathsome being. I suspect he'll slaughter everyone."

"Kenneth, I don't care if you kill me."

"Really?"

"No! Of course I care. But whatever you do to me, you could still help these people! You have a ship, right? It has cannons?"

"Of course."

"You could wipe out Runk and all his men!"

"Without a doubt. To be honest, I probably wouldn't even need my ship. I refer, of course, to my skill with firearms and—"

"So help them! Protect them!"

"Hmm. I never really considered that. Not sure I see the rationale behind that."

"Don't see the *rationale*? You were just talking about how wonderful and talented MaryAnn is, and how you'd just clap your little tentacles together with joy if we became an item! The beings in this community are good, decent people, Kenneth! Doesn't that mean anything to you?"

"Cole, you're familiar with the term *alien sensibility*? That term is applicable to me. I'm perfectly capable of drawing a vicarious romantic thrill from the thought of you finally winning MaryAnn's

heart—it *would* be truly thrilling—and also of leaving this community to its fate."

"She, and everyone here, could be killed."

"Again, it only makes the romance that much more poignant."

"Then at least let me live until after Runk makes his move."

"I'll consider it. But I need to see some real effort. No stalling."

"Effort?"

"Wooing. Romancing. Attempts to win the affections of your
beloved."

"Kenneth, it just doesn't *work* like that."

"Hmmm. Did I mention that my egg supply has continued to
increase since our encounter on InVestCo Three? It's actually getting
rather uncomfortable."

"Right. Wooing, romancing . . ."

"General attempts to capture her heart. Yes."

"Fine. Consider it done. And if I'm successful, you'll let me
live?"

"Well, there is, of course, the matter of the money."

Cole closed his eyes, pinching the bridge of his nose.

"Kenneth . . . ," he said. He hesitated for a moment, just long
enough to bid a final farewell to his imagined future. He took a deep
breath. "I . . . ," he said haltingly, the words hard to wring out of
himself, "can . . . pay you off."

Kenneth chuckled—a rich, layered sound.

"Cole, at this point that's immaterial. And considering the late-
ness of your payment and the attendant interest charges, I find your
assertion dubious at best."

"How much do I owe?"

Kenneth told him the number. The decimal point had inched
over several places since Cole had incurred the original debt. Cole
didn't blink.

"If I pay it, you'll let me live?"

"Hmm," said Kenneth, drumming the countertop with a tentacle.
"That would be quite irregular. Unprecedented, really. As you
know, you were already given a last chance, and Karg is very strict
about these matters."

"Kenneth, do you really do all this for Karg?"

"No, of course not."

Cole stood. "You'll get your money," he said.

"And . . . ?"

"And efforts will be made."

"Fine. I'll give you until the periquartenate realignment of Epios Two and Orvon Seven."

Cole waited.

"That's five days from today, about 4:53 in the morning."

34

It took Cole close to an hour to find Peter the next morning. There had been another near tragedy when the robot had mistaken one of the village's odder life forms for a sandbag and tried to add him to a wall, and Nora suggested that perhaps Peter could go dig some defensive ditches. Where? asked Peter. Wherever you see fit, suggested Nora, as long as it was far away from anyone else.

Cole tracked him down about a kilometer outside of the village in the midst of what had once been a meadow. It now had the appearance of an artillery range, pockmarked with deep craters ringed with irregular mounds of torn-up soil.

Cole wove his way amid the holes, smelling the fresh earth, heading toward a depression at the far side of the field. From it he could see big shovelfuls of dirt issuing forth in rhythmic pulses.

"Hi, Peter," he said when he got to the edge, sidestepping another load of soil that was tossed up from the bottom of the hole. The piles of dirt were interlaced with shredded grass and flowers.

"Oh hi, Cole!" said Peter, about three meters below Cole.

"Wow," said Cole. "Really been doing some digging, huh."

"Yes sir, Sheriff!" said Peter. "Just trying to do my part."

"Yes. Well," said Cole, surveying the moonscape around him, "The bandits will never cross this patch of land, that's for sure." Not unless they took a several-kilometer detour, he continued silently.

"No, sir," said Peter. "Phew!" he added, and then wiped what Cole assumed was supposed to be his brow.

"Sweaty work, huh?"

"Yes sir, Sheriff."

Somewhere nearby a bird chirped. Cole watched some sort of insect crawl over his boot, no doubt wondering what just happened to its cozy underground home.

"Peter, are you by any chance equipped with a gravitometer?"

"Oh yes, sir. I can measure gravitational anomalies accurate to one part in forty million."

I highly doubt that, Cole thought, but continued, "Great. I have a new assignment for you."

It was, he explained as Peter climbed out of the hole, top secret. He needed a full, detailed gravitational survey of the village, highlighting any areas that seemed unusually dense.

"Can you do that for me?"

"Absolutely, Sheriff!" said Peter.

"No need to whisper, Peter."

"Gotcha!"

Off he scurried.

When Cole got back to the village, Kenneth was cheerfully pitching in with the construction of the fence, easily lifting bundles of logs as if they were twigs, chatting breezily with the townspeople as they worked. For their part, the townspeople seemed content to welcome his assistance, no one asking questions about his unannounced and unexpected arrival. Kenneth, spotting Cole, raised a tentacle in greeting. Cole stared back, blank-faced.

"Mighty fine fellow, that Kenneth," commented Mayor Kimber, coming up behind Cole. "Mighty fine. He *is* a fellow, correct?"

"I'm not sure," said Cole. He spat in the dirt. "Wouldn't be too certain about the mighty fine, part, either," he added, walking off.

Cole didn't begrudge the warm reception the townspeople offered to Kenneth—he didn't expect anything less from them. What surprised him was Nora's attitude. He saw the two of them talking animatedly, Nora laughing and patting him on the tentacle, and Cole pulled her aside as soon as he got a chance.

"You realize he tried to kill us all before—several times."

"Oh, c'mon, Cole, he explained everything. It was all a big misunderstanding."

"It was not a misunderstanding, he was trying to—"

"Well, it was all your fault, really. And you never told me how he saved everyone on the satellite, and you just abandoned him there!"

Cole clapped a hand over his eyes.

"Really, Cole, that just seems heartless."

"Arrgh," choked Cole.

"And look at him, he's being so helpful!"

About fifty meters away Kenneth was planting fence posts, holding four of the stout logs in his tentacles.

"I hope he doesn't strain himself," she said.

"Nora, if he was being helpful, he'd go wipe out the bandits!"

"Cole!" said Nora, shocked. "You know about his religious beliefs!"

Cole made more helpless choking noises.

"Hello, Nora! Hello, Cole!" called Kenneth merrily. He waved with one of the logs.

"And you know how I know he's a good person, or good whatever he is?"

Cole had both hands over his eyes now. "Because he has such a nice voice."

"*Such* a nice voice. A bad guy could never have a voice like that."

MaryAnn did her best to avoid Cole the entire day. When they did cross paths she ignored him. A little after noon everyone retreated to the shade for a lunch break, settling along the half-built wall or under the scattered trees that stood near the village entrance. Cole sought her out, finding her sitting alone just inside the main gate, moodily chewing on a sandwich.

"Hi," he said, taking a seat next to her. "I just wanted to—"

That was as far as he got before she stood up and marched off.

"Ho ho ho. You'll have to do better than that, Cole."

Cole twisted around, looking for Kenneth, and finally looked straight up to see an eye peering down at him, dangling from an eyestalk that arched up and over the wall.

"This is your fault," said Cole.

"Oh, tsk. The path of true love, and et cetera et cetera. Onward, young man, onward!"

And so things finally began to acquire the montagelike nature that Cole had desired. But it was instead a nightmarish montage, a string of failed advances and spurned overtures.

MaryAnn continued to refuse to speak with him during the day, stomping off as soon as he got close. Cole didn't press it, fearing a scene in front of the townspeople.

He penned her a humble, apologetic card, agonizing over every word, writing and rewriting it several times before slipping it under her door in the evening. He made the mistake of lingering, allowing him to overhear the violent and extended shredding noises that immediately followed the delivery. Then the door opened just enough for MaryAnn's hand to emerge and toss the pieces in the air. They snowed gently down upon him like cherry blossom petals.

As he was walking away, picking small scraps of paper out of his hair, Kenneth's voice came floating to him.

"A worthy effort! Next!"

The following evening he arrived at her door bearing a carefully selected assortment of chocolates. This got her to open the door a bit wider, if only to tear the box from his hands and fling it into the street, bonbons scattering everywhere.

"Mmm," said Kenneth from somewhere behind him as Cole once again retreated from her door in defeat. "Espresso! Ooo, and nougat! Let's see, what's this? What, no caramel?" Cole kept walking, not looking back. "Hmm. Melon. Not sure I like that."

As Cole reached the end of the street and turned the corner, Kenneth called after him. "Clock is running, Cole!"

The third night a brief ray of light shone down upon the otherwise hopeless, wretched landscape of his existence. He had spent the day in the field, picking wildflowers, trying his best to approximate the bouquet that Daras Katim had given him. It was no match, but even Cole knew it was good. This time MaryAnn opened the door nearly halfway, and regarded the flowers in silence. Then, wordlessly, she took them from him, not ungently, and closed the door without slamming it.

Progress.

He cleared his throat. "MaryAnn?" he ventured cautiously after about a minute. "Hello?"

He was answered by a faint snipping sound, repeated about a dozen times.

The door reopened. She thrust a handful of stems at him and slammed the door.

"Oh, come *on*," he protested, "that doesn't even make *sense*!"

"Ticktock, ticktock."

"Yes, thank you, Kenneth."

The rejection was bad. Having Kenneth silently materialize with each humiliating defeat and chide him for his unsuccessful efforts was worse. What made it sheer torture was Nora.

Each night he'd find her standing in her doorway, waiting for the evening's entertainment to begin. By the third day she had set up a chair and had a bowl of popcorn in her lap.

"Doing great, Cole," she said, her mouth full. "She's gonna cave any moment now."

He flung down the flower stems petulantly and marched across the narrow street to her. "Do you realize that Kenneth is going to kill me if I don't get some sort of response from her? Do you realize that?"

"Oh, c'mon, Cole, be reasonable. I think it's touching how much he cares about you, and God only knows why. Popcorn?"

On the fourth day he checked in with Peter about his gravitational survey.

"How's it going?"

"Fantastic. I've already finished sections one through forty-three," Peter said.

"Oh, great! That sounds great! Er, how many sections are there?"

"Only seven hundred and twenty," said Peter.

Cole did some quick calculations, the result of which equaled him being dead.

"Can you pick it up a bit?"

"Well, I need to be thorough," said Peter, with the air of a professional whose turf was being invaded.

"I agree completely," said Cole. "But can I have you focus on a specific spot for now?"

That evening he stood outside of MaryAnn's door again, ignoring Nora's snickers, aware that Kenneth was watching critically from somewhere, and recited the poem that he had written for her. Well, that he had commissioned for her. Fred had done more of the actual writing.

It was a very good poem. It moved him even as he rendered it into speech, half convincing himself that he was the author. Nora stopped sniggering and fell silent, listening.

When he finished MaryAnn opened the door and looked at him for a long moment, the significance of her sober expression unclear. Then she closed the door softly.

"That was really, really nice," said Nora.

"Thank you," said Cole.

"There's no way in hell you wrote it."

The next morning Cole watched from afar as MaryAnn walked hand in hand with Fred, engaged in what looked to be a heartfelt conversation.

"This doesn't look good, Cole," said Kenneth, slipping a tentacle around his shoulders. "Perhaps your gambit has backfired. You know what they say about the Qx"-x-'--'," he continued, getting the pronunciation perfect.

"No," said Cole.

"Nor I. But I would hazard to guess that this youngster is making a play for your filly. The successful completion of which, I hardly need to add, would constitute an immediate and complete failure on your part."

Cole took Fred aside and established in no uncertain terms exactly where his territorial boundaries stood. Fred, insulted, responded with a short but detailed account of the gender breakdown within his species. MaryAnn, he explained indignantly, had no place whatsoever within the complex, seven-member structure of Qx"-x-'--' romantic life, so Cole could stop worrying and go x-'x it.

That evening Cole went to MaryAnn's cottage empty-handed. It was raining. He was out of ideas, out of gestures, out of hope. He had one final, desperate tactic.

When he arrived at her door he took a moment to arrange his features into what he hoped was an approximation of abject humility and internally rehearsed his speech: MaryAnn, I'm going to be completely and brutally honest with you. You see—and then she opened the door before he could knock.

"Cole," she said, "I need to be completely and brutally honest with you. I can't have you coming here every night. I don't wish to speak with you, I don't want to interact with you, and frankly, I don't even want to look at you. My only hope is that you have at least enough integrity that you're actually going to help these people, and not abandon them in their time of need. Good-bye, Cole."

And she shut the door.

Even Nora didn't say anything to him as he shuffled away defeated. And somewhere, he knew, Kenneth was watching.

35

The rain was pooling on the streets and running along the gutters as he trudged back to the jailhouse. When he went inside, Peter was waiting for him just as they had arranged.

"Please tell me that you have good news," said Cole.

"Oh. I'm not sure that I can," said Peter. "For example, there's something I can't explain. I've discovered a gravitational anomaly right in the middle of the village at the address you gave me. It's very odd: there's something very dense inside there that—why are you kissing me? Will we have sex now?"

Cole said to him, "What if I asked you to write a program for yourself that also included instructions to erase the memory of the program once you've executed it?"

"You mean, like a game?" asked Peter.

"Yes, a game."

"Sure!"

"Okay, let's try something," said Cole. "I want you to take two steps to the left."

Peter took two steps to the left.

"And now?"

"I want you to erase the memory that I asked you to do that."

"Do what?" said Peter. "Why are you dancing around and giggling? Is it time to dance around and giggle now?"

When Cole entered his darkened room on the Benedict, he said, "Hello, Kenneth."

There was a rich chuckle from the corner of the room.

"My, my! How is it you knew I'd be here?" said Kenneth.

Cole smiled to himself. Since leaving MaryAnn's house, he'd been saying "Hello, Kenneth" each time he turned a corner or entered a new space, figuring that eventually he'd be right. Having won the advantage, he pressed on.

"Let me guess, Kenneth: you're here to gloat." He peeled off his wet jacket and sat on his bed to take off his boots, his back to where he thought Kenneth was. "You've come to tell me that I've failed in my attempts to win MaryAnn's heart," he continued, grunting as he got one boot off, "and that tomorrow morning you'll be punching a hole through my skull and so on. But guess what: there's—"

"No, I was thinking of doing it now."

Cole twisted in his seat. "Now hold on! That's not what we agreed! The time limit isn't up yet!"

"Cole, I don't see how granting you any more time would help the matter."

Cole stood and turned to address the darkened corner, the boot still in his hand. "That's cheating, Kenneth. It's not fair!" He hurled the boot to the floor.

"Cole, she has soundly rejected you. To be honest, I think her decision was entirely—"

"Yes, thank you, I know. I'm not good enough for her and I'm a miserable worm, and she made—"

"No, I thought she was being too hasty."

"Really? That's very nice of you."

"She's a wonderful woman, and she'd be stooping low indeed if she were to decide to associate with you . . ."

"I think you've made that point already."

". . . but I believe your feelings for her are genuine."

Two tentacles and an eyestalk extended forward into the light. One tentacle was holding a monocle in front of the eyeball, which was focusing on the object in the other tentacle.

" 'Dear MaryAnn, I don't even deserve to have you read this letter . . . ,' " Kenneth read.

Cole sat heavily back down on his bed and rubbed his forehead. "I don't believe this."

" 'I'm every bad thing you think I am, and probably worse . . .' I think you might be overplaying the humility angle."

Cole flopped backward and stared at the ceiling. "You picked up all those pieces and taped my card back together?"

" '. . . but you once said something wonderful to me, many years ago—"

"Okay, yes, I wrote it, I don't need to hear it again."

" 'Something that I treasure to this day. . . . ' "

"Kenneth, I can get you the money."

"It's a very nice missive, Cole. She really should have given you another chance. But seeing as she didn't—"

"I can get you the money."

"Oh, come now, Cole. Both of us know that's an impossibility."

Cole sat up. "You gave me a time limit and said that if I won MaryAnn over or delivered the money—or something of equivalent value—you'd let me be."

"I was humoring you."

"Humor me some more. Give me until the time limit. I won't disappoint you."

There was a silence.

"If you try to run again, Cole, you should know that I'll be just as happy to deposit my brood in her skull."

"But you like her! You said yourself you think she's wonderful!"

"Alien sensibility, Cole. You have until the deadline. I'm curious to see what you'll come up with." With barely a sound, Kenneth glided out of the room, pausing in the doorway. "Oh, and Cole: there's no need to keep saying 'Hello, Kenneth' each time you enter a new room."

Slightly after midnight Cole rang the alarm bell.

The citizens of Yrnameer came tumbling out into the streets, groggy, disoriented, some half-dressed.

"Everyone assemble!" shouted Cole, standing on the porch of the jailhouse as they milled about. "Hurry up! Let's go! Vern, where's your weapon? Glorf, you're going into battle like that?"

They were a sorry sight, panicked, confused, stumbling about, desperate to know what was going on.

"Fall in! Count off! Let's go! Go go go!"

"Cole, what is this?" demanded Nora, shouting to be heard over the clamor. "Are the bandits coming?"

"This is a drill."

"Now? In the middle of the night?"

"You want to complain, or you want to help?"

She grimaced, but then went about her duties, herding and corralling bewildered townsfolk into their ranks. "Sheriff," said Mayor Kimber, still in his pajamas, "is this really necessary?"

"Is it necessary?" said Cole. "Is it *necessary*?" You're damn right it's necessary, he thought, it's life or death.

"Sorry. Right. Eh . . . ." Mayor Kimber looked about, muddled, then wandered into the commotion, waving his arms ineffectually. Cole saw Joshua, alert as always, darting about and helping to organize. Orwa was trying to calm people. There was MaryAnn, ignoring Cole, whispering into her microphone.

And there was Geldar.

It took them nearly twenty minutes to fully assemble and count off. When they did, Cole harangued them for another twenty for their sluggish, chaotic response, while they shuffled their feet guiltily and tried to hide their yawns.

Then, finally, he saw Peter arrive at the back of the ranks.

"All right," said Cole, "I've had enough of this. Go home. Dismissed!"

Grumbling and muttering, they dispersed.

Nora approached, hands on hips. Cole didn't wait for her.

Cole paced in circles outside the Benedict, gnawing on his nails until Peter arrived. When Cole saw him he jogged to meet him halfway.

"Did you find it?" Cole.

"I found it!"

Cole clapped his hands together.

"Great! Where is it? Show it to me!"

"Show what?"

"The diamond! Where is it?"

"Diamond . . . diamond . . . oh, right. What did I do with it?"

"What do you mean what did you do with it?!"

"Let's see. . . . . I went into Geldar's house during the drill and used the gravitometer to locate it . . . then I picked it up, and then . . . what did I do with it then?"

"Oh, no. Oh, no no no. Peter, how come you can't remember what happened?"

"I got a head start on erasing my memory registers, like you said."

"So you half forgot what happened?!"

"Well, I've been sort of savoring the memories before I discard them. It was all so exciting—like a big caper! What's wrong? Why are you doing that? Does your head hurt?"

A few minutes later they were outside of Geldar's prefab mansion. The lights were off, the streets quiet.

"Well?" whispered Cole.

"I'm not sure," responded Peter in the same whisper. "The gravitometer doesn't seem to show the same reading as before. But it could be still in there."

"Yes or no?"

"Could be.

Cole checked his watch. Four hours.

"Could be?"

"Could be."

The citizens had apparently taken Cole's lecture to heart and reacted much faster the second time he rang the alarm bell. It took them less than half the time to organize themselves into lines and rows that, if not exactly neat, at least qualified as lines and rows. It filled Cole with a certain sense of pride—as well as a certain sense of panic when he realized how much more time he had to stall them for.

"All right," he announced, "I think it's time we learned a few marching songs."

Halfway through the third rendition of "Proudly into Shrapnel," Peter reappeared.

"Good! We're done! Go home and get some rest!"

"It's not in there?"

"I don't think so."

Cole checked his watch. Two hours.

"Does your head still hurt?" asked Peter.

"Peter, you have to think. Where did you put the diamond?"

"The diamond. The diamond. Think. Thinking. Ah!"

"What?"

"I know why I can't remember—I erased that memory! Or did I tell you that already?"

"Peter, we have to find that thing, and we only have a few hours to do it."

"Right! We should split up!"

"Peter, I don't have a gravitometer."

"No, but both of me does!"

There were a few soft clicking noises, and suddenly the complex, shrimplike part of Peter separated from the simple, blocky Peter.

"Wait a second—didn't you tell me half your brain is in each robot?" said Cole, alarmed.

"Did I say that?" said the shrimp. Then a moth flew by. "Oo, pretty!" said little Peter, and he was off, scurrying erratically into the night in pursuit of the insect.

"Peter!" hissed Cole. "Peter, come back!! Dammit!"

Cole turned to big Peter, who actually contained only twenty-seven percent of Peter's already nondevastating intellect.

"Duh . . . durrrh . . . duhuh . . . ," said big Peter.

"Oh, no," said Cole.

Cole ran alongside big Peter, saying, "What about here? Measure here!"

"Uh . . . I dunno . . . ," big Peter would say. The other thing he kept saying was "MaryAnn . . . MaryAnn . . ."

Finally Cole said, "Are you saying you put the diamond in MaryAnn's house?"

"MaryAnn," said big Peter.

Another check of the watch.

This time Cole didn't stick around, leaping off the porch of the jail-house and skedaddling the instant he rang the alarm bell. Tomorrow, if he were still alive, he'd tell the mayor that it must have been a practical joke—blame it on that youngster Joshua, for example, full of high spirits and lacking judgment.

It was 3:57 in the morning, less than an hour before his rendezvous with Kenneth. Cole made a wide berth to avoid Main Street, where the citizens were already gathering, big Peter clomping behind him. They got to MaryAnn's cottage in about seven minutes.

The door was open, the lights off.

Cole went in, followed by big Peter, who could barely fit through the door frame. The front door opened into a small living room, the kitchen through another door in the rear. There was a stairway to the right, going up to the bedroom, Cole figured. Cole held a small flashlight in his mouth as he searched the living room, gingerly at first and then with increasing determination. Nothing.

"MaryAnn," big Peter said. "MaryAnn."

"Yes, I know," said Cole.

She had a small writing desk against the wall to the left. He opened and shut all the drawers, knowing as he did so that it wouldn't be in there, because a neutron star diamond would tear a hole through the wood. He jerked open the last drawer. It was stuffed with what looked like personal correspondence. He shut it.

And opened it again. The first letter on top was in a masculine hand, starting, "Dear MaryAnn. I miss you a great deal. . . ."

"MaryAnn . . .," said Peter.

Cole scanned down the text until he reached "Love always," but whatever name was written below that was beyond the crease where the paper was folded back on itself.

"MaryAnn . . . ," said Peter again.

"Yeah, yeah, MaryAnn, MaryAnn," said Cole, reaching to flip the letter over.

"What are you doing in here!" demanded MaryAnn from the doorway. Cole jumped, sending letters flying.

"I'm not reading them!" he shouted, as sensitive personal information gently settled around the room.

"Get out of here!"

"MaryAnn—" said Cole.

"MaryAnn," echoed big Peter.

"Get out!"

"Let me explain! I'm not here to go through your drawers—I mean, I'm not here to read your letters, I'm here to steal . . ."

He paused. They stared at each other. He gave up.

"Okay, I'll go," he said.

He walked back to the ship, big Peter padding after him, saying, "MaryAnn . . ." Cole didn't have the energy to tell him to shut up and go away.

He didn't bother looking at his watch. The sky was starting to brighten on the horizon. He knew what time it was, and what would be waiting for him.

He could ring the alarm bell for the fourth time, and maybe the citizens of Yrnameer would respond yet again, this time to defend their sheriff against Kenneth.

Kenneth would wipe them out.

He could run again.

Kenneth would find him.

He wondered what would happen when the bandits came. He wondered if MaryAnn would be all right. He wondered if what was about to happen would hurt.

Kenneth was waiting for him outside the ship. Little Peter was darting around at his feet like a lapdog. His voice grew in volume as Cole got closer.

"And then he flew this way, and I was like, hold on, whoa, and then he flew that way. . . ."

"Mmm-hmm . . . mmm-hmmm . . . ," Kenneth was saying in response.

"Hi, Sheriff Cole!" said little Peter when Cole was close. "I saw the coolest bug!"

Cole smiled wanly.

"I don't suppose you have the money," said Kenneth.

"No."

Kenneth sighed. "Unfortunate. I was almost rooting for you." He held a tentacle up to an eye. The tentacle had a wristwatch on it.

"Well, then . . . ," said Kenneth.

"Yep," said Cole.

"Quite a journey since our meeting in the alley."

"Sure was."

"Any preference?"

"Left eye, please."

"Fine."

"Sheriff Cole?" said Peter. Cole turned. Big Peter and little Peter were one once more.

"Yes, Peter," said Cole.

"I just remembered something," he said.

"You did?!"

"Yes. MaryAnn said I shouldn't trust you."

"Oh. That's why you kept saying . . ."

"MaryAnn. Yes. Just couldn't quite remember it."

"Okay. Thanks for telling me that."

Cole turned back to Kenneth.

"Left, was it?"

"Right," said Cole. "Or, correct. You know what I mean."

He and Kenneth shared the sort of wry chuckle that might be shared when one party was about to lay his eggs in the other's skull.

"Okay, then," Kenneth said, and drew back his ovipositor to strike.

"Sheriff Cole?" said Peter behind him.

"Yes, Peter."

"I remembered something else."

Cole heard the steamy, hissing noise of an air-locked compartment opening.

"Goodness, what would that be?" said Kenneth. Cole turned. From the middle of Peter's blocky body extended a small, drawer-like compartment that Cole hadn't noticed before. In it was what looked to be a Lucite cube, and at the very center of the cube was a tiny, brilliant point of light.

"I remembered where I put the diamond," said Peter. "Why are you kissing me again? Should we have sex?"

36

It took Kenneth two tentacles to lift the cube, which was no larger than an apple.

"It certainly has the appropriate mass," he said. Then he produced a jeweler's loupe from somewhere and examined the glimmering gem in the center. "Hmmm," he said, "standard brilliant cut, well executed . . . okay, thanks."

And then he glided away and was gone.

The next morning Geldar came to the jailhouse, fidgety and discomfited.

"Can I help you with something?" said Cole.

"Uh . . . well, yes. You see . . . I'm missing something. Something of great value."

"Huh," said Cole. "Can you describe it?"

"It's . . . well . . . you know, I'd really like to make sure this stays private. . . ."

"Of course. What's the item?"

"It's . . ." He paused, his three eyes observing Cole searchingly. "Sheriff Cole, Cole, be honest with me. Have I met you before? I feel like I might have. Before. Do I know you?"

Yes, Stirling, you farging well do, you bastard, and I know you and what you've done and I took your diamond and you deserved it.

Is what Cole thought. What he did was shake his head and say with deep sincerity, "No, I don't believe so."

"Ah," said Stirling who was Geldar. Cole waited patiently. "Perhaps I just misplaced it," said Stirling.

"I see. If you can't find it, come on back, and we can file some sort of report."

"Yes."

"Thanks for stopping by."

"Yes."

Stirling/Geldar left.

37

It was like any Terday evening, with Orwa, a white shawl draped over his various gas bladders, delivering the ecumenical sermon from the podium at the front of the town hall. But everything was different. Tonight the pews, usually sparsely populated, were over-flowing. Townspeople stood against the wall, filling every available space. The mood, if not somber, was solemn. This, everyone knew, might be the last Terday sermon, because in eight days the bandits would come.

"Yrnameer is about the dream of peace, the ideal of compassion," Orwa was saying. "But in a few short days our oppressors look to shatter that peace."

Cole, standing against the back wall, scanned the crowd. He felt a sudden and unexpected upwelling of affection for these people, his fellow citizens of Yrnameer.

"In this time of strife," continued Orwa, "we need to join together, and look to whatever god—"

"Or gods," someone suggested.

"Or gods—" said Orwa.

"Or no gods," said someone else.

"Or no gods, as the case may be—"

"The universal mother!" said a third.

"Yes, yes, of course," said Orwa. "The point is, we look to a higher power for the strength and wisdom—"

Cole sighed and slipped out the door. He stood on the porch, rocking on his heels, gazing up at the three moons.

"Beautiful evening," said Mayor Kimber.

Cole turned. The mayor had stepped outside onto the porch and was filling his pipe.

"That it is," said Cole.

Cole listened to the sound of the match being struck and Kimber drawing on the pipe. From inside the hall came the opening notes of a hymn. After a few moments, Kimber said, "Now, I've asked you this before, Cole, so forgive me for asking it again. But how do you fancy our odds?"

Cole took in a deep breath, smelling the rich aroma of the brrweed. He exhaled.

"Someone recently advised me I should give up gambling, Mayor."

Behind him he could hear the mayor take a few even pulls. He turned to look at him. The mayor returned his gaze, waiting.

"Well, Mayor, we're outnumbered and outgunned, and so far there's been twelve self-sustained injuries during training. . . ."

The mayor, puffing on his pipe, furrowed his brow.

"I'd say the odds are good, Mayor. My money's on the good folks of Yrnameer."

The mayor slapped him on the shoulder. "That's what I like to hear!"

As the mayor turned to reenter the hall, Cole remembered something. "Mayor?"

Kimber turned. "Yes?"

"Just out of curiosity, when the bandits came here before, when you helped them, how did they carry the crops they took with them?"

"Hmm," said the mayor, chewing on his pipe stem as he thought back. "I guess they had some sort of levitating transport to lift it. Something big and red. What? That surprises you? You look like you stepped on a fire migi."

"A Big Red Lifter?" asked Cole, trying to control his excitement.

"Yes, I suppose you could call it that."

"No no no. Was it that model? A Big Red Lifter?"

"Well, I'm not sure. How would I know?"

"Was it big and red, with BIG RED LIFTER, trademark, on the side?"

"Why, yes, I guess it was. Is that important? Hey, where you going?"

The next morning Bacchi was gone. He took with him a baiyo, a gun, food, and water. More tellingly, he'd also taken the coordinates that Kenneth had provided that indicated the location of Runk's encampment.

"I knew it," fumed Cole, pacing the floor of the jail. Nora, Joshua, and Mayor Kimber watched him silently. "I *knew* it! I shouldn't have trusted him!"

He angrily kicked the door of the cell shut, then had to catch it when it rebounded back in his face.

"Stupid door!" He slammed it again with the same result, then repeated the gesture a third time.

"Here, Sheriff, let me get that for you," said Joshua as Cole wound up again, gently taking the door from him and easing it shut.

"You think he'll come back?" asked the mayor.

"Come back? Come *back*?" said Cole. "Yes, he'll come back, with Runk and all his men."

"You think that's where he went?" asked the mayor.

"Where else," said Nora. "He's saving his own skin."

"He sold us out," said Cole. "He's heading to Runk right now."

"Cole," said Nora, "he knows everything. All our plans, everything."

"I. *Know*."

"So what do we do?" asked Kimber.

Cole stopped pacing and turned toward them, meeting their expectant gazes. "I—"

"You're going after him!" blurted Joshua.

Cole grimaced in frustration. "Joshua . . . ," he said, his eyes closed. God, the kid could ruin a moment. He shook his head and took a moment. "I'm going after him."

"I *knew* it!" said Joshua.

Mayor Kimber agreed that it would be best to keep it quiet for now.

"We'll keep it simple," he said.

Cole knew Joshua would want to come, and was ready for it. You have to stay, he was planning to say. While I'm gone, you'll have to be in charge. Except the kid had disappeared, gone off somewhere to sulk.

As he walked out the front gate, leading a baiyo, Cole murmured to Nora, "You're in charge."

"Of course," she said.

Cole waited until he was several hundred meters away from the village before he tried to mount the baiyo. On his fourth try he got it, lying forward on its neck and clinging tightly until it stopped spinning in agitated circles. He then rode unsteadily away toward the east.

About a kilometer outside of town he passed a copse of trees. About ten minutes after that, Joshua silently led his baiyo out of the grove and climbed effortlessly onto its back. Then he set out after Cole, taking care that his pace matched that of the sheriff.

It was a hard three days' ride, leaving Cole sunburned and exhausted and so sore that the agony of staying in the saddle was exceeded only by the agony of walking. The landscape grew increasingly harsh as he moved eastward, the green fading to green brown to brown green and then finally just to brown. He did not catch up to Bacchi.

By the evening of the third day he was past the foothills, the mountains rising before him to jagged, unfriendly peaks. Massive boulders littered the landscape, remnants of some past seismic event. The vegetation was sparse and spiky.

He had paused by one of the boulders to drink from his canteen and check his coordinates when he heard the Firestick 21 ("Scare them just by chambering a shell"). He took the appropriate action, which was to freeze.

"Looking for something?" said a voice.

There was a gun pushed against the side of his head. He wasn't sure what it was, but it was big and heavy and at this range the caliber probably didn't matter so much.

Runk's face loomed in front of his own. It was an exceptionally repellent face, pockmarked and scarred and disfigured, like something that had been gnawed on and spat out and had emerged tougher and angrier for the experience. It was an outer ugliness, Cole knew, that did not quite do justice to what lay within.

The lookout who captured him had roughly tied a blindfold over his eyes and marched him up a narrow rocky path, prodding him in the back with the Firestick 21 as Cole stumbled along, trying to spot stones and rough spots through the small space between the blind-fold and his nose. After a while the path grew steeper, then leveled out, then descended, switching back and forth several times. Cole heard voices and laughter and was aware of a commotion around him as Runk's men gathered to examine the captive. Then the blind-fold was removed and he was face-to-face with Runk himself.

"Well well well," said Runk. "Hello, Cole."

Cole fought to keep from gagging on Runk's breath.

"Hello, Runk," he wheezed.

"And good-bye, Cole," said Runk. "Shoot him."

38

Cole heard the hammer pulled back and squeezed his eyes tight, then yelped as the firing pin hit an empty chamber with a loud *click*.

Runk and his men roared with laughter, falling all over each other at the hilarity of the scene.

"*Ha ha ha ha ha!* I was just playing with you, Cole!" said Runk, slapping him several times on the cheek in a friendly manner. Cole barely felt the blows—Runk's hand was about the size of a small coin. In this it was proportionate to the rest of his body, which measured slightly more than twelve inches in height. But perched as he always was on Altung's massive, rocklike shoulder, his eyes were level with Cole's, and about three feet higher if Altung got off his knees and stood up. They were, thought Cole, the carbon-based version of Peter the 'Puter.

"Ohh, damn, it's just like old times, huh, Cole?" said Runk, still laughing.

"Yep. Boy, I sure miss those halcyon prison days . . . ," said Cole.

"So, tell me," said Runk, "what is this I hear about making a deal?"

It was later and they were sitting by a campfire. They'd offered him rotten bread and stringy dried meat and harsh liquor and some qhag to chew if he wanted it. He declined. The rest of Runk's men where sitting around their own fires, eating, cleaning weapons, discussing whatever desperate criminals discussed in the requisite coarse voices.

The camp was in a flat, sandy depression, surrounded on three sides by towering cliffs that were dotted with caves. The only way in was through a narrow pass, easily defended. The living quarters consisted of ramshackle structures set randomly throughout the camp, half building, half tent. It seemed senseless to Cole to set up in such a barren, hostile environment, but that was Runk.

Cole had looked around but hadn't spotted Bacchi. He casually asked Runk if he'd seen him.

"No," said Runk. "But I'll kill him if I do."

Earlier, the Yoin had noticed him and approached.

"Why, it's the poet!" he said.

Someone else laughed.

"He's not a poet."

The Yoin turned sharply toward the cynic.

"Have you ever heard his work?" demanded the Yoin, his hand moving toward his weapon.

"Well, I—"

"HOW do you KNOW he's NOT a POET if you HAVEN'T HEARD HIS WORK?"

"It's just that—"

The Yoin equivalent of an angry letter to the editor broke out. When it was over and the erstwhile critic was being carried away, the Yoin turned to Cole and said, "My apologies. May I have your autograph?"

"So tell me," said Runk, pausing to spit out a tiny droplet of qhag-stained saliva. "Why would I trust you?"

He was sitting on Altung's lap now. From somewhere up above, Altung expelled a large blop of qhag juice, which hit the fire with a heavy splat and sent steam hissing forth.

"Careful, idiot!" said Runk. Altung rumbled something in response. Cole was never sure if he could actually speak, or even think. He had, however, once seen him punch his fist directly through a singulite-reinforced safe door.

"As I was saying, why should I trust you?"

"Because you know me, Runk. I'm as dishonest as you are, and a complete coward. Why would I take a risk for these people?"

Runk laughed, then spat again. Altung followed suit, sending another gout of steam up from the fire.

"Idiot!" said Runk. "Still, why should I help you?"

"Because I'll be helping you."

"Why do I need your help? Those people are weak. We could ride over there now and kill everyone, barely break a nornog."

Cole wasn't sure what a nornog was, but he understood the general gist.

"You're wrong," said Cole. "You don't know what they have planned for you. They've got tricks and traps and all sorts of stuff. You'll lose a lot of people."

Runk appeared to think about it. He looked around the camp, as if calculating acceptable casualties.

"A *lot* of people," said Cole again. Runk was still thinking. "And you might not come home with the food."

This appeared to have some effect.

"Do it my way," said Cole. "You still get to have your fun—you ride in there, terrorize everyone, maybe shoot one or two if they resist, and in the end? You get the food. Or maybe they're not interested in that?" Cole jerked his head in the direction of Runk's men. "Maybe they're patient enough that it doesn't matter."

Cole watched as one of the creatures sitting close to a nearby fire took a bite out of his meal, growled, and dumped it on the flames.

"Nah, they probably wouldn't mind," said Cole.

Runk spat. Altung spat, splattering Cole's boots.

"So what do you want?" asked Runk.

"You have a Big Red Lifter. They built them with a spare Artemis coil. I need it to repair my ship and get off the planet."

"And in return?"

"You get your food and have your fun, risk free."

He told them everything. The plan, the preparations, the traps, everything, drawing diagrams so there would be no mistakes. The next morning they sent him on his way. Altung, at Runk's direction, handed him the Artemis coil, the device about the size and shape of a doughnut.

"Thank you," said Cole. "Now remember: they're expecting you in five days. I take the watch the night before the fourth day. You come in the morning, early. The gate will be open. No one will be awake. They won't have time to mount a defense. But listen," he said, and leaned in close so he could whisper to Runk, "I'm leaving. But if you break your promise and hurt anyone, I'll be back."

He leaned back. Runk was staring back at him with a flat, dead-eyed expression.

"I'm *kidding*!" said Cole. Runk's laughter was still ringing in his ears as he rode off.

Joshua saw it all.

He had followed Cole the whole way from the village, always staying just barely within sight, doubting that Cole would bother to look back and see if he was being followed. At night he shivered under a blanket, not wanting to build a fire. Every so often Cole would get too far ahead and Joshua would dismount, searching the horizon with the binoculars and scanning the ground for tracks. By the second day it occurred to him that Cole hadn't once done that himself and he wondered at it, trying to figure out how Cole was able to track Bacchi with such confidence, and why he wasn't riding faster.

A few kilometers outside of the camp he dismounted. He took the saddle off his baiyo and hid it between some boulders, along with his bag. Then he let the baiyo wander free, knowing it would come when he whistled.

He slipped into the camp when Cole was captured, using the commotion to pass unnoticed. When Cole had his conversation with Runk at the campfire, he had been hiding in the shadows of one of the tents. When Altung was handing the Artemis coil to Cole the next morning, Joshua was perched on a rock, peeking over the edge, heart pounding.

He didn't want to believe it. He couldn't.

Tears were rolling down his cheeks as he watched Cole ride off. He waited for Altung to carry Runk away, then rolled over to get up. There were three gun barrels pointing at him.

Bacchi was waiting for Runk in his tent when he returned. He was sprawled out on a pile of rugs and pillows, pouring himself some wine from a flagon. He barely looked up when Altung pulled back the tent flap and entered, depositing Runk on a specially constructed chair.

"Enjoying the wine?" asked Runk.

"You know where that cute little detour he outlined takes you?" said Bacchi, ignoring the question. "Right past the afterburners of his ship. He's not planning to fly anywhere. He wants the Artemis coil so he can fire up the engines just as you pass, and then fry all of you." He sipped the wine. "This stuff is crap."

They threw Joshua onto the dirt in the center of the camp. A ring formed around him, the men laughing and jeering at him. Someone kicked him in the ribs and he gasped, curling into a ball. Another kick landed. Someone else produced a long, curved knife.

"Enough!" he heard a voice say. "Get him to his feet."

Altung reached down with one hand and lifted Joshua to his feet by his head. Runk examined him, scowling.

"Who are you?" he said, but Joshua's gaze was unfocused, looking off to the side. "Who are you!" Runk repeated.

"Bacchi," whispered Joshua. Runk squinted in confusion, then followed Joshua's gaze to Bacchi, who was trying to conceal himself behind another of Runk's men.

"Bacchi!" said Runk. After a moment's hesitation, Bacchi stepped forward. "You know him?"

"That's Cole's deputy."

"You sold us out," said Joshua. "You sold us out!"

"Yeah, there's a lot of that going on," said Bacchi.

Joshua went to spit on him and missed, scoring a direct hit on Runk. It was quite a soaking, considering Runk's size.

"Argh!" said Runk, and viciously backhanded him, producing a tiny slapping sound and no apparent effect. "Hit him!" he screamed at Altung. Altung hit him. That had a very apparent effect.

Runk glared down at Joshua's unconscious form. He jerked his head at one of his men, a creature with short, bristly fur and hard, gemlike eyes.

"Throw him to the uk," he said. He turned to Bacchi. "You help him."

"Sure, why not," said Bacchi. "I want to watch."

Joshua woke up to the feeling of sand and gravel scraping painfully up his back and the back of his head. In front of him was the night sky. He realized he was being dragged by his heels.

A boulder with a thick vertical crack in it drifted by to his left. Still woozy, he reached out and stuck his hand in the crevice and held on. He jerked to a stop.

He felt a few impatient tugs on his legs, and then they were thrown violently down. An alien voice spit out something angry and staccato.

"Oh, you awake now?" This time it was Bacchi speaking. "Well, you better get up and walk. Or he says he's going to shoot you in the ninga."

The bristly alien grabbed his wrist and yanked him up to a sitting position. Joshua pulled his wrist out of his grip and got to his feet on his own. Bacchi, behind him, shoved him forward, the touch burning the abraded skin on his back.

"Keep going."

As he staggered ahead, Joshua again said, "You sold us out. You both sold us out."

Bacchi chuckled. "See, the thing is, if you really knew Cole, you wouldn't be surprised by that. If you were smart, you'd know that you should never trust a word he says."

Joshua kept walking. To his right the ground fell away steeply down to the camp. Below him he could see Runk's men making preparations for the ride to Yrnameer.

"Did you hear me?" said Bacchi. Joshua didn't answer. "Did. You. Hear. Me," repeated Bacchi.

"I heard you," muttered Joshua.

"Do you understand me?"

Farg him, thought Joshua. He wasn't going to answer.

The path was turning now, a sharp switchback that cut through a narrow corridor in the rock that Joshua hadn't seen from the camp. Bristly stepped to the side before entering, and gestured with his gun for Joshua and Bacchi to go first, then followed them into the passageway. The walls were close enough that Joshua could touch each of them without straightening his arms. High above him he thought he could see the jagged aperture where the walls opened to the sky.

He slogged forward, still dizzy. Now the walls abruptly ended as the three of them emerged into a roughly circular opening, about twenty meters across, the rock stretching to the sky like a giant chimney.

In the center of the circle was a pit. As they got closer Joshua wrinkled his nose at the stench rising up from it. He heard a gargling, growling sound. His heart started to thump.

Behind him, he heard Bristly giggle.

"End of the line, Joshua," said Bacchi. He held out his hand to the alien for the gun. "May I?"

The alien said something.

"What?" said Bacchi. "Are you kidding?!"

The alien said something else.

"Whoa, whoa, whoa, let's take it easy, pal," said Bacchi.

Again the alien talking.

"Runk said *what*?!"

Joshua risked looking over his shoulder. He only had a brief moment to register the sight of Bristly pointing his gun at Bacchi, who had his hands in the air, and then Bristly thrust out a leg, his foot catching Bacchi in the chest and sending him stumbling backward and over the edge. He screamed on the way down, and then Joshua heard the thump, and then horrible growling and screeching and tearing and more screaming that ended abruptly. Something sailed out of the pit and landed with a dull thud on the ground. Joshua jerked his head away, gagging. It was a foot-long section of Bacchi's tail.

Bristly was speaking to him now, the gun pointed at his chest.

"No," said Joshua, trying to back away, his feet inches from the edge. "No!" he repeated, as Bristly gestured again. The alien let out an enraged honking sound and clubbed at Joshua's head with the pistol.

Joshua reflexively ducked into a deep crouch. Bristly stumbled forward, carried by the momentum of his own swing, and tripped over Joshua.

Joshua didn't hear the thud, but the screaming was even louder this time, a bloodcurdling trilling noise, mixed with snapping and crunching and gurgling, and then the trilling stopped. Another object was ejected from the pit, reaching the apex of its flight just above and in front of Joshua. As it dropped he automatically reached out a hand and caught it. Bristly's gun.

39

MaryAnn wouldn't come to the door when Cole rapped softly on it, then knocked harder. Now he was nearly pounding on it, hitting it as hard as he dared, hissing, "MaryAnn. MaryAnn!"

It was a few hours before dawn. The streets of Yrnameer were silent. They'd be coming soon.

He had ridden for two days straight, often falling asleep in the saddle and jerking back awake, stopping only when the baiyo was too exhausted to take another step. When he got to the village he rode to her door, dismounting the baiyo without tying it up.

The sky had started to brighten on the horizon when she finally answered, opening the door the merest crack to peer at him suspiciously.

"What do you want?" she said.

"You have to come with me."

"What? No," she said. "What's wrong with you? Are you—?"

"No, I'm not drunk. MaryAnn, please, I need you to come with me."

"Go away." She started to shut the door. He stuck his foot in it.

"MaryAnn, wait, please, wait."

"Get your foot out of the door!"

"MaryAnn!" he shoved against the door, forcing his way inside. She stepped back, not cowering exactly, but looking at him like she didn't know him, not expecting this behavior. He found himself at a momentary loss for words.

"Please, just come with me. Please. I'll explain as we go."

"Cole, I'm not going anywhere. What is wrong with you?"

"MaryAnn, remember that time, a long time ago, when you told me you had faith in me? You remember that, right?"

She hesitated, but then she nodded, a small movement.

"I need you to have that faith now."

She stared at him, silent. But this time she shook her head. "I can't," she whispered.

It seemed very quiet in the room. He nodded slowly. "I understand," he said. "Sorry to wake you."

Then he left.

He was nearly around the corner, walking fast, when she called out to him.

"Cole. Wait."

They were running now, heading toward the main gate.

"Where," she said, trying to catch her breath, "are we going?"

"Gotta get to the ship," said Cole. "Come on!"

They didn't say another word until they were at the base of the passenger ramp, gasping for breath.

"Cole, what's happening?" she managed.

"Just . . ." He gestured for her to follow him up the ramp. "Not much time."

She followed him through the corridors of the Benedict, catching up to him as he clambered up into the escape pod.

"Cole—" she said again as she climbed into the pod.

"They're coming," he said. "Have to hurry." As he talked he was hitting switches and manipulating the controls.

"Cole, what's going on. What are you doing?"

"Yes, what exactly *are* you doing?" demanded Nora from right over his shoulder.

"*Argh!*" said Cole. "Where did you come from?"

"I followed you two from the house. So that's what's happening, huh? You two are running?"

"Nora!" said MaryAnn.

"We're not running!" said Cole.

Nora jabbed a finger at MaryAnn. "I trusted you! I thought you were a nice person!"

"I *am* a nice person!"

"She *is* a nice person!" seconded Cole.

"So what are you doing? Get away from those controls!" said Nora, pulling at Cole's hands.

"Nora, let go of me!" said Cole, trying to fend her off. "We don't have time! I've got to get the engines online!"

"Because you're running!" said Nora.

"No!"

"You're running?!" said MaryAnn.

"I'm not running!" shouted Cole, pulling his wrist from Nora's grasp.

"So why the engines?" said Nora. "Why?"

"Because he's running," said Joshua.

He was a sight: sunburned, his eyes red, his hair full of sand and dust. He had dried blood on his face. He glared at Cole balefully, holding the gun on him with a hand that trembled from fatigue and adrenaline.

"I saw you," he said, his voice a whisper. "I followed you there. I heard what you told them," he rasped.

"Joshua," said Cole, keeping his tone as even as possible, "we don't have time for this."

"Joshua," said Nora, "what happened to you? What are you talking about?"

"I believed in you," said Joshua, his gaze fixed on Cole. "We all believed in you."

"Joshua," said Cole, "please. We've got to hurry."

"Cole, what is he talking about?" said Nora.

"He sold us out," said Joshua. "He sold us out. Bacchi was right—you're just a liar and a thief and a cheat!" He was crying now, and he angrily wiped the tears away with his forearm. The gun stayed aimed at Cole, though.

"Cole, what is he saying?" said MaryAnn, looking at him in horror.

But Cole wasn't listening. He was looking at one of the monitors, the view from the most distant remote camera that he had set up. He'd placed it in one of the trees that bordered a field a little over a kilometer to the northeast of the village. As he watched, the first of Runk's men marched into frame. And then there were more of them, and more.

"Joshua, we *really* don't have time for this!" said Cole.

"Joshua, what are you saying?" said Nora. "Explain what you mean."

"I followed him! To the hideout! He made a deal with them! He's leaving everyone to die!"

MaryAnn and Nora looked at Cole. "Cole?" said MaryAnn.

Cole jabbed his finger at Nora. "It was her idea!" he said.

Joshua turned to her, confused, and Cole lunged forward and grabbed the gun, punching Joshua in the nose with the other hand. Joshua tumbled back, sitting heavily on his rear end. When he tried to get up, Cole was pointing the gun between his eyes.

"Nobody move!" said Cole.

Nobody moved.

"Now you listen to me," Cole said to Joshua. "You get in my way and I will farging shoot you in the farging head. Understand? Understand?!"

Joshua nodded, wide-eyed.

"Good," said Cole. "Hold this."

He shoved the pistol back in Joshua's hand, jumped back into the control chair and let his momentum pivot him around to face the controls, extended a stiff-arm blindly at Nora just as she was opening her mouth—"Save it!"—and got to work.

"Cole . . . ?" said MaryAnn.

"Just listen," he said. "Bacchi's right. I am a liar and a thief and a cheat, and much worse than that." His eyes were on the control panel as he hit a rapid succession of keys. "But I'm not running. And I wanted you here, so you could see that."

He glanced up at the monitor. Runk's men filled the screen. He pointed to it with one hand while he typed with the other. "See that? That's them. They're nearly here."

"Oh my God!" said MaryAnn.

"We have to warn everyone!" said Nora. "We have to wake everyone up, or they'll be slaughtered!"

"She's right! I'll go!" said Joshua.

"No! You wake them up and they'll be slaughtered anyways, and half the casualties will be from shooting one another," said Cole. "Nora, you know it's true."

"So what are you going to do?" she said.

"See that?" said Cole, pointing to a second monitor, showing another field, this one unpopulated. Peter's field, the one he had torn to shreds, and then, at Cole's direction, very carefully repaired. But not before making some important additions.

"I have to get the engines to fire by the time they get to that field, or they'll make it to the town."

"The engines?" said Joshua. "But—"

"The fuel cells," said Nora. "You buried the fuel cells in the field. And then when they walk through it—"

"Nothing, unless I can get the engines online." He turned his attention back to the controls. "Okay, here we go." He hit a button, then pounded his fist on the panel, swearing. "Why does nothing ever work for me when I need it?" He massaged his forehead, trying to think. "Why won't they respond to *oh farg me with a whutger, that's why*!"

He leaped out of his seat and rushed past them, practically jumping into the open hatch. He was halfway down the ladder before he reversed course and sprang into the escape pod again, raced to the control panel, and pointed to a large button.

"You see this? When you see this turn red and light up, you push it. Got it?"

"Got it," said MaryAnn and Nora.

"Right," said Joshua.

"Good," Cole said, and ran the two steps back to the hatch. Before he disappeared from sight he stopped again. "It lights up, you push it." Speaking to all of them, but directing it at Nora.

"Got it," she said.

"I mean, no matter what. Understand?"

She stared at him, the import of what he was saying sinking in. She nodded.

"Yes," she said.

"Good."

And then he was gone.

And then he was back again, scrabbling up into the pod and marching across to MaryAnn, pulling her into his arms to kiss her, hard.

When he released her she let out her breath in a little rush, speechless, her fingers on her lips.

"Thanks," he said quietly. "Thanks for your faith."

Then he turned to Nora, grabbed her, and kissed her, too.

"Just to be fair," he explained as she blinked at him, stunned. He turned to Joshua. Joshua shrank back. Cole stuck out a hand. "You're a good kid," he said when they shook.

And then he was gone again, this time for good.

"What's a whutger?" said Joshua.

Item number seven on Cole's checklist, underlined twice: make absolutely sure that the Traifo interface is correctly aligned and connected.

There was no check mark next to it. He cursed himself.

He switched to cursing Joshua as he struggled to undo the knot that tied Joshua's baiyo to a tree near the Benedict, aware of the seconds ticking away. Frustrated, he pulled out his knife and cut the line. The baiyo wheeled and shied, leaving Cole pivoting in tight circles as he tried to mount, giving him yet another target for his curses.

"Oh for God's sake, would you please just stand still?" he finally said. The baiyo suddenly stopped resisting and stood stock-still, trembling. Cole shook his head in wonder and hoisted himself into the saddle, grunting with the effort.

"All right, let's go!" he said, spurring the baiyo on, and it took off like a shot.

In the escape pod they watched him on one of the monitors as he galloped out of frame.

"He's going the wrong way," said MaryAnn.

A moment later the baiyo galloped back into frame and continued on in the other direction.

"That's better," said MaryAnn.

"To the right of the trees! This way!" Runk shouted at his men from the skimmer. "Careful with the lifter! You smash it up and we'll eat your guts for dinner!"

There were over a hundred of them, some mounted on baiyos, some trudging along on foot, their weapons clanking dully. They walked alongside and behind the Big Red Lifter like it was a parade float, the giant flatbed hovering a meter above the uneven ground. Runk darted around on the skimmer, which listed slightly to one side due to Altung's weight. The lifter could have easily carried the men who were walking, but early on there had been several arguments over who got to sit where, one of which ended in gunplay. After that Runk made everyone get off.

It was light enough now that Runk barely needed a flashlight to check the map that Cole had sketched for him, showing what Cole claimed was the safest route to the town. Bacchi had drawn over it, a red line indicating a detour that took them to the north before they descended on the town's flank. Then they'd blow a hole in the fence and the fun would start.

"All right," said Runk. "No more talking from here on out. Everyone check your weapons. We're close."

Cole was close, too. When he was a few hundred meters from Peter's field he hopped off the baiyo and ran the rest of the distance, figuring he would be harder to spot that way. He got to the edge of the field just as Runk's men were coming into view to his right. Cole dropped to the ground, hoping the grass would give him enough cover.

He wormed forward like they'd taught him in the space marines, keeping as flat as possible. In his mind he could hear the drill sergeant screaming at them: "Heads and asses down, space marines," and then Farley saying, "Space marines? Don't it seem weird to you that they call it . . . ."

Cole was just a few meters away from where he'd hidden the Altex remote box, which took the signal from the ship and relayed it through the Traifo interface to the Artemis coil, and then to a series of hardwired connections to the fuel cells. He could hear Runk's men now, the low hum of the lifter, the higher whine of the skimmer, a few scattered *clacks* as weapons were prepared.

He got to the spot where he'd placed the—wait, wasn't this the spot? Where was the damn Altex box? Over there, under those branches! No. Here? No. Oh, for farg's sake, he didn't have time for this. . . .

He scrambled back and forth, going from spot to spot, yanking away matted grasses and vegetation. About half of Runk's men were in the field, nearing the blast area, close enough that he could hear the occasional murmur and then a stern *"Shh!"* from Runk. The Big Red Lifter was a stone's throw away.

Where did he put the stupid thing? He pulled himself forward. If one of Runk's men looked this way, he would almost certainly see the grass waving about.

It wasn't going to work. At this rate, even if he found it in time, they might be past the field, and then it would be too late.

He clawed aside a pile of dead grass. Not there. Not to the left. Not in that—wait. He could see the little blue box now, about a body length away. He started creeping toward it, then froze. One of Runk's men had broken off from the main group and was walking directly at him, his weapon held ready at hip height, scanning back and forth for danger.

Cole tried to wiggle lower into the earth. As the man got nearer Cole could see him better. It was the Yoin. He was just steps from Cole, getting closer, slowing as he did, then stopping, one foot nearly stepping on the Altex box. Cole, facedown on the ground, could now only see as high as the Yoin's shins. If he reached out, he could just about touch the Yoin's toes. The Yoin had to see him. Cole held his breath.

In the escape pod they could see it all. They could see Runk's men, moving across the field. In the lower corner they could see Cole, scuttling back and forth in the grass.

"Something's wrong," said Joshua. "He can't find something!"

"He's got to hurry," said MaryAnn. "They're almost all in the field."

Then they saw the Yoin split from the main group and walk toward Cole.

"Oh, no," said MaryAnn.

"Get out of there, Cole!" hissed Nora. "Get out of there!"

They watched, barely daring to breathe, as the Yoin stopped in front of Cole.

Cole heard the Yoin shifting his weight, and then adjusting his weapon. Farg it. If he was going to die, he might as well go out swinging. He got ready. One, two, *ttthhhr*—or maybe if he begged, the Yoin would spare him long enough to . . . no, just go for it. One, two—

The Yoin began to urinate.

"What's he doing?" whispered Joshua, squinting at the image of the Yoin.

"I'm not sure," said Nora. "I think he's—"

Oh, they all said at the same time.

About two minutes later, when the Yoin was still at it, Joshua said, Wow.

Cole knew that his perception of time was probably somewhat askew. But even so, it did not seem physically possible that the Yoin could have so much of his internal real estate devoted to bladder. Nor did it seem possible that he couldn't see Cole, lying nearly at his feet.

There was another saying in the Yoin language. It went, "Big bladder, bad night vision." It rhymed better in Yoin.

The Yoin was humming something and, from the sound of it, was now drawing designs or signing his name. A thick, dark rivulet began to meander toward Cole's face. Cole tried to shrink back without making a noise.

After what seemed several hours, the Yoin sighed contentedly. The rivulet had turned into a small pool four inches from Cole's nose. Cole heard various adjustments and then squishy splashing noises as the Yoin turned to walk away. Cole released his breath. Then the Yoin grunted and stopped.

"Why is he stopping? Did he spot Cole?" said Nora.

"He's picking something up," said MaryAnn.

The Yoin's hand entered Cole's field of vision. It reached down, prodded the Altex box, grasped it, turned it over, then lifted it up and out of sight.

Cole closed his eyes. It was over.

He heard the Yoin grunt again. "Hmm," said the Yoin.

Then there was a mucky splash and some warm droplets splattered Cole's face. The Yoin walked off.

Cole opened his eyes. The Altex box was lying in the mud in front of his face.

"He's leaving again! He's going!" said Joshua. "What's Sheriff Cole doing?"

"That box—it must be connected to the fuel cells," said MaryAnn.

"Wait," said Joshua, "when we push the button, won't Cole . . . ?"

Cole grabbed the box, trying to ignore the wetness. Now he had to find the Traifo interface plug. He got into a crouching position and scuttled forward, detouring around the small lake that blocked his path. Runk's men were in the field, and in a few moments they'd be beyond it, and all this effort would be for naught. There it was. He stooped to grab the Traifo plug and tried to insert it into the 89-pin connector in the Altex box, his hand shaking. That's when the Yoin heard him and turned.

"Hey," he said. "It's the poet!"

"Hey!" said Cole, giving him a little jock nod with his chin while he kept trying to insert the plug. "How are ya?"

"I'm okay," said the Yoin. "What are you doing here?"

"Just," said Cole, twisting the plug and trying to get the thing aligned, "you know . . ." He smiled.

"Huh," said the Yoin. "Maybe I should shoot you."

"Uh . . . can you hold on a minute?" said Cole, jabbing the plug desperately at the socket.

"Hmm. I don't know. . . ."

The plug clicked into place.

Cole sighed.

"Okay," he said, "I guess you might as well shoot me."

In the cockpit of the escape pod the button went red and lit up.

"No," said Joshua, shaking his head, his eyes tearful.

"Don't look," said MaryAnn, and tears were streaming down her cheeks.

Nora placed her fingers on the button. Her hand was shaking.

MaryAnn closed her eyes.

Then opened them. Nora's hand was still poised on the button. MaryAnn realized Nora was crying, too.

"I can't," Nora whispered. "I can't do it." She pulled her hand away.

"We have to," said MaryAnn, and she pounded the button.

40

Nothing happened.

MaryAnn pounded the button again.

Nothing.

The Yoin calmly took the safety off his gun and racked the slide.

"Uh . . . ," said Cole, "can you wait a little bit longer?" With his other hand he jiggled the connection, then slapped the box.

"Sort of in a rush," the Yoin said, then took aim and fired.

The bullet plowed into Cole, knocking him backward and spinning him around, the Altex box flying from his hand, and as he fell and all went dark his final thought was that he had failed.

The impact of the bullet carried his body backward, landing on a thick mat of vegetation that gave way under his weight, allowing him to fall through to the deeper hole hidden underneath, the one hole in the meadow that Peter had failed to fill. The Altex splashed down into the puddle of urine, inert.

Then, with a small *pop* and a few sparks, it shorted out.

The explosion was huge.

Only two bandits survived the blast.

Runk and Altung were beyond the field when the fuel cells went off, the shock wave nearly knocking the skimmer from the sky.

Runk didn't wait to check to see who was wounded and who was dead. His mind was filled with rage, the desire for vengeance blotting out all other thoughts.

The skimmer screamed through the sky above the village, the townspeople stumbling about in confusion and fear, roused from sleep by the violent concussion of the explosion. Runk fired down on them, overwhelmed by bloodlust, simply hoping to kill as many as possible.

Neither he nor Altung saw the projectile that struck the rear intake vent of the skimmer, knocking out one of the two engines and destroying the lateral stabilizer. The burning skimmer slashed a thick charcoal line of smoke against the pale blue of the dawn, disappearing from view to the west of the village. Somewhere over the horizon there was an explosion, followed by a black column that rose lazily upward.

Even by gralleth standards, it was an incredible shot.

41

There was a well-attended memorial service, with much sniffling and crying. Orwa spoke eloquently about the heavy toll of violence and hatred. Afterward the townsfolk lingered in and around the town hall, talking quietly in small groups, exchanging hugs and comforting one another.

The bandits might have been the enemy, but they deserved mourning just the same.

Cole was dreaming.

Once again, he was dreaming of the woman he loved, the only woman he had ever loved, and she smiled her radiant smile and all was poetry and songs and spring and wonder, and she spoke to him again:

Cole.

MaryAnn, he whispered.

Yes, Cole, it's MaryAnn.

And once again he felt the serene warmth filling him and bringing him back to life, and even though a tiny warning bell was going off somewhere he still tried to reach out to her, except someone was holding one of his arms down, so he extended the other toward her dreamy dream breasts—

"Cole!"

"Wha?!" he said, just before another pitcherful of water shlapped into his face.

Oh, God, no, he thought.

He apprehensively opened his eyes a crack.

MaryAnn was standing at his bedside, one hand on her hip, the other holding a now-empty pitcher. Next to her were Nora and Joshua.

The band kicked in.

Flashbulbs popped.

Cole closed his eyes again.

There was another party, almost as good as the first, except this time Cole had his arm in a sling and his singed eyebrows hadn't grown back yet. He also drank much less at this party, and the pats on the back made him wince.

He found himself once again searching for MaryAnn, then spotted her across the floor. As he made his way across, Mayor Kimber got ahold of his arm, pulling him into a small circle with Orwa and the purple rug thing.

"So tell us again," said the mayor, who looked and smelled tipsy. "Bacchi was part of it from the beginning?"

"Uh, yes, yes he was," said Cole, looking around for MaryAnn without success. "All part of the plan."

"How'd you figure that all out?" asked the purple guy.

Cole gave up on MaryAnn for the moment.

"Well, I knew that Runk wouldn't trust me, no matter what, so if I told him to do something he'd know it was a trap. But someone with a grudge double-crossing me? Runk understands that idea. He trusts it. To him, that person is reliable. You see, you have to understand how the criminal mind functions."

Ahh, they all said.

"Excuse me for a moment," he said, catching sight of MaryAnn again.

He'd gone about a step before Nora grabbed his good elbow.

" 'Understand how the criminal mind functions'—I wonder how you manage that." She hiccupped and grinned. She seemed a bit tipsy herself. "I guess congratulations are in order," she said.

"Just pretending to do my job, ma'am," said Cole.

"You did good, Cole," she said, and patted his cheek. "You're a really rotten guy, but you've got hongos."

She gulped some more beer. "Why didn't you tell anyone what the plan was?"

"Really? You have to ask?" he said. "You know if I told them the real plan, they would have been accidentally shooting each other in the flippers and tripping on one another's eyestalks. That, or someone would have gone out to the field and planted a warning sign, to make sure none of the bandits got hurt."

"Why didn't you at least tell me?"

"Would you have gone along with a plan like that?"

She smiled. "You did good, Cole," she repeated. "Good kisser, too," she added. Then she gestured toward the other side of the room. He followed her gaze, spotting MaryAnn.

"I think your girlfriend is waiting for you," Nora said, then patted him on the cheek again and walked away, glancing back to grin at him in a manner that could only be construed as saucy.

Cole edged through the crowd toward MaryAnn's most recent location, accepting handshakes and more painful back-pats along the way. He passed Peter, who was describing his contribution to the plan: "Then I went to work on hole number fourteen. I went scoop, scoop, scoop scoop scoop—or was it, scoop scoop, scoop? No, hang on. . . ."

Cole finally caught MaryAnn's eye and waved, redoubling his efforts to swim his way to her: "Pardon me. 'Scuse me. Pardon. Sorry. Thank you, that's very kind. Ow—arms's still a bit sore. Thanks. Pardon me. . . ."

When he reached her he was visited by a sense of déjà vu, as the old awkward feeling welled up again. He slowed, shuffled, hemming and hawing for the last few feet of his approach, casting about for the right words.

"Hi," he said.

"Hi," she said.

"Sorry about the—"

"Forget it."

He smiled, did some more shuffling.

"We've had this conversation before, huh," he said.

"Cole, I wanted to tell you this: I've never seen anything so brave before. You were prepared to sacrifice yourself for everyone, and I can't tell you how admirable that is."

It was nothing, Cole nearly said, or, There was no choice, or, A man has to do what a man has to do. . . . Instead he said, "Actually, I didn't think the explosion would be that big. I thought I had a pretty good chance of surviving."

She smiled again.

"You're being honest."

"I'm a little drunk."

She laughed. "Cole . . . ," she began.

"Sheriff! Sheriff!"

Joshua came running up, face flushed, excited.

"Hi, MaryAnn! Sorry! Sheriff! Sheriff!"

"Do you perhaps have something to tell me?"

"They found the skimmer! It was in a ravine beyond the foothills, all crashed and burnt up!"

"Ah. Remains?"

"They're not sure. It looked like a bad fire."

"Ah."

"What if Runk survived, Sheriff?"

Cole thought about it.

"He's right," said MaryAnn. "What if he did?"

"He might come after you, Sheriff!" said Joshua.

Cole chuckled and put a hand on Joshua's shoulder. "No. You don't know Runk. If he's alive, he's gone for good."

"Okay," said Joshua uncertainly. "If you say so, Sheriff."

"Joshua!" boomed the mayor. "Come here, young man!"

Cole and MaryAnn watched as the mayor dragged Joshua off to receive his own share of adulation. Cole turned back to MaryAnn, suddenly feeling very tired.

"You know, I think I'm going to head out," he said.

"You want me to walk you home? It might be dangerous out there. Bandits, you know."

He smiled. "Sure."

As they turned to walk out, she said, "You really think Runk is gone?"

"Long gone," he said.

42

They walked at an aimless, leisurely pace for a few minutes, the lively sounds of the party slowly fading behind them.

There was a lull in the conversation, but a pleasant lull, the expectant pause before something important and meaningful is said. MaryAnn took a deep breath.

"Cole," she said, "what I've been wanting to say is this: I *erk*!"

Cole kept going for a few steps before he realized MaryAnn was no longer walking next to him.

"MaryAnn?" he said, confused, looking about for her. *"Erk!"*

"Hi, Cole," said Runk.

Cole's sense of déjà vu returned. He was once again upside down in an alley, dangling by an ankle, except this time it was Altung who was holding him, and MaryAnn was dangling next to him, struggling to free herself.

"Hey!" she yelled. "Let me go!"

The way Altung was holding her, she was facing away from him toward the wall. She twisted, trying to see her attacker and saw Cole.

"Cole? Cole!"

He reached out and grabbed her hand, the two of them steadying each other.

"What is this? What's happening?"

"It's all right, MaryAnn."

"Not really," said Runk.

"Who is that!" she demanded. "Is this some sort of joke?"

"This is my good friend, Runk."

"Runk?!"

"Last person you'll ever meet, sweetie," said Runk.

Runk was standing on a rain barrel next to Altung, pointing a very small gun at them. It was an act that struck Cole as rather redundant.

"Is that a Firestick 2?" asked Cole.

"Sure is."

"Let's see. Firestick 2 . . ."

" 'Small, but Oh My.' "

"Right."

"Remind you of anyone?"

"Hmm. No one really comes to mind. . . ."

MaryAnn interrupted.

"I don't care who you are, but if you don't put us down right now I'll scream," said MaryAnn.

Runk chuckled. "Go ahead and scr—"

"*Helllllp!!!!*"

"Go ahead. Scream all you—"

"*Helllllllp!!!!*"

"See, it doesn't bother me at—"

"*Helllllppppp!!!!!*"

"Okay, that's starting to get on my—"

"*HEELLLLLLLPPPPPP!!!!!*"

"Altung, shut her up."

"No, wait," said Cole. "MaryAnn. It's okay."

"It is?" she said.

"Yes," he replied.

His tone was calm and reassuring, with a quiet confidence. It matched what he felt.

"It's not okay," said Runk. "I'm going to kill you both. And I'm going to kill her first, and it's going to hurt, and I'm going to make you watch."

MaryAnn began breathing faster. Her hand squeezed his.

"Yeah . . . I don't think so," said Cole. He couldn't remember when he'd last felt so relaxed. "When all this is over, I'll probably be dead, but I think she's going to be just fine."

"Cole, what are you saying?" said MaryAnn.

"Plug your ears," he said.

"What?"

"Trust me."

She plugged her ears.

He didn't have two good arms. He couldn't plug his. He'd have nightmares for weeks about the sound.

Altung jerked spasmodically, his grip spiking sharply, causing MaryAnn to cry out at the sudden pain. Then his hands relaxed completely, spilling them on the ground, MaryAnn yelping again as they fell. Altung sagged down onto his knees and hung there as if suspended, while Cole and MaryAnn scuttled frantically backward until their backs were against the wall.

"Oh, my God," whispered MaryAnn.

"Don't watch!" said Cole, placing his hand over her eyes to block out the horrific scene.

There was a slurping, popping noise, almost as revolting as the first noise. Then, slowly, Altung started to pitch forward, like a tall tree cut down at the base, picking up velocity until he collapsed with a heavy thud in front of Cole and MaryAnn. Before Altung's face slammed into the hard-packed earth, Cole caught a sickening glimpse of the ragged hole where his left eye had been.

"Ah," said Kenneth, wiping his ovipositor, "I feel *so* much better."

Runk had not moved. His tiny eyes were wide with shock as he regarded Altung's prone form, the giant's left leg twitching slightly. Then his view was blocked by the dozens of eyeballs that surrounded and scrutinized him from every angle.

"Kenneth," said Runk, still stunned.

"Runk! How wonderful!" said Kenneth. "An *amuse bouche* for the kiddies!"

A tentacle swept him up. Cole closed his eyes, not wanting to see what happened next.

"Cole, what's going on?" said MaryAnn.

"You don't want to know," said Cole.

There was another wet, popping noise, like a cork being shoved into a watermelon, or a small creature being shoved into a hole in a much larger creature's head.

"There, that should keep things in place," said Kenneth, and Cole heard him slapping his tentacles together like a workman finishing a task. "Oh, Cole—I have your change."

43

"Full house, jacks high," said Cole, laying down his cards.

"Crud," said Joshua, tossing his hand in.

"Mmm-hmm," said Bacchi, in the tone of someone who had just confirmed something he had been suspecting.

"Why do I keep losing?" asked Joshua.

"Because Cole is cheating," said Bacchi.

Joshua looked at Cole.

"It's true," said Cole, shuffling the deck with his one good hand, his other arm still in a sling. "Consider it a life lesson."

It was a quiet afternoon, edging toward the evening. The air was getting crisp. They were sitting on the porch of the jailhouse, Cole and Bacchi smoking cigars and drinking shersha. Joshua had a citron-ade with ice.

Bacchi had staggered into the village the day after the party, bedraggled and dehydrated, missing most of his tail.

"But, that thing, in the pit," said Joshua. "I saw you fall!"

"He spat me out," said Bacchi. He sounded somewhat insulted.

At the moment he was watching Cole deal the cards. When Cole finished, Bacchi reached over and picked up Cole's cards, swapping them for the hand Cole had dealt him. He fanned the cards, examined his new hand, and sighed.

"You knew I was going to do that," he said.

"Mmm-hmm," said Cole out of the corner of his mouth as he puffed on the cigar.

"That's impressive, with one hand," said Bacchi.

"Mmm-hmm," said Cole.

Bacchi shook his head and tossed the cards into the center of the table. Joshua followed suit.

They'd been playing for about an hour, low stakes, and Cole had managed to approximately double the amount of money he'd received from Kenneth, meaning he now had slightly more than six NDs in front of him.

First there was the principle of the debt, Kenneth had explained, plus interest, handling charges, transport costs, food, fuel and lodging, bribes. . . .

"That diamond was worth tens of millions," said Cole.

"Oh, yes, definitely, even with the confiscatory fee I had to pay to fence the thing."

"So what happened to the rest?"

"I donated it to my favorite cause!" said Kenneth.

"Don't tell me. . . ."

"Yes!" said Kenneth happily. "Would you like a tote bag?"

In the end, there were enough IPR tote bags for everyone in the village. Even Stirling accepted his, at first scowling, guessing where the funds might have come from to support such largesse. Then he smiled.

"You know what?" he told Cole. "I sort of like this."

Cole checked his watch. MaryAnn would be there soon for their date. He smiled at the thought. Their Date. He put down his own cards to tap the ash off the cigar. Joshua watched him as he examined the glowing tip, then put it back in his mouth.

"Can I try one?" said Joshua.

"No," said Nora.

"Where'd she come from?" said Bacchi.

"She does that," said Cole.

Nora climbed up the steps of the porch and pulled up a chair to the small card table, obliging Cole and Bacchi to move to the side to make room.

"Deal me in," she said. Cole reached for the cards and she stopped him. "On second thought, I'll do it."

As she dealt, she said, "Philip was looking for you, Joshua. You're supposed to be on the farm helping the other kids."

Joshua looked to Cole for help.

Cole chewed on his cigar. "Come on, now, you don't want to take my deputy from me, do you?"

Joshua smiled, then looked anxiously at Nora. She was concentrating on her cards, reordering them. "No," she said at length, "I don't suppose I do."

"All right!" said Joshua. "Give me one of those!" he said, reaching for the cigars. Nora slapped his hand away.

"No."

"Okay. Sorry."

Bacchi sniggered.

"Shut up, Bacchi," muttered Joshua.

"That's the spirit," said Cole. He tossed in his bid. "Gotta be careful with this one, Joshua," he said, inclining his head toward Nora. "She's nearly killed me about three times so far."

Nora, eyes on her cards, raised him. "How do you figure that?"

"Well, I count at least twice on the way here, and then you go pushing a button while I'm in a field surrounded by high explosives." He checked the stakes. "I raise you five."

Bacchi and Joshua folded.

"You've been misinformed. I wasn't the one who pushed the button."

Cole looked up from his cards for the first time. "What?"

"Wasn't me. I call. Three queens."

Cole lay down his pair of tens. As she scraped the pot over to herself he said, "So who?"

"Hi, Cole!"

He stepped down from the porch to greet MaryAnn, hesitating this time not from awkwardness but from distraction.

"Hi, MaryAnn," he said, and leaned in to kiss what turned out to be her cheek.

"Hi," she said, then leaned back to smile at him. A complicated smile, the eyes sending a different message than the mouth. And sure enough: "There's something I need to tell you."

"If it's about the button, I already—"

"The button? Oh, right. Yes, I pushed it, just like you told me."

"Oh. Well, that's very . . . brave. That must have been very hard for you."

"Oh, no," she said, waving a hand dismissively. "That was easy. It was clear that had to be done. But that's not what I wanted to talk about."

"Right," said Cole, aware that everyone on the porch was observing them intently. "Maybe on our date—"

"That's what I wanted to talk about."

"Right. The date. Okay. Uh . . ." He glanced over at the porch again, then placed a hand on her shoulder and ushered her several steps away from their audience, then a few more just to be safe.

"So," he said.

She took a deep breath. "Cole, there's no other way to say this. I told you before that I came to Yrnameer after a painful relationship. My boyfriend and I had such ups and downs, such good times and hard times. . . . Well, I've been in contact with him, and it's clear that he's grown a lot. He's a different person now. You see, Teg's realized that he—what? What's wrong? Are you okay? Cole? It's very hard to talk to you through that."

Cole, his voice muffled because he'd pulled his collar up and over his head like a turtle, said, "You're going to tell me how handsome he is."

"Oh my God! Do you *know* him?!"

Cole made a grunting noise. He was now deflating into a squatting position, jacket over his head like he was shielding himself from a blast.

"That's amazing!" said MaryAnn. "You know, he used to have a ship just like yours? It even had all those stickers and decals on it! How wonderful that you know him! Don't you think he's handsome?"

Cole, under his jacket-tent, said, "Yes. He's very handsome. Very, very handsome."

MaryAnn gave him a fond, lingering hug, her breath warm in his ear as she whispered, "Thanks, Cole. I knew you'd understand."

They watched him walk heavily back to the porch and drag himself up the three stairs like he might not make it to the top. He lowered himself with effort into the chair that Joshua scrambled to position for him, accepting the glass of shersha from Bacchi and draining it without a sideways glance.

Then he sat, blinking slowly, his eyes focused on nothing. Finally, Nora said, "Cole?"

When there was no response she said it again: "Cole?"

He turned his head lethargically to look at her. Her expression was full of concern and compassion.

"You all right?" she said.

He stared at her dully for several slow, deep breaths. Then a little shudder ran through him—once, twice, a third time, and he shook his head and rubbed his face and looked around at his surroundings like a man waking from a trance. He realized they were all watching him.

"Of *course* I'm all right!" he roared. "Deal 'em up!"

"That's the Cole I know!" said Bacchi, clouting him on his bad shoulder as he refilled his glass.

"Deputy," said Nora, dealing the cards, "I believe the sheriff needs a cigar."

"That's right!" said Cole. "The sheriff needs a cigar!"

Nora took the cigar from Joshua and lit it, taking a deep drag before popping it into Cole's mouth. And as Cole picked up his hand and chomped on the cigar and felt the shersha smoothing out the rough spots in his brain, he glanced at his tablemates, and then out at the peaceful town, and then up at the sky, and thought, This is good. This is right. He was the sheriff.

"What'd you say, Sheriff?" said Joshua.

"What? Oh, I guess I said, this is g—"

He was interrupted by a crashing noise coming from somewhere down Main Street. Then another crashing noise. Then some smashing, followed by some growling, mixed with screaming.

"Oh, for farg's sake, what now," said Cole.

Mayor Kimber came running up to them, out of breath.

"Sheriff," he said, panting, "Ed's gone quagga!"

"What? What does that mean?"

"It's the interaction of the moons with the rin grass and bad yog juice! That's what it does to Hennies! They change!"

"Change?" said Cole, standing up. "What do you mean—*whoa*!" He'd just caught sight of a large, white-furred creature with fangs and claws and burning red eyes, wreaking havoc at the other end of Main Street. "That's *Ed*? Has this happened before?"

"Of course! What do you think happened to our first sheriff!"

"You had another—"

"You've got to do something, Cole!" said the mayor, grabbing Cole by the arm and pulling him down the steps and shoving him toward Ed, who was now holding the carved wooden himphyn that decorated the outside of one of the bookstores over his head.

"That thing has to weigh five hundred pounds," said Cole, just before Ed heaved it through the air.

"Sheriff!" said Kimber.

Cole looked up at Nora, Joshua, and Bacchi.

"Go get him, Sheriff," said Nora.

"Right," said Cole.

"You need help, Sheriff?" said Joshua.

"Nope," said Cole, unholstering his gun.

"No guns, Cole, that's Ed!" said Kimber.

"Right. Of course." He looked at his gun, sighed, and handed it to the mayor. "Farg me," he said, took a deep breath, squared his shoulders, and marched resolutely toward Ed.

"All right, Ed, this is your sheriff speaking. Ed, come on. Ow! Leggo! Ed, be reasonable! *Ow! Owww!!!! Ed! I'm the sheriff!!!*"

Elsewhere, more trouble was brewing.

acknowledgments

I would like to offer my deepest thanks to my agent, John Silbersack, to his assistant, Libby Kellogg, and to everyone else at Trident Media Group; to Marty Asher at Vintage/Random House for his great enthusiasm, Jeff Alexander at Vintage for his insight and advice, and Dan Frank at Pantheon for thinking hardcover; to Paul Kaup, Steve Wilkinson, Chuck Graef, Kosta Potamianos, and Kathy Egan for always being my first and most enthusiastic readers; and to my parents, family, and friends for their wonderful support.

Meet with Interesting People
Enjoy Stimulating Conversation
Discover Wonderful Books